INTO THE ASHES

LEE MURRAY

SEVERED PRESS
HOBART TASMANIA

INTO THE ASHES

Copyright © 2019 Lee Murray

WWW.SEVEREDPRESS.COM

ISBN: 978-1-925840-57-5

ACKNOWLEDGEMENTS

It is time to blow kisses to the lovely people who have supported me in the writing of this book. Firstly, to Clarks Crit Group, three valiant and loyal musketeers, who laboured on this manuscript from its conception until the last full-stop – I cannot thank you enough for your unwavering support and your genuine belief in me, and for labelling all correspondence to me 'Writer Extraordinaire' to boost my morale. To thriller writer, Ashley L Knight, author WA Cooper, and NZDF weapons expert Rock Chesterman, thank you for your valuable comments on the final draft. I appreciate the generous gift of your time and expertise. To my sensitivity readers, who I have not named, but to whom I am grateful for their considered advice. Any shortfalls in the work are my own. To my son for the title, and my family – David, Robbie and Celine – for your patience and your pride. I love you all.

Lee Murray, 2018

CHAPTER ONE

Tongariro National Park, Central Plateau

At the whump of a distant chopper, Otago University volcanologist Robert Clague lifted his eyes from the EDM and looked to the summit. That pilot had to be one brave bastard given the conditions.

Adjusting the bandana covering his mouth and nose, Clague searched the skies for the aircraft. The white ash was getting thicker, so thick he could barely see the conical peak of Mount Ngāuruhoe across the Mangatepopo Valley. It wasn't the lack of visibility that made flying hazardous. Taking off in hot volcanic ash was like greasing your engine with molten lava, not to mention the abrading effect on the blades. Whoever he was, the pilot was taking his life in his hands. With nothing to see, Clague turned back to his work, the drone of the departing chopper fading.

The earth rumbled beneath him.

Not again.

Clague dropped to the ground and curled into a ball, his arms crossed over his chest. Being a turtle, his daughter Kayla called it, when her preschool had instigated drills after the big quake in Kaikoura a year ago. She'd giggled when she showed him, getting down from the dinner table to hide in her shell on the tiles, her chin tucked to her chest and her head cradled in her chubby little arms. Enduring any quake on the mountain was no laughing matter. This wasn't a big one, and yet the earth heaved, the shaking seeming to go on and on. Small stones and debris, worked loose by the tremors, tumbled down the mountainside. Eyes down, he didn't see them, but he heard their rattle well enough as they bounced from one tabular lava layer to the next. Clague kept his breathing even, grateful for his hard hat. Seconds passed. His heart thumped. Still Clague waited for the grumbling to stop. He should be used to it by now: the quake one of many, part of the ongoing earthquake swarm they'd been experiencing over recent weeks and for which they had no answer.

And no choice other than to wait them out.

Finally, the shaking eased. Out of precaution, Clague remained crouched. Sometimes one quake would set off another.

"Clague?" a voice came at his shoulder. "You okay?"

Clague unfurled his body, squinting as his colleague, seismologist Taika Thompson, hovered into view. Despite the ash, the knobs of andesite rock higher up the mountain glistened behind him. "I'm fine. That was a long one."

"Yeah," Thompson agreed, his stance wide to brace himself against the hillside. "Feels like they're getting bigger."

Clague got to his feet. More frequent, too. Luckily, the tripod had stayed put, its feet lodged tightly in the stone.

A flake of ash floated from the sky to rest on Thompson's moustache. "I came to tell you we have to go." The ash bobbed as his mouth moved. "Keira got a call through on the satellite phone. The government's called a state of emergency, Volcanic Alert Level 4. The university has ordered us off the mountain."

"What? No way. They need us here. The data we're providing—"

"I don't need an EDM reading to tell me the ground moved, do you? Anyway, it's out of our hands," Thompson said. He rubbed at his nose, dislodging the flake of ash. "The Beehive is all abuzz: someone with a higher pay grade did some modelling and decided this swarm could be a warm up for the big one."

"Fuck," Clague breathed, his bandana puffing outwards.

"Yeah. Tell me about it. Anyway, Keira and Ahmad are packing up the gear. Keira said to tell you we'll be moving out in fifteen minutes."

"Okay. I'll be down in a sec. I want to check the strain meter," Clague said.

Already, Thompson was leaping over the rocks, off down the mountain. "Don't take too long," he called back over his shoulder. "Much more of this ash and we'll be breaking out the snowshoes to get to the road."

Clague turned back to the tripod to take a last measurement, then started dismantling the equipment. A wave of nausea hit him. He ought to get out his gas mask, but he was going to be packing up in a few minutes anyway.

Higher up the mountain, rocks clattered. Clague froze. Another quake? But the ground was still. Hairs lifted on the back of his neck.

Through the drifts of ash, a figure was climbing the mountain. A warrior? It looked that way: Clague spied flashes of muscled skin glistening with sweat. And was that a *patu*-club he was carrying? What the hell was he doing up here, dressed in a *piu piu* as if he was part of a tribal war party?

"Hey!"

The man kept climbing.

"Hey, you can't go up there! It's too dangerous. There's a state of emergency…"

If the warrior had heard him, he didn't show any sign of it, striding up the mountain to the summit.

Bugger.

Even if this wasn't the big one, the whole area was a hotspot. Clague couldn't leave him. No one should be out here alone, not without protective gear.

Clague twisted to take in the campsite on the plateau below. All but one of the tents had been dismantled, but their gear was still scattered about the site. A few minutes remained until his colleagues would be ready to leave. If Clague hurried, he'd have time to catch the warrior. Thrusting the EDM and his computer into the plastic suitcase, he snapped the locks closed. Then he left the case and the tripod propped against a rock and took off up the slope after the stranger.

"Hey!"

The warrior kept going, slipping in and out of the drifting ash, all the while putting distance between them. Clague picked his way carefully. An experienced mountaineer, he wasn't afraid of heights, but new vents were appearing in the ground everywhere. It wouldn't do to step in one.

When the warrior dropped below the crest, Clague put on a burst of speed. The ash was heavy, and it was getting harder to breathe. There! Clague caught sight of the warrior as he disappeared behind a huge boulder.

"You there. Hey!"

At last, the warrior turned and Clague saw his mistake. It was a woman, her shoulders as broad as any man's, her legs muscled. There was something striking about her. Something compelling…

"I don't know if you know about the state of emergency—" His voice sounded nervous, like an infatuated schoolboy.

The woman smiled, revealing stained teeth sharpened to points. She hissed softly, and took a step towards him. She lifted a finger…a talon…and pointed it at the ground at his feet.

Clague's eyes widened.

A fissure was opening, the earth cleaving! A shot of steam lunged for him, snorting and spitting. Clague jumped clear. Rocks flew over his head. He staggered, and righted himself.

Holy shit!

He clutched his head. This couldn't be happening. He should've taken the time to put on his gas mask. Without it, he was sucking in the fumes of Hades that were seeping up through cracks in the earth. They were taunting him, making him woozy and playing tricks with his brain. The fumes were the reason the woman looked feral, like a *furie*, forsaken for years in the bleak environment of the plateau. No one actually had teeth like that. And the fissure – Clague shook his head to clear the fuzz – a coincidence, nothing more. With all the volcanic activity they'd had lately; fissures were inevitable.

When he looked again, the woman was still there, her dark hair tinged grey with ash and billowing on the air. She raised her fingernail again, creating another fumarole and calling forth a second burst of steam, which spewed and spat into the ashen air.

This time, Clague wasn't fast enough. The steam touched him, searing his lower leg raw. He screamed. *For the love of God!*

Clague turned to run, and came face to face with a second warrior woman. He stopped in his tracks, his chest heaving. Equally dark, this woman was stunning, with cheekbones like mountain ridges and lashes that swept her cheeks the way pīngao sedges sweep the sand dunes.

He backtracked. One step. Two. The hiss at his back reminding him that way was blocked. Neither of them could be real. They couldn't be! Yet the pain throbbing in his leg was real enough.

"Look, I don't want any trouble, okay? I just came to warn you…" Clague edged sideways, towards the ridge, towards the others, his heart thundering beneath his ribs.

The warrior woman in front raised an elongated index finger, her movement languid and nonchalant, as if she had all the time in the world. Fathomless dark eyes fixed on his and slowly, slowly, she extended the digit in his direction, the way the alien did in that old ET movie poster. Clague had the strangest feeling he wouldn't be going home. He was incapable of moving. How could he have thought the woman beautiful?

When she grinned, her smile was malevolent.

*

Clague didn't descend the mountain as agreed, so Thompson left Keira and Ahmad and climbed the slope to where the volcanologist had been sampling. Clague's gear was there, packed and propped against a rock, but the volcanologist was gone.

"Clague!"

A shout came from over the crest. Suddenly, stones hurtled down the mountain. Thompson flung an arm up to protect himself. It wasn't random debris either. Some of the projectiles flying past were the size of small cannon balls.

What the hell?

Another shout galvanised him. Something was wrong. Thompson scrabbled up the slope, weaving and diving as he ducked tumbling boulders. Just as quickly, the rain of rocks ceased, and the mountain quieted enough for Thompson to hear his own boots crunching on rock and his breath in his ears. "Clague! Where are you? Come on, we're shipping out."

On a waft of ash, there was the faintest mewling. Like a kitten.

"Clague!"

Mewling again. Weaker this time. Where was it coming from? Thompson strained to hear over the wind. Over the pounding in his chest. Had Clague called his name? Thompson dashed up the ridge, vaulting blackened crags, putting his hands down to clamber across a ditch.

"I'm coming."

Through the haze of grey-white ash, he caught sight of Clague's boot up ahead. It was sticking out from behind a boulder, his foot folded back on itself. Shit! A broken ankle. How the hell were they going to get him down the mountain with a broken ankle? The options scrolled in Thompson's head. They were limited. Keira was strong enough, but Ahmad was a runt. Fat chance of the student carrying even half of Clague's weight. If they were to have any hope of getting him out, they'd have to dump the equipment, and even then, they could hardly do it without jostling him, possibly even dropping him. The pain would be excruciating... Thompson rounded the boulder.

He drew in a breath.

Jesus!

Clague lay prone on the rock. At least, what remained of him.

Thompson staggered back a step. Clague's yellow hard hat was melted to his skull. His body was puckered and blistered, scorched to the muscle – to the *bone* in some places. His lower jaw jutted through blackened flesh, bubbles foaming at his ruined mouth. He was still breathing, his torso trembling as he sucked. One eye rolled upwards, showing white, and Clague mewled again. Barely a gurgle, yet Thompson heard it as a scream.

That smell – *like roast pork.*

Thompson emptied his stomach on the ground.

CHAPTER TWO

Rangipō prison, three days later

Karl Pringle put in the call, eventually getting the Civil Defence controller, who wasn't having a good day despite the early hour. "There are no buses," the man railed on the other end of the line. "Every vehicle that isn't a unicycle's been commandeered for the evac, every road out of Taupō in gridlock – State Highway One, Napier-Taupō Road, Earthquake Gully – and there's bottlenecking at bridges crossing the Waikato River. Go south and Tokaanu village is practically empty. Turangi's a ghost town."

"Not all of Turangi," Pringle interrupted. "We still have men here."

"And I've got a rest home to evacuate. The Prime Minister's great aunt lives in that home. You want to be the one to tell her we can't get dear old Auntie Joan out because a bunch of fraudsters and rapists need a ride?"

It was an exaggeration. Despite its tough rep, Tongariro was a low security facility, but Pringle wasn't about to debate the issue. "What are you saying? That we should just bugger off and abandon them?" Like the prison's director. The arse-wipe had fled into town yesterday, promising to come back as soon as he'd checked on his family. That was the last they'd seen of him.

"Hey, I'm not telling you to do anything," the controller said. "But there's a civil emergency in force. Times like these, you gotta make some hard decisions for the greater good. What about the guys on the ambos? You think triage is easy? Playing God: deciding who's going to make it and who isn't?" He lowered his voice. "Look, I'm not going to lie to you: things are bad. Forty minutes ago, a massive sinkhole appeared in the road heading out of Kinloch. Swallowed six cars before anyone had time to tap their brakes. It's a real-life monster truck rally out there. All crunching metal and breaking glass. Women and kids screaming. A couple of our guys are on site, trying to rescue the survivors, and meanwhile the rest of Kinloch are driving on by. Right now, I haven't even got an ambulance to send. I told my guys to give it an hour, two tops, and see what they can salvage. The NZDF are doing a final sweep: maybe one of their choppers will be freed up by then, although the way the ash is, who knows…"

"All I need is a vehicle."

"Yeah, you and everyone else in a hundred and thirty thousand square kilometres. We've got the entire central plateau to evacuate, and the men you're talking about aren't exactly pillars of society, are they? If they'd wanted a seat in first class, maybe they should've bought a ticket... Hey, not that one!"

Pringle held his cell away from his ear while the controller bellowed instructions to someone. Outside, ash fell like the first flurries of snow on the green roofs of the facility.

The controller came back on the line. "...Godspeed to you too, mate... Rangipō, you still there?" he said, referring to the prison's local name.

"Yeah."

"Well, you shouldn't be. You need to haul arse out of there. The way things are going, who knows how much time—"

"*Help* us, then. So you haven't got a bus. What *can* you give me?"

There was a pause. "A mini-van. Unless something better turns up, it's the best I can do."

A mini-van. Pringle stepped to the desk, and, pulling up the manifest on the computer, counted the names. Besides him and Lewis, there were thirty inmates left at the facility. Plus, they'd have to make room for a driver. Even if they ripped the seats out of the van and didn't carry any gear, they'd only be able to evacuate half that number...

"How soon will it be here?" he demanded.

"Just as soon as I can find you a driver," the controller replied.

"When?"

No answer.

Beneath the office, the ground rumbled impatiently. Pringle dropped to crouch beneath the desk. "How long?" he demanded.

A sigh. "I don't know. No one wants to come south."

The controller was still listing excuses when Pringle swiped the phone off.

When the rumbling eased, Pringle came out from under the desk.

Andy Lewis entered the office, the fire doors swinging behind him. "Did you get hold of Civil Defence? When can they get here?"

"No go. We're on our own."

"Fuck." Lewis clapped his hands to his head and blew out hard. "The bastards. What are we supposed to do? We still have men here!"

With six hundred men on site, everything with wheels had been deployed to get them out. All the staff had gone too, including the prison chaplain. Now only Pringle and Lewis were left to get the remaining inmates clear.

Pringle clicked print, then crossed to the printer to collect the manifest. "We'll have to take them out on foot," Pringle said, folding the print-out and stuffing it into his pants pocket. "I reckon our best bet is to head towards Waiouru. It's a 52 km walk." He held up a hand to stall Lewis' protest. "Before you say anything, I know it means walking right underneath the mountains, but at least it isn't backed up with vehicles like the road around the lake. And the Civil Defence guy said the army are doing a final sweep of the area. With a bit of luck one of their trucks will pick us up on its way back to the barracks."

Lewis' face was grim. "I suppose if the mountain goes up, at least we'll see it coming."

"We're *not* going to die. When we get to Waiouru, we'll cadge a ride south."

"What if we can't?"

"Then we keep going on foot." Pringle grabbed a key card and slipped it into his shirt pocket. "You'd be amazed what people can achieve when their lives depend on it." Bring down a submarine. Slay a kraken. He didn't say it, but Pringle had seen men face incredible odds and survive. Yanking open the heavy fire doors, he strode into the corridor.

"Wait," Lewis waved towards the storeroom. "We're going to need supplies: water and food. And first aid gear."

They took a quick detour, stuffing eight small backpacks with gear. Pringle added a couple of torches, before hurrying to the common room. Pringle was about to scan his key card when Lewis swatted away his arm. "Hang on. We should probably grab some guns."

"Guns?" Pringle stared at him.

"There are two of us and thirty of them. What if they don't like the plan?"

The thought had never occurred to him. Rangipō's isolation meant there wasn't much need for force. Offenders all knew the facility was surrounded by forest on one side, farmland on the other, and beyond both of those was the central plateau desert, the army's training grounds. Escape attempts weren't worth the bother. Any runner would be picked up within hours. "I really don't think…"

Lewis had already dumped the backpacks and was racing back down the corridor to the firearm store. "I'm getting them."

Pringle could hardly argue. Lewis was a senior corrections officer. His role was to ensure the containment of the prisoners, whereas Pringle was just an instructor, an IOE; teaching the men a trade so they had a chance of a job, and a future, when they'd served out their time.

Within minutes, Lewis was back, carrying a couple of Bushmaster M4 carbines and rounds. "Okay, open up."

The inmates turned as they entered. There was silence.

A big Samoan named Taliava, stood up. "You going to kill us, then?" he asked, tilting his head in the direction of the guns.

"What?! No, of course not!" Pringle said.

"So, why the guns?"

"Standard procedure in an evac," Lewis lied.

"I don't believe it," said Barnes, the scrawny man dwarfed beside Taliava. He tugged nervously at his hair. "They're going to take us outside and shoot us. No one will miss us, will they? A bunch of crims."

Several men got to their feet. Pringle recognised a few: McCready, Pope, Ants. His stomach churned. On second thought, the guns had been a bad idea.

Thankfully, Taliava turned to face the men, the big Samoan raising his hands in the air, demanding calm. "No one's getting shot. It's like Lewis said, the guns are standard in an evac. They're just doing their jobs."

"Exactly," Lewis said. "If we'd wanted you dead, all we had to do was leave you in your cells. Think of us as the A-Team, here to save your sorry arses." He kicked a couple of backpacks towards the prisoners. "Some of you need to carry these because we're walking out."

"Why? Is the road blocked?" a fellow named Rutledge asked. "How bad can it be? It was just a small quake."

"There are no vehicles left," Lewis said. "Civil Defence couldn't give us a bus. It's okay though, because the army are doing a sweep. All we have to do is get on the road and they'll come along and pick us up."

"What about the bus in the workshop?" Taliava interrupted. "We could take that."

"What bus?" Pringle said.

"One of the farm buses. It was rattling and shit. The tutor said the boys could take it apart in the workshop. Mechanics class was working on it the day before yesterday. Maybe they fixed it and it's already gone; I don't know. Maybe it's still there."

Lewis grinned. "Well, lace up your boots, boys, looks like our odds of getting out of here just doubled."

CHAPTER THREE

New Zealand Defence Force Army Base, Waiouru

Major James Arnold studied the tussocked wasteland of the central plateau. Beyond the bleak rolling plains of tundra, the snow-capped peak of Mount Ruapehu dominated the skyline, magnificent despite the flurries of ash on the window pane. It wasn't the first time Arnold had borrowed the office or stood in this spot, yet never had the situation been so grave.

A knock at the door. "You wanted to speak with me, Major?"

Arnold turned to greet Private Karen Dawson, wishing, once again, that he were a younger man.

"Ah yes, Dawson," he said, gesturing to her to take a seat on the other side of the burnished kauri desk. He waited while she sat down. "I wondered if you'd thought about evacuating?" Arnold hoped he didn't sound patriarchal, or misogynistic or whatever the word was these days. Yes, yes, he knew you weren't supposed to treat women like women anymore; only in Arnold's day you were taught to put women and children first and he wasn't about to unlearn it now.

If Dawson was offended, she hid it well. "I'd prefer to stay at my post." It was a soldier's response. Arnold had expected no less.

Still, he gave it one more go. "There's no guarantee we won't end up buried under a mountain of ash, even here in Waiouru. Civil Defence say the whole area could go up at any time."

"Until then, we need personnel close by. A rescue operation like this one takes a lot of organisation."

She really was a very pretty girl: reminded Arnold of Brenda, back in the happy days before she'd got cancer. Perhaps that was why he had a soft spot for the young private.

She gave him a wide smile, her eyes twinkling with mischief. "And with all due respect, Major Arnold, a couple of my colleagues couldn't organise themselves out of a paper bag."

Arnold almost snorted. It was true there were a few hopeless cases in every organisation, even the NZDF. "You realise if you change your mind, I'm not sure I'll be able to arrange for—"

"That's fine, sir. I appreciate your concern. I'm determined to stay on for as long as I'm needed. I've contacted my parents."

"They're somewhere safe, I hope?"

"In Dunedin, sir. If they're not safe there, nobody is." She got up, the chair scraping on the polished floor. "If that's all, I have Sergeant McKenna waiting for you in the corridor."

"Yes, yes. Send him through."

She left the room, that magnificent rear swaying as if she were a fifties screen siren. Arnold looked away, embarrassed. For crying out loud; he was old enough to be the girl's grandfather!

"McKenna, sir."

Sergeant Taine McKenna entered the room and approached the desk. Arnold took him in. A veteran of Timor-Leste, Afghanistan, and Egypt, at thirty-six years old and two metres tall, the man wouldn't have been out of place in a Netflix action movie: he was all coiled strength, chiselled cheekbones, and skin like polished rimu, the latter inherited from his Māori mother. Grace of a panther and not an ounce of conceit in him. Not an ounce of flab either. Arnold resisted an urge to suck in his stomach as the sergeant came to attention before the desk.

"Major Arnold."

Arnold gestured for McKenna to park his arse where Dawson's delicious rump had been just moments before. "McKenna. At ease. Good to see you, son."

"Boss." McKenna used the SAS nickname for a commanding officer.

"Good to see you've been keeping out of trouble."

The steel blue eyes creased at the corners. "What can I say? Trouble finds me."

Arnold grinned. "Like a guided missile, no less." He crossed the room, checked behind the door for Dawson, then closed it quietly.

He returned to the desk and sat down. "How's Hine's training coming on?"

The Tūrehu woman had joined McKenna's section last year, one of only a few survivors of the legendary ghost people. The remaining members of the tribe were hidden deep in the wilds of southland. With incredible abilities, Hine had the makings of a formidable soldier – a super soldier – but her skills attracted attention, increasing her chances of discovery. And when that happened, certain parties would go to great lengths for her DNA, would pay billions to capture her.

One almost had.

But with the help of the Minister of Conservation, the NZDF had been able to hide her in plain sight within McKenna's section. Information about the tribeswoman was classified, distributed strictly on a need-to-know basis.

"She's already learned our language," McKenna replied, "and she's taken to the training like, well, like a fish to water."

His elbows on the desk, Arnold rested his chin on his hands. "Any trouble keeping it under wraps?"

"Jules Asher and a few others from Conservation know." McKenna's jaw twitched. "And Matt Read. We've told the rest of her section that she has a birth defect and is waiting on a surgery date from the public health system and that's why she wears gloves. People tend to clam up after that. Makes them uncomfortable, I guess."

Yes, Arnold knew all about uncomfortable silences. In the later stages of her illness, Brenda had concealed her baldness beneath a lilac headscarf. That tiny scrap of fabric had been like a beacon, announcing her pending death to all and sundry. Brenda, being Brenda, had accepted it, accepted that *other* people couldn't cope, but Arnold had despised the world for its hushed rooms and averted gazes. It was for Brenda's sake that he'd held back, stopped himself from screaming: "Look at her, look at my beautiful wife!" Yes, he could definitely understand how *other* people's discomfort could work in Hine's favour.

Pushing back his chair, he got up and returned to the window. Breathed deeply. Outside, ash floated in swirls on the wind. Mesmerised, Arnold watched the eddies dance across the plains. Several minutes passed. He was grateful for the silence. Eventually, he turned. "The quakes haven't abated."

McKenna merely waited.

"Seems the government has finally got off its bony arse and called a state of emergency."

McKenna straightened his back. "We're ready to deploy. It's why we're here."

"The idiot suits have left it too late, haven't they? The scientists are saying the super-crater could erupt. And not just a little rumble either. They're talking about an event like the Lake Taupō eruption 1800 years ago," Arnold said, although McKenna had to know it already. Let's face it, it was all over the news.

"What's the brief, Boss?"

"Transport, security, search and rescue. Evacuate any remaining citizens." Two steps had Arnold standing before a topography map pinned to a cork board on the wall. McKenna stood up and joined him. "Your section is to sweep the epicentre of the quake swarm – this region from here to here." Arnold circled the area on his map with his finger. Even on the map, it seemed huge. An impossible task.

A task McKenna would kill himself to carry out.

Already the sergeant had turned on his heel and was making for the door. "I'll alert the men. We'll move out immediately."

Arnold followed him. "Dawson has your orders. And McKenna…tell the men to phone their families."

McKenna nodded.

"Will you take Hine?"

The sergeant stopped, his fingers on the doorknob. "That'll be up to her."

Moments later, he was gone.

Fucking suits, safely tucked away in the capital. Arnold kicked himself for not shaking McKenna's hand.

CHAPTER FOUR

New Zealand Defence Force Army Base, Waiouru

Taine strode into the barracks in a swirl of ash. Three of his men were there, the rest were probably in the mess hall having breakfast. Privates Adrian Eriksen and Eddie 'Lefty' Wright looked up from a game of draughts.

"Boss?"

"We're moving out. 0800 on the parade ground. Tell the others."

Eriksen stood up and made for the door. "Parade ground in fifteen. On it." Taine knew they'd be there; the section had been geared up and ready to deploy since Civil Defence had issued the warning 48 hours ago.

Twisting, he called over his shoulder, "Eriksen, tell the boys to take a minute to call home. The major says things could get ugly."

"Right."

Still seated, Lefty was lacing his boots. "We taking a chopper?"

Taine shook his head. "No choppers. There's too much ash. The army's worried the birds will drop out of the sky. They've given us a Pinzgauer and a couple of old Unimogs."

Taine's new corporal, thirty-year-old Australian ex-pat, Shane Harris, had been reading in his bunk. Standing up, he shoved his feet into his boots, then shuffled to his locker and slipped on his DPM smock. "Evacuation?"

"You guessed it." Taine tossed their orders onto the corporal's bunk, then walked a few paces to his own, where he gathered up his gear. "I got the impression Major Arnold isn't happy. Reckons the CDEM left it too late."

"No fucking kidding." Harris had been with the section for eight months and Taine still hadn't warmed to him. The man hadn't done anything wrong. In fact, his skills were solid, with eight years in the Sydney constabulary before he'd switched codes and retrained. His Kiwi wife had been keen to get back across the ditch and closer to her family. Already, Harris had proven he had a good head on his shoulders and he'd established a good rapport with the rest of the section. The men called him Hairy for the Greek origins which had blessed him with a decent follicle count, on his back as well as his head. Taine wouldn't say he *disliked* Harris. There was nothing not to like. He just wasn't Coolie.

"Normal kit, then?" Harris said, grabbing his helmet out of his locker.

"Yeah, normal kit." Taine picked up the pūrerehua from the locker beside his bunk and unravelled the flax string. It wasn't normal kit, yet there were times when the little bullroarer offered him more strength than the collective firepower of an entire section. Taine never went anywhere without it. He slipped the carved wood over his head, tucking it inside his clothes, close to his chest.

"Not the j-hat," he said to Lefty. "We're going into an earthquake zone. Bring your helmets everyone. Harris, see you outside." Taine quit the barracks.

In the quadrangle, Read was hurrying out of the mess tent, Hine and Eriksen following him.

"Read, we'll take the Pinzgauer," Taine called. "Eriksen, you and Lefty will come with us…"

"What about Hine?" Read asked.

The pale-skinned Tūrehu tribeswoman had already clambered into the back seat of the vehicle and was fumbling with her seat belt, her nu-text gloves slipping on the shiny metal.

"Hine, you shouldn't—" Read said. He took a couple of paces towards her, then broke off and rushed back to Taine. "McKenna, the orders…surely, they can't include her? Tell her she has to stand down. It's too dangerous. There are…" He lowered his voice so only Taine could hear him. "There are few enough of her kind as it is. What if, you know, the big one happens, like everyone's predicting? What if she dies?"

The rest of the section converged on the vehicles in a collective thump of boots and shouts, their MARS-L modular assault rifles slung over their shoulders, helmets hooked at their elbows. Taine called out their orders: "Privates Miller, Parata and Bahr, you'll ride with Corporal Harris in the Unimog." That done, he turned back to Read. "Matt, think about this. Hine's here because she wants to live. She left her family and her tribe because she didn't want to spend the rest of her life cowering in a cave and jumping every time a tramper passed by."

"I know that, but she's—"

"She's got skills we should use. This isn't the 1950s. We both know Hine can look after herself."

"But—"

"Read, she's going. That's the end of it."

"You wouldn't say that if it were Jules," Read said.

"Jules isn't a soldier."

Read snorted.

Taine adjusted his helmet. "Do we have a problem, Read?"

Lifting his chin, Read gave Taine a hard stare. "No sir," he said, and turning, he hoisted himself into the Pinzgauer.

Taine understood Read's concern. And he was dead right. If it were Jules and not Hine in the Pinzgauer, he'd be hauling her out of the truck and putting her on the quickest ride out of here. At least, he'd *want* to. But, like Hine, Jules didn't take orders from anyone. Jules had proved she could hold her own too, even saved Taine's life more than once. Taine made a note to keep an eye on Read; concentrating could be tough when you were worrying about a loved one's safety.

Damn. Now he was thinking about Jules. Arnold had told them to call their families. Maybe he should call her? Even though they hadn't spoken for months, he'd caught news of her from Jug, and snippets from his old friend Temera on the rare occasion he'd seen him.

What did it matter? She'd made it quite clear it was over. What purpose would it serve, phoning her now when he hadn't called her in all this time? Oh, he'd thought about it. He'd thought about it so often that he'd made himself delete her name from his phone. It hadn't helped; he knew the number. Knew it by heart, like the sound of her voice...

Taine shook his head. What was he thinking? She'd be too busy to talk, anyway. Her friend, Sara, lived in Rotorua on the outer fringes of the evacuation zone. As well as having Brocas Aphasia, Sarah had partial paralysis of her legs, so moving her would take time. Ever practical, Jules would've insisted on getting her somewhere safer...

"Lefty's got a hard on for his ex," Eriksen's voice cut in.

Taine roused himself from his daydream.

Lefty had turned a glorious beet colour. "I have not!"

Taine checked his watch. Two minutes. He rounded the Pinzgauer, pulling open the driver's door. Lefty and Eriksen trotted behind him.

"Her name's Lisa, Boss. She's in Tokaanu. I contacted her."

Eriksen snorted. "You contacted her instead of your sister?"

"I already talked to Sheryl! Right after you did. In any case, she and little Ed are miles away; Lisa's right in the middle of the quake zone."

"Why didn't she leave when everyone else did?"

"She thought they could wait it out. Didn't want to go to all the trouble of moving on account of a bit of smoke. She's supposed to be on bedrest. Preggars."

"Oh geezus." Eriksen hooted. He slapped Lefty on the back. "You sly dog. What have you been up to, Lefty? Did you creep in there and do the dirty with your ex? Are you gonna be a daddy?"

McKenna arched an eyebrow. It was rich coming from Eriksen, given that he'd gotten Lefty's sister pregnant a couple of years back.

Normally mates, the pair had fallen out over it, but in the end, the baby – little Ed – had won them both over.

Lefty swatted at his friend. "Just can it for five minutes, will ya, Adrian? I'm serious. I don't know the details, Boss. All I know is, she's still there. Her mother's with her, only the old lady doesn't drive."

"What about her new squeeze? Where's the baby's daddy then, huh?" Eriksen said. "Why doesn't he step up?"

Lefty turned, his fists clenched. "I don't know, do I? I didn't ask. It's none of my effing business. All I know is she's stuck there in the evac zone."

"Okay that's enough, both of you," Taine said, stepping between them. "Eriksen, get in the damned vehicle."

"Right."

Taine put his foot on the tyre and swung himself into the Pinzgauer. He shut the door, leaning out the window to speak to Lefty. "Get Parata to put a call through to Lisa and her mother and tell them someone will come through and pick them up. If not us, then one of the other sections."

"Thanks, Boss." Lefty jogged away to the Unimog and the section's communications officer.

Taine had just started the engine when Jug Singh appeared. "Hey, Boss. I heard you were pulling out. I stopped by to wish you good luck." He passed his hand through the window and Taine shook it.

"You too. Stay safe."

Riding shotgun, Read leaned across the console to speak to the doctor. "You're not coming with us?"

"Sorry, no can do. The medics are spread thin enough as it is. All the panic to get out over the past few days has meant a spate of accidents. Some of them pretty bad. We've set up an emergency hospital for casualties in the tunnels."

Taine caught Eriksen's murmur from the rear, "I hope you've got an obstetrician, 'cause it sounds like you're going to need one."

Jug thumped the side of the vehicle. "Stay safe," he said.

Taine pulled out.

CHAPTER FIVE

Maungapōhatu, Te Urewera Forest

It was morning and Rawiri Temera was in his childhood bed. He lay there a moment. Enjoying the dawn cacophony going on outside, he wiggled his toes under the covers. Milky sunlight stole through the gap between the curtains. It played on the walls, revealing spots where the old wallpaper was peeling away. He breathed deep. The house had been shut up for years, and yet the scent of the forest permeated every corner. Or maybe it was the pine disinfectant Pania had squirted everywhere the weekend she and Wayne had brought him out here. That girl had spent hours and hours scrubbing surfaces and washing the bedding. Said she wasn't leaving until the house was habitable, which meant getting Wayne to haul the kitchen rug outside, hang it on a tree, and beat the living shit out of it. Good thing, too. Temera could've grown potatoes in all the dust. He smiled. She was a good kid, that Pania. His nephew had done well to nab her.

Of course, the pair of them had headed out on Sunday afternoon to go back to work. Neither had been happy about leaving him here. They'd reminded him that the whole point of moving into Rotorua was so they could look after him. Even Temera had questioned his decision more than once. He was eighty-five. No spring chicken, as Wayne put it. And there was no hospital out here, no corner store and the neighbours were twenty minutes away on a goat track.

On the wall, the triangle of sunlight widened and brightened. Temera turned on his side and cradled his head in the pillow.

That was the problem though, wasn't it? They *had* looked after him. Too well. He'd been like a pig in mud, living with the pair of them. There was Pania with her roast chicken dinners, chats in the back shed, and visits to the doctor, and Wayne taking him to the footy or to Bunnings Warehouse when he wanted a bit of timber for a project or some snail bait for the veggie garden. This time of the morning, at their place, Pania would've knocked quietly on his door and brought him in a cup of tea.

Except in town, my gift failed me.

Well, he might have lost his gift, but he could still see well enough to know that if he wanted a cuppa this morning, there was no one here to get it for him. Grunting, he swung his legs over the side of the bed and slid his feet into his slippers. God, it was cold. Taking his dressing gown from the hook on the door, he slipped it on and went into the kitchen to put on the kettle.

When the jug had boiled, Temera took his mug, the teabag still in it, out to the porch. Sitting in the rickety fold-out beach chair, he wrapped his dressing gown around him against the chill. Then, he lit up a cigarette, took a deep drag and leaned back. The cicadas were singing full tit. He loved that buzzy chirping sound. Relaxed him more than any of the rubbish they played on the radio. Although, he didn't mind that Lorde-girl. She'd done well for herself, hadn't she? For a youngster. Temera exhaled slowly, the smoke curling into the porch rafters.

It was good to be home. The mist maiden Hine-Pūkohu-rangi had released the mountain ranges from her soft embrace, revealing the twisted face of the mighty Te Maunga for the first time since his return.

Te Maunga, sacred mountain of the Tūhoe people.

How could I have lived so long without you?

Nearby, a morepork called.

Temera grabbed the windowsill with his free hand and hauled his old bones upright. The little owl hooted again.

Was it his spirit guide?

He leaned forward in the chair, straining to see the bird through the foliage. A flash of grey plumage. Temera held his breath. His heart raced. Please, let it be her... There! The bird bounced from one branch to another. Their eyes met, her big saucers checking him out before she disappeared into the deep green of the canopy. Temera's hope faded. It *was* a morepork, a welcome visitor to the isolated homestead, just not his childhood friend. That little owl had drowned, washed up on the beach, her neck broken. Temera's old eyes pricked. She'd been the victim of a battle with a sea monster. He sent up a karakia-prayer for the bird's spirit to make a safe journey to Cape Reinga, back to her island resting place in Hawaiki.

Temera leaned back in his chair and took another drag on his cigarette.

He missed her.

And he missed his gift.

His ability to see the future had perished with the little bird. She'd been his connection to the spirit world. At night she would come to him, her mournful song reaching into his dreams, and he would wake as a nine-year-old boy to run in the forest with the wind at his back. She had always led the way, flitting gaily through the canopy, waggling her tail feathers. It had been that way since his childhood. Now, his friend, and his gift, were gone, his wairua-spirit had been cast adrift. He was no longer a matakite, a seer. He was just a man. And an old one at that...

On the edge of the yard, a warrior maiden stepped from between the beech trees. Broad nosed and broader shouldered, she was as solid as a tōtara trunk, yet she moved like lava, smoothly closing the ground between them. "Remember me?" she said.

Temera lifted his chin. "You're Te Pūpū, sister of the chief Ngātoro-i-rangi, and a daughter of Hawaiki."

She tilted her head and smiled coyly. "And what else?"

"You're a fire—" About to say demon, Temera stopped himself in time. "—goddess," he said quickly.

Her laughter crackled like the spit of burning wood. "Well said, seer, well said."

She stepped onto the porch and circled the fold-out chair, her finger on the back rest and her body so close to Temera that a strand of her hair brushed his wrist. His skin tingled where it touched. When she leaned her torso towards him, he felt her heat against the morning chill. "You've gotten old," she whispered with breath of smoke.

He trembled. "Yes." His voice was strangled.

Abruptly, she stepped away. Her back to him, she looked up, searching the porch rafters. "Where's your little bird-friend? She's usually nearby. Did I frighten her off?"

Temera winced. "She's not here."

The demon nodded as if she'd been expecting the answer.

"So, you've lost your guide, then? We could help you…"

Something stirred in Temera, something ancient and primal. He pushed it back.

They're offering to help me.

The idea filled Temera with dread. He gripped the plastic armrests.

"Why are you frightened?" the demon asked. She gestured to the trees where a second warrior woman hovered in the shadows. "My sister, Te Hoata and me, we helped you once. Do you remember?"

Temera nodded. "I remember. You warned me about the geyser that was about to explode in my brother's yard, under his boy's sandpit."

"That's right. We didn't have to tell you, but we did."

"It was a long time ago."

"Not so long."

What did they want? Had they come to demand payment for the favour?

"Ask him how the boy is," the sister-demon shrilled from the trees. Temera could not see her clearly; darkness obscuring her face.

"He's fine," Temera said. "All grown up. A good man."

"Hmmm." Te Pūpū touched the pillar holding up the porch roof and let the digit linger. A wisp of smoke spooled into the air. She giggled and lifted her finger, the wood scorched black.

Temera couldn't bear it any longer. "Why are you here?" he blurted.

In two fluid steps, Te Pūpū crossed the porch. She curled a pointed nail under his chin as if he were a child. "We can't come and visit an old friend?" she hissed.

She pushed her face close to his.

Her smile burned like ice…

Temera woke, his heart thundering. He was still on the porch, his mug of tea stone cold beside him. He drew in a breath, then breathed out long between pursed lips, his chest slumping. It was nothing. He'd nodded off and had a bad dream, that's all. No need to wet his pants over it. It must've been a deep sleep, though; he still had the cigarette clutched between his fingers, burned to an elongated tube of ash. Lucky for him, the embers hadn't dropped onto the lawn, not with the grass so high. He sighed. Well, that was today sorted. He'd have some breakfast, then drag the hand mower out of the shed and see what he could do about taming the grass.

Temera didn't move.

Instead, he stared at the pillar, and the blackened mark where the fire demon had scorched the wood.

Desert Road, Central Plateau

At the roadblock, Jules pulled to the side of the road. Her engine idling, she pressed the button to lower her window and waited for the Civil Defence worker to approach the Toyota.

The man rested an orange sleeved forearm against the window frame, lowered his sunglasses, and leaned in. "I don't know if you've noticed, sweetheart," he drawled, "but you're going the wrong way."

Jules had noticed. She'd have to have been an idiot not to. Since leaving Waiouru, apart from the occasional army vehicle, she'd had the northbound lane to herself. Meanwhile, the other side of the road had been bumper-to-bumper with cars, local earthquake evacuees all heading south, away from Lake Taupō and the mountains.

"I'm on my way to—"

Chugging sounded behind her.

The Civil Defence worker glanced up. "Hang on a sec, love." Putting his sunnies back on, he stepped away from the Toyota.

Jules checked her rear-view mirror. An army Unimog. So, the government had brought in the big guns to round up the stragglers. They must think it's serious.

Maybe her coming here was a mistake. The whole trip was a long shot, prompted by a hiker's photograph posted online a week ago, the image showing a specimen which resembled the Chesterfield skink. About the size of the hiker's hand, the skink in the photo had been speckled with rust-brown lateral markings. It could be nothing, of course. Most likely she was mistaking it for one of the other fifty-odd cryptid varieties, but if the photo was evidence of the critically-endangered Chesterfield skink, a treasured taonga, then it was a huge find. Jules had to follow it up. Her colleagues hadn't agreed:

"Let you go in there now? No way. I'm not signing any authorisation."

"Look, Jules I get it: the little skink's on its last legs, but if I sign this, I could be signing your death certificate. Sorry."

Desperate, she'd phoned her former boss, Richard Foster of Landcare. Richard hadn't even bothered to reason with her; he'd just hung up.

In the end, she'd taken her case to the top, to the Minister, explaining how, up until now, the shy little creature had only ever been seen on the beaches on the west coast where it had developed in isolation, cut off since the ice age.

"You got all this from a photograph, you say?" the Minister said, the capital's town belt providing a lush green backdrop through the window behind her.

"Yes, ma'am."

Standing up, the minister had steepled her hands on the desk and leaned towards Jules. "Bloody hell, Asher, you do know what you're asking? I've come straight from an emergency meeting of the house. They're saying the whole plateau is a ticking time bomb. The government is doing everything it can to get people out, not send more in."

"Yes, I realise that, ma'am."

"You realise that." Shaking her head, the Minister stepped out from behind the desk and paced the outer curve of her Beehive office, her Merino skirt brushing against her boots. "How on earth did the skink land itself there in the middle of the country? There are nearly one thousand kilometres between these two sites, not to mention the Cook Strait."

"Five million years ago, there might still have been a landbridge."

The Minister snorted. "What exactly are the odds of finding a second population so far away?"

"I admit, it'd be a miracle. But the latest survey suggests there are only thirty-four left anywhere in the world. Thirty-four, ma'am. Once they're gone, there is no going back. So, if there's the slightest chance of recovering a second population..." Jules trailed off. She nibbled her lip.

"And if this picture is just some everyday skink?"

Jules said nothing.

The Minister sat heavily in her chair. Folded her arms. "How many of you idiots intend to go?"

"Just one idiot, ma'am. You said it yourself: the area is a ticking time bomb. We shouldn't risk any more lives. All I need is an hour on the ground."

The Minister sighed. It wasn't the first time Jules had come begging a favour.

"Thirty-four live examples," Jules said softly. "The species is all but extinct. The Chesterfield skink is our version of the white rhino – a single adult could make a difference, the second chance the species needs to survive."

"All right, all right." The Minister scribbled her autograph on the page. "You can go. But be careful," she said, and folding the document in half, she handed it to Jules as if it were a prescription. "Let me know how you get on."

Jules tapped her fingers on the steering wheel. So far, she was getting nowhere fast, the Civil Defence man taking his sweet time. When the Unimog had rumbled past, and the roadblock reinstated, he ambled back to Jules.

"I have to—" Jules said.

"I'll tell you what you have to do, love," the man interrupted. "You'll have to turn around and go back the way you came. There's nothing for you in there. Everyone's leaving." He thumped his palm on the roof of the vehicle, signalling the end of the conversation.

"I have an authorisation from the Conservation Minister." Jules passed the letter through the window.

"Authorisation, huh?" The man lifted his sunglasses, then unfolded the letter. He pursed his lips. "Says here you're going to Lake Rotopounamu?"

"It's a tiny lake south of Turangi and west of Rangipō prison."

"But that's right under the bloody mountains!"

"It's important. There's been a sighting of a Chesterfield skink—"

The man sucked air over his teeth. "You're kidding me, right? You're going to risk your life for a skink? One of those little lizard-thingies…"

Jules had heard all the arguments. "I really need to get through, please. Every minute I sit here is a minute wasted. As you can see, the Minister authorised my travel so if you could please move the roadblock…"

"All right, all right. Keep your pants on." Passing the paper back to her, he gestured to his colleague to move the vehicle blocking the northbound lane.

Then he turned back to Jules. "Look lady, whether you find your little beastie or not, make it quick. Get in and get out, that's my advice. If you get into trouble, look for the army boys." He shook his head. "Failing that, you're on your own."

"I understand." Jules didn't thank him when he waved her through.

She raised the window and carried on.

CHAPTER SIX

Central Plateau, heading north from Rangipō

When they finally got the bus running, it sounded like a dying bull. Lewis left it idling as the prisoners filed on.

"Doesn't sound like the mechanic boys fixed it," Pringle said, drily.

"It'll have to do." Lewis pulled a man out of the line. "Moses, you're driving." Nodding, the man climbed into the driver's seat.

Pringle sat up the front, facing the aisle. Lewis stood at the rear, his hip against a seat back, the rifle resting on his thigh. "Let's go," he shouted.

The bus stalled twice before they even left the prison grounds. The second time, Moses flooded the engine trying to restart it and they had to wait ten minutes to have another go. It felt like hours. Ash swirled at the grubby windows and the men fidgeted and whispered in their seats. The ground rumbled beneath them. Pringle gripped the barrel of his rifle and clamped his mouth shut. Nothing he could say would get them out of here any faster.

Finally, Moses coaxed the engine into a rumble and they moved off, leaving the prison compound and taking a left onto the highway. The sky ahead was cloudy with ash. No doubt the ground was still rolling and jolting beneath them, but the way the bus was rattling, who could tell? It was a small mercy. Everyone was on edge as it was.

They made slow time through the hairpins until they reached the straighter roads of the plateau. Moses opened the throttle. So far, the road was empty, the promised army absent. Pringle prayed the bus would hold together.

The mountains loomed to their right. Everyone looked through the dusty windows. You couldn't help it. In front was Ruapehu flanked with its mantle of pink and grey, its white caps thrust into a murky sky. From the road, with the soft focus of the ash, you could almost believe those slopes were gentle. Alongside Ruapehu stood Ngāuruhoe, with its too-perfect cone, and then Tongariro, the sprawling granddaddy volcano with its tendency to flare up over the slightest little thing. Somewhere in between them, like a peahen amongst the peacocks was Pīhanga, the she-mountain who supposedly set all the others afire in an age-old winner-takes-all booty story. All of them perched on the rim of an enormous caldera, Lake Taupō. All of them being shaken by this ongoing earthquake swarm. Who knew what was going on beneath the earth's crust? Usually, when Pringle drove through here, the mountains uplifted and inspired him. Today, his teeth ached.

Suddenly, Moses slammed on the brakes. The bus lurched forward, then stopped dead in the middle of the road. The men groaned.

"What the fuck, Moses!" Lewis screamed from the back. "Get this bus moving!"

"Sorry! I couldn't help it. There's a bloody big crack in the road!"

Standing up, Pringle took a gander, his forehead pressed to the window. It wasn't a massive crack, not like gouges that had sliced up the road into Kaikoura in 2016. Still, it was the perfect width to wedge a bus tyre and send them all flying. Moses had done well to stop when he did. Only, it was a really bad place to stop. They were right under the mountains. Sitting ducks.

A few seats back, by the window, Taliava piped up. "There's a gap over here." He pointed out his side of the bus.

Pringle craned his neck to look over the big Samoan's shoulder. There was a narrow strip of gravel between the end of the crack and the bank.

Moses got up and had a look. "I dunno," he said.

"We're not going back now," Lewis said.

"Well, don't go blaming me if we get stuck," Moses said, swinging himself back into the driver's seat. It took some manoeuvring, Moses cursing the whole time, but eventually Moses squeezed them around the crack and back on the road. The men cheered.

They were picking up speed, when Pringle took his seat at the front again. He puffed the air out of his cheeks.

Thank God.

He checked his watch. Getting around the crevasse had taken an extra fifteen minutes. On the plus side, they still had a ride and the mountains hadn't blown. Looked like they'd been granted a reprieve.

The bus jolted. Metal screeched. A hiss. Someone shrieked. Pringle grabbed at air. Tumbled. A blur passing his face. His head hit something. Everything exploded in pain.

*

When he came to, Pringle was lying on his back in the tussock. Too winded to move, he counted his limbs. All there, although his arms were outstretched as if he was being prepared for a ritual sacrifice. His head throbbed, and his chest felt like the bus had run over him. Maybe it had. Still, he counted his blessings: he was sore, but he was alive.

He was about to raise his head, when the air shattered with the sound of gunfire.

Fucking hell!

His head screaming, Pringle flipped onto his belly and scrambled for cover behind a couple of low boulders.

He peered out.

The bus lay on its side in a twisted wreck, a streak of metal smearing fifty metres back along the road. Somehow, he must have been thrown free through the front door, or maybe through the windscreen, when the bus spun out of control.

He wasn't the only one to be ejected; those others hadn't been so lucky. A couple of people lay on the ground. Motionless.

A posse of men came around the back of the bus. Pringle counted twenty of them, Barnes and Taliava in front, carrying the rifles. Pope was among them. Ants Chizmar.

Shit.

"All I'm saying is, there was no need to kill Lewis," Taliava said.

Jesus! They shot Lewis?

Pringle sucked a breath.

"We were already on our way out of here," Taliava said. "Now, we're stuck in the middle of nowhere with no vehicle and a dead guard."

Pringle hunkered down. A lone guard without a gun against twenty desperate men? He didn't have a death wish. Instead, he hugged the earth as Barnes turned on Taliava, got his face right in the Samoan's, forgetting that Taliava had a rifle too, forgetting that he was a bantam weight and Taliava could probably put down Dwayne Johnson if he had half a mind. "I felt like it, that's why," he snarled. "You going to argue?"

Barnes? The guy was scared of his own shadow.

Apparently not.

The big man backtracked. "Nah, nah, chill man. I'm not arguing."

"Look, nobody gives a shit about Lewis," McCready interjected, taking the heat off Taliava. "He was a pig. But nobody told you to shoot him, either. No way I'm taking the rap for that."

The rifle roared. Pringle stifled a yelp as McCready crumpled. Shot point blank, his head almost separated from his neck.

"Like I said, anyone going to argue?" Barnes sneered.

The other men shuffled backwards.

Taliava stood his ground. "Hey, come on, Barnesy," he said. "No need for that. No one's objecting. We're all just trying to stay alive here."

"Well, that proves how effing short-sighted you are," Barnes said quietly. "We've got a chance here to do more than just stay alive. You did see how they abandoned us, right? Left us sitting in that prison to die."

"Lewis and Pringle didn't leave us—" Ants said.

Pringle wanted to scream at him: *Don't challenge Barnes, for heaven's sake. Can't you see the man's a simmering psychopath?*

Barnes dug the barrel of the rifle into Ants' chest. "You. Shut the fuck up."

Ants backed away, his palms up, the sheen of sweat on his forehead visible in the murk. "Hey, I wasn't saying..."

"Barnes, think about this," Taliava said, clearly trying to calm the waters. "It's not the end of the world. We can still go on to Waiouru. We'll tell the authorities that Lewis' gun went off in the crash. They'll believe it. Especially if we all—"

"Shut up. You're not getting it. Why should we tell the authorities anything? The government, society, every-fucking-one of them left us out here in the middle of a shit storm. Right now, they're so busy playing hero and saving the *civilised* folk, they couldn't care less if we live or die. What are we, anyway? A bunch of useless crims. We could fall off the face of the earth and no one would give a piss."

"So, what are you saying?" Taliava said.

"I'm saying this is the perfect opportunity to make a run for it while no one's paying us any attention."

"Make a run for it?" Pope said. "When they're saying the whole place could go up like freaking Vesuvius."

Barnes snorted. "They've moved people before. Always comes to nothing. Anyway, it'll give you fuckers an incentive to walk faster, won't it?"

Taliava rubbed his throat. "Where exactly are we going to go?"

"Everyone's evacuated, right? The place is empty. We walk back into Turangi, or Tokaanu, one of those little towns, and we find ourselves some clothes and some wheels..."

"Passports," Ants said.

"And some passports. That's right, some passports. And then we go—"

"We'll need money."

"We'll get some money. When they evacuated, they didn't take the ATMs with them, did they?"

There was some laughter, but it felt canned. They weren't all buying it.

"I don't know, mate," a man named Perenia said quietly. "I'm fine with you doing that, for sure, but I've only got two months to go before I'm released. I'd rather not risk another sentence."

Barnes nodded. "Yeah, that's fair enough. Anyone else in that boat?" Two men raised their hands. "Well, it's a free world. If you guys can keep your traps shut, I don't see why you can't carry on to Waiouru."

Pringle's spine tingled. What was he playing at?

"Let's just run through it, shall we?" said Barnes. "What happened here?"

The three men looked at one another, then one said, "Something happened, and the bus rolled. I heard a gun go off, and when the smoke cleared we found Lewis with a bloody great hole in him."

Barnes laid the barrel of the gun on Perenia's shoulder. "You?"

Perenia shifted his feet. "Yeah. Absolutely. That's what I saw, too."

"Musta gone off accidentally," the third man said quickly.

"And what happened to the rest of us?"

"You decided to head towards Taupō," Perenia blurted. "You reckoned there was a better chance of getting picked up that way. The three of us didn't agree, and that's why we split up."

"Good man. Okay, you guys can bugger off. But if I hear some other story circulating, I'll come looking for you. Got that, Perenia?"

"Yeah. Sure thing. You can count on us, Barnesy."

"Well, then." Barnes flicked his head towards Waiouru. "Get the fuck out of here."

They set off down the road, each of them looking over their shoulders warily.

"Get the backpacks out of the bus," Barnes said to Ants, his eyes fixed on Perenia and his mates.

They'd almost dropped out of sight in a dip in the road when Barnes lifted the firearm and squeezed the trigger. Pringle hadn't known he was so proficient. Four shots and three men lay like piles of laundry on the road.

Ants climbed out of the bus and dropped the backpacks at Barnes' feet. Barnes bent and picked one up, slinging it over his shoulder. "Right, now that the loose ends are tied up, we can get out of here," he announced.

"Wait! What about Pringle? He isn't in the bus," Taliava said.

Pringle felt his balls shrink. He pressed his head to the ground. Held his breath.

"I saw him fly out the window in the crash," Ants said. "I reckon he's under the bus. He'll be ground flatter than a chapati."

Barnes' laugh echoed across the plain. "I always hated foreign food," he said.

*

When they'd moved off, Pringle waited for another quake to pass, then crouch-ran across the road. Keeping out of sight in case one of Barnes' lot decided to look back, he circled the vehicle's ruined carcass, checking the bodies, feeling for their pulses in case any of them were still alive.

This one was dead.

Dead.

Dead.

Nothing.

Please, no. Lewis wasn't just dead. Barnes had blown his genitals off, the guard's beige cargo pants soaked at the crotch in blood and gristle. His eyes were open. Glassy. It was his hands that made Pringle shudder. They were covered in blood where Lewis had tried to staunch the bleeding.

Pringle leaned his back against the bus and struggled to get his breathing under control. All this time, he'd believed Barnes was a nervous-nelly. A man who hid sidled up to the biggest man in the prison for protection. Scared to squeak in case he offended someone dangerous. Not the kind of man who could blow away a guard's genitals and let him lie there while his lifeblood seeped into the tarmac. Clearly, Barnes wasn't what he seemed. Had the other prisoners known? Probably, but there was a code, wasn't there?

Pringle stared out across the haze to where Barnes and his men were just visible. Thank God they hadn't found him.

Time to check inside the bus.

Pulling his sleeves down and wrapping his hands in the fabric, he climbed in through the shattered windscreen. Lying on its side, the interior was a mess of blood and glass. Moses was crushed in the driver's cab, sandwiched when the seats behind had concertinaed in the crash. Pringle clambered over the mangled benches. All up, he counted four bodies and a severed leg. Ants was right, a couple of the men could well be under the bus. Slipping his hands free of his shirt cuffs, Pringle pulled the manifest out of his pants pocket and marked off the names of the dead men.

He was tucking the list back in his pocket when he spied the smear of blood on the glass above him. Finger-marks. They almost looked innocent, like a painting a child would bring home from kindergarten. Those marks meant someone was alive. Whoever they were, they'd swung open the emergency hatch and crawled out. Pringle braced his feet on the upended seat and hauled himself through the gap, wincing as he bumped and chafed places he hadn't known were hurting. He crabbed the last bit, his feet swinging wildly until he was on the roof. Avoiding the window panes in case they'd been loosened in the crash, he lay on the top and scanned the plain again. In the distance, the view was blurred with ash. He couldn't see Barnes and his men. He stood up slowly. Still no sign of Barnes.

But up here there were other things to look at. He let his eyes follow the blood smear, the scuffs in the dirt and the crumpled tussock grass, eventually locating the missing casualty. He was about twenty metres away, tucked in a hollow and hidden by a clump of alpine heather. Up here, Pringle could see – any lower and he might have missed it.

He recognised the man's slight frame. Man. He was little more than a boy. Paul Brooker. Twenty, twenty-one tops. Quite bright: he'd taken a liking to carpentry and shown quite an aptitude. Pringle couldn't remember what he was in for, but his future was promising – provided he was able to keep his nose clean.

Mind you, Pringle had been wrong about Barnes.

Hunkering down to slip front-first off the bus, Pringle dropped to the ground and crept forward through the scrub.

"Who's there?" The voice was full of panic.

Pringle squinted through the clump of heather.

On the other side, Brooker was sitting up, his back propped against a small rise. His face was streaked with tears. "I know you're there!"

"It's okay, Paul," Pringle said standing up and stepping over the heather to join him in the dip. "It's me, Pringle."

"Fuck. I thought you were dead," Brooker said, his shoulders slumping in relief.

"I got thrown from the bus in the crash."

Brooker nodded. "I climbed out through the roof. Barnes shot Lewis." Brooker's eyes welled. Pringle looked away while Brooker got himself under control. He could hardly blame the boy. He'd come close to having a panic attack himself when he'd seen the body.

"It's okay, I know."

"I saw him do it. He stuck the gun right in his nuts and squeezed the trigger. And he laughed. I was so scared I nearly fell off the bus. I waited until they went around the other way, then I slid off the side and hid."

"You did the right thing. If you hadn't, you might be dead now."

"What are we going to do?"

"We're going to do exactly what we were doing before the crash. Move away from the epicentre. Only now, there'll just be you and me and no comfy bus."

"I can't. I can't go anywhere!" Brooker said, his face white. "I twisted my leg when I was getting down from the bus. I think I heard it crack, and now it hurts like buggery."

"Let's have a look."

Brooker pulled up the leg of his overalls. There was no obvious swelling, but that didn't mean there wasn't a fracture. Maybe more than one.

Brooker sucked the air in between his teeth. "Fucking oath!"

"Sorry."

"Is it broken?"

"It could be, or it might be a bad strain."

Brooker craned his neck back and closed his eyes. "I'm fucked, aren't I?"

"No, you're not. We're going to sort this. I need a few minutes to think, that's all. Wait right here. Don't go away," he said.

Brooker laughed nervously.

Pringle went back to the bus. He climbed in through the windscreen, clambering over the seats again, searching for something he could use. Underneath the bus' back bench seat was the broom. Pringle tossed it out through the emergency exit. It bumped as it hit the roadside. He kept looking. Barnes had taken all the backpacks, so there was no food or water. There'd be water in the bus engine, but it'd be full of antifreeze. Even if it wasn't, he couldn't carry a container and support Brooker too.

He whooped out loud when he found the first aid kit at the back of an overhead luggage tray. Admittedly, it was pathetic: one of those plastic lunch box jobs where the scissors are always missing, but thankfully there were still a few dressings inside. There was even a foil strip of Aspirin. Only four left. Hey, beggars couldn't be choosers. On the way out, he grabbed Jones' jacket from beside him on the bench, thanking the dead man quietly as he tied it around his waist.

Even with the swirling ash, Pringle could see the relief in Brooker's face as he crossed the tussock the second time. He must've thought he'd desert him.

"I found this." Pringle held up the first aid kit.

"Bloody awesome."

While Brooker punched out two of the white discs and ate them without water, Pringle leaned the broom against a rock and stamped on it, breaking the handle in two. He splinted Brooker's leg with batons on either side, securing them with bandages from the kit. When he'd finished, Brooker's forehead was shiny with sweat.

"You okay?"

"Aspirin'll kick in in a minute."

"Let me help you up."

Brooker hooked an arm around Pringle's neck. They probably looked like a couple of boys' college students practising for the school dance. With some awkward manoeuvring, they got Brooker to his feet.

"Can you put your weight on it?"

Brooker put his foot down gingerly and took a couple of steps. He bit his lip. "It's painful, but it's okay." He pushed away from Pringle and limped a couple of steps towards the road, his arms stretched wide like a trapeze artist to stop himself from falling.

Narrowing his eyes against the ash, Pringle looked up the highway towards Waiouru, the empty road and drifting ash like a scene from a Christmas card. There was no way Brooker was going to be able to walk forty kilometres on that leg. They had no food, no water and as far as Pringle could tell, no chance of being picked up.

Brooker turned, his face anxious. "Pringle? You coming?"

Pringle shook his head. "Paul, let's go this way," he announced, flicking his head back towards the mountains. "We'll find a farm. There'll be a tractor. A first aid kit. Maybe a landline."

"What about the earthquakes?"

"If our time's up, it's not going to make much difference if we're here or ten kilometres away, is it?"

"I guess not." Brooker turned and hobbled back. It was painful to watch. Pringle regretted making him suffer even those few extra steps.

"Pringle?"

"Yeah?"

"What about Barnes?" Brooker whispered.

"Same as the earthquake," Pringle said grimly. "We'll have to take our chances."

CHAPTER SEVEN

Lake Rotoaira, Central Plateau

Barnes smiled at the cheap wooden signs on either side of the road. The words, Lake Rotoaira, were scrawled on both signs in peeling blue paint. They were bolder than the township deserved, given how pathetic the place looked. At least it wasn't another 1960s turquoise weatherboard on a scrubby back country farm. How many shithole farms had they checked so far? Four? Five? All of them lonely places with rutted gravel driveways running through uneven paddocks where sagging fences failed to hold back the advancing bush.

The whole area was deader than jail visiting hours on a long weekend. Everyone had cleared off. They hadn't left as much as a skate board, let alone transport for twenty men. Which made this little town with its tired blue tourist signs their best hope yet. There had to be around thirty houses here, and a better chance of finding a vehicle.

Maybe more than one.

"Pope, take a couple of guys and do a circuit of the town; see what you can find."

"Sure, Barnesy."

A group of five men peeled away after Pope, heading for the dirt tracks that flanked the township.

"Pete, you and Climo wait here. Keep an eye out."

The two men slipped into the bushes at the side of the road.

Barnes and the others strolled into town. Other than the crunch of their boots on the gravel, it was eerily quiet. Ash drifted about them like the first snowfall of the season. Barnes led them down the middle of the road, not bothering to keep to the shoulder. What was the point? They hadn't seen a fucking car since they'd left the bus.

At the lake end, the road opened onto a small camping ground where a dozen caravans sat in the long grass, their slumbering frames fanned about a concrete toilet block. On one end of the toilet block, the word WAHINE was written alongside a stick figure with a triangle skirt. A couple of the men ducked through the door marked TANE at the other end.

Covered in lichen, a rickety jetty extended into the lake. There was a mooring post, but no sign of a boat.

"Looks like everyone's buggered off," Taliava said.

"No kidding, Sherlock," Ants replied.

"No Sherlocks either," Barnes said. It was the perfect getaway, seeing as the cops had cleared out, too.

Not quite perfect.

He frowned as a Beagle Boys cartoon popped into his head, three masked escapees, each with heavy jowls and serious five o'clock shadows, all of them dragging a ball and chain. Barnes' chain had twenty balls on it. It was fine for now, but at some point he'd have to cut the others loose. There was no other choice. Did they really think twenty crims could skip the country together? Just rounding up that many passports – with photos which would pass muster – was fantasy enough. They'd have to hack into the airlines for the flights. And then there was face recognition software to get past. A single individual stopping at a customs officer might make it through, because humans made mistakes, didn't they? Especially at the end of a shift. Whereas machines didn't get tired and they didn't make mistakes.

A small building near the lakefront looked to be the local grocery store if the faded Coke poster and Rachel Hunter ice cream ad were anything to go by. The door had been padlocked shut. Barnes kicked at it. The padlock rattled. "Find something to open that up," he said.

"On it," Ants replied. He took off to the lake, coming back with a couple of rocks, which he and Rutledge used to attack the padlock, going at it one after the other. Thump, thump, thump. It was enough to give a man an effing headache.

Suddenly, the ground rumbled and shook.

Barnes' stomach lurched. He drew in his breath as Taliava grabbed him by the forearm, the big man steadying him with his weight.

Barnes grinned. Whatever happened, Barnes could count on Taliava to protect him. The Samoan would pluck him from the fires of hell if need be. Throughout their incarceration at Rangipō, Taliava had made himself extremely useful and no doubt he'd continue to be useful, so long as Barnes had eyes on Taliava's wife and daughter. In fact, it'd be in Taliava's interests to make sure Barnes got to a phone sometime in the next three days.

The shaking eased. Taliava let go of Barnes.

Rutledge and Ants resumed their ridiculous drumming. They weren't making much headway with the lock. Already, the door was a fucking mess of dents and scrapes.

Taliava sighed. "Here, let me." Elbowing Ants and Rutledge out of the way, he put his shoulder to the door and heaved, splintering the wood, and breaking the padlock off at the hinge. When he stood back, the metal lock swung gently on its hook like a Christmas bauble.

"Let's see what we've got, shall we?" Ants pulled the door open.

Inside, rough-cut wooden planks lined the walls, the shelves covered with tins of tomatoes and beetroot and things in packets – chili mix and cup-a-soups mostly. There was a fridge in the corner. It had been turned off, so the drinks were warm.

Ants snatched up a bag of chips, ripping the metallic package open and cramming his hand in. "Thank God. I'm starving." He stuffed a handful into his mouth.

Leaning his gun against the wall, Barnes checked behind the counter and found the stack of cigarette packets alongside some roll-your-own kit and a box of cheap Bic lighters. Slipping a packet into each of his back pockets, he opened a third, took out a cigarette and lit up.

The other men, seeing the booty, started to crowd in.

Barnes shook his head. "What the fuck is this?" He stepped forward and blocked the doorway. Exhaled a long plume of grey smoke in their faces. "Some of you go check the caravans. Look for passports, money. Jesus, how are you gonna make it out of here if I have to fucking tell you everything?"

A couple of them hung around, but a bunch did as they were told and slouched off towards the caravans.

Barnes grinned. Mentioning the passports had been a nice touch. Of course, he wasn't stupid enough to think everyone would be buying that story. The ones who didn't like it – the smart ones – knew to shut the hell up and go along with his plan. They'd all seen he wasn't shy about using a gun. Well, it suited him, too. For now.

"Barnes!" A shout pierced the quiet.

Barnes turned as Pope and two others emerged from between a couple of run-down baches. Hang on. There had been five men with Pope. What had happened to the others? Barnes felt his pulse lift. Would Pope be the one to challenge his leadership?

He kept his voice even. "Where are the others?"

Pope waved an arm, pointing back in the direction he'd come. "We left them back a ways. We found an old tractor parked up in a boat shed."

"Awesome." Ants spoke through a mouthful of chips.

"Any boats?" Taliava asked.

"Nah. A boat wouldn't do us any good anyway," Pope said. "Lake Rotoaira doesn't go anywhere. It's just a big puddle."

His pulse quietening, Barnes took another suck of the cigarette. "And how do you know that?"

"Went looking for the tractor keys in the nearest house. There's a map of the plateau on the wall. Turns out Lake Rotoaira is smaller than my thumb. Like someone spat in a carpark."

"We'll take the tractor, then," Ants replied. "We can use it to pull a caravan or a trailer. Load some of us in the back."

Pope grimaced. "Yeah about that. The problem is, it won't start. Smithy and Knife are taking a look at it now."

Barnes narrowed his eyes. What was to stop Smithy and Knife cranking up the tractor and pissing off out of here? If that tractor was leaving town, Barnes planned to be on it. "Taliava, go check on them," he said.

"They're about a hundred metres along. Shed's next to a red house," Pope said.

Taliava hitched the rifle on his shoulder and ran off along the track.

Pope strutted forward and cupped his hand to his mouth, as if he was about to give away a bit of gossip. "I haven't told you the best bit, Barnes. We didn't just find a tractor. We also found this!" From a canvas bag at his hip, Pope lifted a bottle of whisky, three-quarters full of golden liquid. "The house we went in has a bar!" he announced.

"No shit," Ants said, flinging the empty chip packet on the ground and wiping his hands on the back of his pants.

"True. Takes up half the living room. Bloody thing's full of grog."

"Is that so?" Barnes dropped his cigarette, twisting it into the ground with his boot. "Well, we have a little time while Smithy and Knife check out the tractor; maybe we should investigate. Which way?"

Pope pretended to take off an imaginary hat, sweeping it low to the ground. "This way, sir."

"Grab some food first," Barnes said.

The remaining men collected as much packaged food from the store as they could, stuffing it in cheap plastic grocery bags before following Pope to the miracle house.

"It's this one here," Pope said.

It was the biggest property around, possibly the original 1930s farmhouse from the looks of it, a veranda running the length of the building on the lake side, with a couple of modernish extensions added at the back, and not by a master builder. Inside, it smelled of old furniture and cheese. Surrounded by green-gold loop carpet, the bar did take up half the living room.

Ants lined up a row of shot glasses and filled them with vodka. He'd barely finished pouring the last one, when the first shot glasses were banged down on the bar, the men demanding more. Pope threw himself into a faded orange sofa, glugging from the whisky bottle in his hand.

Let 'em drink. Just as long as it keeps them happy and pliable.

Leaving them to it, Barnes turned to the map. He checked the date. 1990. Pretty old. Still, it was better than nothing, and the area was mostly National Park so maybe not too much had changed. He yanked it off the picture hook, prised open the clips behind the cardboard backing, and pulled the map out of the frame. He was folding it up, when there was a noise from outside.

Someone arriving. Smithy and Knife? Had they got the tractor running?

Leaving the men at the bar, Barnes snatched up his rifle and stepped out onto the veranda. A woman's voice carried across the hamlet. Barnes peered down the track as the group who'd been searching the caravans headed his way, pushing a young couple ahead of them.

So what have we here, then?

"We found these two hiding under the squabs in one of the caravans," one of the men, a fellow named Grant, said.

"They've got passports," said the man next to him. The guy had a monobrow like that muppet. Monobrow opened the red booklet. "This one here is Brigitte Calmet, and the bloke is Alain de la Fontaine. Posh names. Says here they're French."

"Yes, yes, we are French," Alain interrupted. "We visit New Zealand on a WWOOF exchange."

"What's that then?" Barnes asked.

"WWOOF. It is a programme where workers volunteer on local farms in exchange for food and lodgings."

"Yeah?" Barnes said.

Monobrow raised his eyebrow. "Barking fucking mad."

Ants giggled.

Barnes took another cigarette from the packet in his pocket and tapped the filter end against his palm. "What were you doing hiding under the beds, Alain? Didn't you hear that the area is being evacuated? In case you hadn't noticed, the mountain is set to blow up."

"Yes, yes, but we don't think it is so bad. Just a lot of ash. We thought we will wait until it goes away. So we waited. Then Brigitte, my girlfriend, she changed her mind. But everyone has already gone, and we have no way of leaving." Alain kicked at the ground.

Barnes stepped closer. "If you wanted to leave, why hide from my men?"

"There's something they don't want to tell us," Grant chanted.

Monobrow punched his finger on an open page of one of the passports. He smirked. "I think they forgot to tell us that their Visas have expired."

Alain bit his lip. His shoulders slumped. "We saw the guns. We know you are the authorities. You will deport us for overstaying our Visa."

Grant cackled. "We're not the—"

Barnes flashed him a look. Grant trailed off.

Taking his time to dust the ash off the veranda rail before he leaned on it, Barnes flicked open his lighter and said, "You say you've been volunteering on New Zealand farms. You know anything about engines, Alain?"

"A little bit."

Flick.

"Tractors?"

"Yes."

"Well, as it happens, we've had some trouble with our vehicle, so we need a new one. There's a tractor here that we could use, if we can get it going. What say you help us out and maybe we can look the other way about your Visa?"

Flick.

"You won't report us?"

"All I want is for everyone to get out of here safely."

Alain looked at his girlfriend, then nodded. "Okay, I help you."

Barnes opened the French door to the lounge and gestured to Pope to join him on the veranda. "Take Alain, here, out to the tractor. Seems he might be able to help the boys get it going."

The girl, Brigitte, moved to follow her boyfriend, but Barnes caught her by the arm, stopping her. "No need for you to stand over a greasy tractor. There have been a few nasty shakes lately. Stay inside where it's safe."

The girl hesitated. "Alain?"

"It's okay. Go inside, Brigitte."

Flicking the lighter closed, Barnes slipped it into his pocket. He smiled widely. "We'll take good care of her."

Desert Road, Central Plateau

Taine got out of the Pinzgauer and walked the length of the Unimog, pushing through the cluster of soldiers to get to join Harris on the road at the front of the convoy.

"What's the hold up?"

"Some slightly unusual road furniture, Boss," Harris said, stepping to one side and allowing Taine to take in the scene.

In a dip in the road, three men, two in orange overalls, were sprawled face down on the road, their legs overlapping as if they'd been tripped up while playing some macabre game of Twister. On their backs, dark stains were visible through a fine coating of ash.

Shot? And in the back. Taine dropped to his haunches, checking for firearms.

"If you're looking for a gun, we've already swept the area. Nothing. Whoever did this, took the gun with them," Harris said. "You know what they say about killers: they like to dispose of the murder weapon."

And they always return to the scene of the crime.

His skin prickling, Taine scanned the surrounding tussock. "Keep your eyes sharp. Whoever did this could still be in the vicinity."

Hine and Eriksen lifted their rifles, the soldiers automatically turning outwards to survey the area.

Harris nodded. "I've already sent Miller and Bahr forward to scope out the road."

Read crouched to check the pulse of the man in track pants. "This one's gone, Boss," he said.

Lefty checked the two in overalls. "Same here." He rolled the body nearest to him over. Thirty-something, the dead man reminded Taine vaguely of a cousin. Thank the gods it wasn't, because the man's overalls had gaped open showing his obliterated chest and shoulder. Dark brown blood was congealing on the road where he'd been lying, sprinkles of ash already settling on the surface. "Body's still warm," Lefty observed quietly as he set the dead man's head gently on the tarmac.

The soldiers in Taine's section were no strangers to death, but a cold-blooded attack like this? It was the sort of thing that affected even the hardest men.

"Any clues about who they are?" Harris asked.

"Not that I can see," Read replied. "I can't find any ID on this one. No phone either."

"No ID here either," Lefty said. He twisted a ring off one of the men.

"Hey, what are you doing?" Read said.

"Checking for an inscription," Lefty said. He brought the ring close to his face, squinting as he looked inside the band.

"Anything?" Read asked.

"No." Lefty slipped the ring into the man's pocket.

"The orange overalls should help narrow it down," Harris said.

"Not really," Taine replied. "Lots of people wear them for work these days. Transport employees and forestry workers, for example."

"Or they could be Civil Defence volunteers," Eriksen said without turning back. "The entire plateau has been crawling with them for days."

Read got to his feet. "Civil Defence workers would carry ID."

"They were on foot. Maybe someone ambushed them and stole their vehicle. Maybe they took their IDs, too."

Lefty shook his head. "These men weren't killed at close range. They were shot in the back from a distance." He nodded up the road in the direction they'd been heading. "And from that direction."

Harris sighed. "Civilisation is like a thin layer of ice upon a deep ocean of chaos and darkness," he said.

Lefty raised an eyebrow. "Whoa, Hairy, that was deep. Who said—"

A quake hit.

Read and Harris threw their arms out, Hine steadying herself against the Unimog as Taine dropped to the ground. The earth grumbled like distant thunder. The earthquakes were gathering force. They were wasting time.

When the shaking slowed, Taine said, "This mystery will have to wait. Let's send a message to HQ and get these guys bagged up for now. I don't like leaving them here, but we'll need space in the vehicles for evacuees."

"Boss!"

Taine turned.

Miller was coming back towards them at a run.

"The road's blocked up ahead. We're going to need a heap more body bags."

Five minutes later, the convoy slowed. This time, Taine didn't need to walk past the Unimog for a status report.

Lake Rotopounamu, Tongariro National Park

Jules pulled her scarf up over her nose and mouth and examined the sky. White flakes swirled like dandruff on the air. She giggled. Someone should tell that old mountain, Tongariro, he ought to change his shampoo. She tightened the knot at the back of her head, securing the scarf, then turned back to her search amongst the driftwood at the edge of the little beach. All at once, the sand pitched beneath her feet. She froze, her hands clutching at air and her breath trapped in her throat, while she waited for the tremor to pass. Her heart hammered. Another big one. That made four sizeable shakes in the past hour. The area was really hotting up. She should leave while there were only shakes and flakes to deal with. Who knew what was happening elsewhere in the park? Lahars, toxic gases, fissures. It was possible the roads had already been cut off. Further up the mountains, came the rumble of shifting stones.

The Chesterfield skink is our version of the white rhino.

She'd give it another fifteen minutes. The skinks deserved that much.

She crouched again, picking up the tempo as she sifted through the jumble of vegetation at the edge of the beach, lifting rocks and stones, and examining the sand under low-lying bushes, hunting for the wiggly tracks left by the animals' tails.

A low grumble announced the start of another quake, water lapping at the edge of the lake. The sand shifted. Only metres away, a tree toppled, the splitting of its trunk like gunfire before the canopy plunged into the lake. Water rushed in.

Jules jumped to her feet, her ribs heaving. Moments ago, she'd been searching right there, where the tree had fallen across the beach. That was too close. She was out of time. *Sorry guys, gotta go.*

She picked up her pack, slipping it over her shoulders and clipped the straps together. Then, scanning the beach one more time for any sign of the little skink, she turned and started out on the two-kilometre trek back to the car.

*

Jules trudged out of the trees onto the road, relieved to see the Conservation Department twin cab Toyota waiting, intact, where she'd parked on the verge. Had she given up the search too soon? The trembling seemed to have abated in the half hour since she'd left the tiny beach. It was the falling tree that had spooked her. What if she went back and searched for another hour? She hadn't had a chance to search the treeline for narrow crevices where the lizard might hide out during the day. She should have started her search there, instead of grubbing about in the driftwood.

A sudden waft of drifting gas caused her to cough. Sulphur dioxide. Her eyes watered. She wiped them with a patch of clean fabric on the inside of her scarf.

No, maybe not.

Unclipping her pack, she opened the driver's door and clambered in. She started the vehicle and pulled out, heading north to Turangi with the mountains at her seven o'clock. The car radio, which she'd had on for emergency updates, crackled and hissed. A fat lot of use that was. She turned it off. The cab was unnervingly quiet. This stretch of road was never very busy; the buses carrying tourists to the Tongariro Crossing preferring to take State Highway One out of Turangi. Today though, it was so quiet it was like the aftermath of an apocalyptic movie – not a single vehicle anywhere. She recalled the Unimogs on the Desert Road on her way in. While she'd been searching the beach, the boys in their MCUs must have rounded everyone up and shepherded them out of the region.

MCU: multi-terrain camouflage uniform.

In the silence of the cab, she snorted. That's what happens when you date an NZDF sergeant for sixteen months; you end up using their army jargon.

Had Taine been among the sections evacuating the locals?

There was no one in the car with her and, still, she couldn't help but roll her eyes. *Of course*, Taine was here on the plateau. It was dangerous, wasn't it, and New Zealand citizens were at risk, so naturally he'd be in the thick of it.

Unless he was somewhere else, somewhere even worse.

Jules tried not to think about that. It was too late to call him now anyway. She'd wanted to, had almost phoned him before she'd left Wellington. How many times over the last eight months had her resolve nearly crumbled? No matter how much it killed her, she'd stuck to her guns.

He hadn't called her either. Maybe he'd moved on? Met someone else? She was still in contact with Read and Jug and surely they would've said something? No, they were too loyal. The soldiers in Taine's section would jump through the fires of hell before they betrayed him.

And why not? Taine would do the same for them.

So, there it was: New Zealand was in a state of national emergency with the supervolcano system beneath Lake Taupō threatening to blow its top, only erupting with a force 1.3 million times the nuclear load on Hiroshima on its last outing, and neither Taine nor Jules had picked up the phone to call one another. *I guess that means we're really over.*

Jules sighed. Well, it was what she'd wanted, wasn't it?

She tightened her grip on the steering wheel and peered at the road stretching before her. Ash drifted like summer snow across the tar seal, while on either side of her, the trees crowded in. Jules shivered. It was weird, knowing you could be the only one around for miles, while the mountains spewed and rumbled at your back. Still, it was only another kilometre or two before she'd hit the township where there would likely be a few die-hard anti-authoritarians hanging about, dragging their heels over the evacuation order.

She rounded the corner and saw a lahar, a deathly wash of mud and stones as wide as a bus is long and who-knows-how deep, sweeping across the road.

Jules sucked in her breath and slammed on the brakes, the car slewing to one side, tyres shrieking as she fought to keep the vehicle under control. Then, for a tiny instant, the world stopped on its axis, her vision a blur of green and grey and there was nothing she could do but wait and hope. Would the car stop, or would she be swept up in the cascade? Her foot hard to the floor, she gave herself over to fate: closed her eyes, and thought of Sara, her mum, Taine…

The vehicle halted, jerking her sideways, and back. She opened her eyes and breathed again. Side on to the river of grey-black silt, the twin cab was barely a finger's breadth from the heaving tide, a whisper from being swallowed up in the mountain's effluent.

For the shortest instant, Jules sat there, her hands on the wheel, and panted with relief.

The car had stalled. Fingers trembling, she restarted it, praying the engine wouldn't flood. She exhaled deeply when it hummed to life and made a tight turn to face the mountains. There was no way across the lahar, and no route through the dense bush. She would have to head south, back the way she'd come.

Still, if there was one lahar, then there could be others. What if the road was blocked this way, too? She could be trapped between two black rivers of rubble. Or worse, she could be entombed here, buried alive beneath the detritus.

Jules shook her head. The Minister had been right to call her an idiot. Here she was panicking at the first sign of trouble. She'd narrowly avoided an accident, but apart from a bit of mild shock, she was fine, the vehicle was intact, and this wasn't a dead-end road. She'd drive slowly, keeping her eyes peeled for falling trees, debris, fissures, and any other crap the mountain might throw at her and if she met another lahar, then she'd abandon the vehicle and go on foot. All she'd have to do was cut through the bush, skirting the lake until she got ahead of the flow, then head south-east to meet the main highway where she'd have the best chance of catching a lift.

There, already she felt better. Having a plan B always helped.

At the corner, she glanced in the rear vision mirror, taking a last look at the lahar. Wait. She squinted through the drifts of ash and mist. A dark-haired woman stood at the edge of the churning current. Jules gasped. Where had she come from? Jules had been there, where the woman was standing, less than a minute ago. How had Jules not seen her? She had to go back, or the woman would be bowled away, sucked up in that greasy, roiling tide.

She stomped on the brake, threw the stick into reverse, then twisted to look back through the cab. The woman had vanished, the road empty.

*

At the turn-off to Lake Rotoaira a man in orange overalls stepped into the road and flagged her down.

Not bothering to pull over, Jules stopped the Toyota and wound down the window. "Hello. Jules Asher, Conservation Department. Is everything okay?" Lifting her chin, she grinned. "I mean, other than the sky falling on our heads."

The man's smile put her in mind of Lost in Space's Dr Smith. "No, but we're going to need to commandeer your vehicle, Miss."

"Of course." Jules shoved her pack into the footwell. "I have room for three or four in the cab, and space for a few more in the back if people don't mind sitting on the flatbed. How many are still to be evacuated?"

"Maybe twenty."

"Twenty! I didn't know Rotoaira had that many inhabitants." Jules had stopped in to use the public toilet block once. The place was miniscule; a handful of beach baches and a summer motor camp.

"Yeah, well it does, doesn't it?" the man snapped. He sniffed, wiping under his nose with the back of his hand. "Are you going to help us or not?"

Jules' skin prickled. There was no need to be rude. Still, people didn't always react well in a crisis. She'd nearly flipped out herself after coming face to face with the lahar. She could be the last hope of a ride out for the people stranded here; it was enough to make anyone's nerves fray. She gave the man what she hoped was a reassuring smile. "I'll take as many as I can, Mr—" She raised her eyebrows in the quintessential Kiwi question mark.

The man hesitated, then shrugged. "The name's Climo."

"Pleased to meet you. What happened to your own vehicle, anyway?"

Climo rolled his tongue around his mouth. "We…um…donated it, didn't we? To get the civilians out."

Jules' nodded. "You're Civil Defence?"

That pause again. "Sure. Let me get our controller." He signalled with his head to someone concealed in the trees. "Pete, you wait here with her. I'm going to get Barnes."

"You might want to tell him to hurry," Jules called through the window after him. "The road was washed out a couple of kilometres back. Makes this the only way out."

Climo nodded, then turned and ran down the road to the hamlet, while Pete, who was also wearing orange overalls, took his place standing in front of Jules' vehicle. The man's stance made Jules shiver. Why the sentry? And why had Pete been hovering in the bushes in the first place?

Jules puffed out her cheeks. Now, who was being paranoid? Stranded without transport, naturally the Civil Defence controller would want to be sure any passing motorist didn't spook and run before loading up with evacuees. And as for Pete hiding in the trees, more likely he'd simply stepped into bushes to relieve himself. She pursed her lips. *Something* was making her uneasy and it wasn't just the pitch and roll of the earth or grand-daddy Tongariro having a hissy fit up there in his mountain throne-room. Still, whatever was putting the wind up her, there was nothing she could do about it, not unless she was prepared to mow down a man in cold blood. She'd have to wait until Climo returned with his controller.

Jules chewed the inside of her cheek. She hoped they didn't take all day about it.

She glanced at the sentry. His arms folded across his chest, Pete stared back at her as if he hadn't eaten in a week.

Remote Farmhouse, Central Plateau

The walk up the driveway to the farmhouse had been interminable. With the muscles of his back and sides on fire and his neck chafed raw by his companion's overalls, Pringle had practically dragged Brooker the length of the winding gravel lane and up the stairs onto the deck, setting the boy down at the wooden BBQ table, while he caught his breath.

His hands on his hips, he bent over and breathed deeply.

Hell's teeth. He was completely wasted. His legs felt like the globules in one of those psychedelic lava lamps. If he survived this, he was going to get himself in better shape. It's not as if they'd walked that far. Maybe five kilometres on mostly-managed forest tracks. He might be slight, still the youth's weight had tripled with every kilometre until Pringle could have sworn he was hauling King Kong's carcass across the uneven ground. He'd almost cried out with relief when he saw the winding driveway and the rural delivery letterbox, and yet he'd hesitated to bring them here. It was the first house they'd come across, which meant there was a good chance Barnes and the others had seen it too. If Barnes discovered they were alive, after what they'd seen, they were as good as dead.

Not willing to take a chance with the boy's life, Pringle had propped Brooker against a tree while he'd crept closer to the house to check. Twenty minutes had passed with no evidence of Barnes' rabble. There'd been no sign of anyone, in fact. Not that he'd expected the residents to be here. They'd be long gone, safely evacuated by the authorities. Pringle and Brooker couldn't stay either; any respite the farmhouse had to offer would be temporary. If this earthquake swarm provoked the supervolcano enough to lose its rag, their bodies would be immolated to dust, their crumbled remnants flung to the winds to be picked up by the swirls of ash. Still, neither he nor Brooker were in any state to go on. They needed to rest up and consider their options.

"You okay?" Brooker asked, his voice ragged.

"Sure," Pringle panted. "You?"

The kid's face was ashen, his skin slick with sweat. "The aspirin has worn off."

"I figured. Let's get you inside, then I'll have a hunt around, see if I can find a first aid kit to sort that leg of yours, and maybe get you something to drink. How does that sound?"

The boy's eyes brimmed with tears. Embarrassed, he turned away. "Yeah, that'd be great, man. Thanks."

Pringle glanced around the deck for something to break open the door: a tool or a stone or something. There was nothing nearby. A kettle BBQ which wasn't much use for anything. Maybe under the deck, there'd be a piece of left over decking timber.

"Pringle."

"Yeah?"

"Try under that pot." Brooker nodded to the far side of the deck where a ceramic planter sported a tired red flax flocked with ash.

Pringle smiled. The planter wasn't centred and the circular water ring on the wooden deck beneath it was slightly askew as if someone had moved the planter recently. He nudged the pot to one side. No key. Maybe it had fallen through the cracks in the wood. Or maybe the owners, in a hurry to evacuate, hadn't bothered to leave one.

"Tip it up," Brooker suggested.

Pringle tilted the planter, ash fluttering onto the deck like petals in spring. Pringle ducked his head to look. The owners had duct-taped their emergency key to the bottom of the pot. "Eureka," he said.

"Told you," said Brooker.

"You did." Pringle unlocked the door, pushing it open. "Hello?"

Brooker laughed. "You sound like my mum."

"Yeah, well keep that up and someone will end up crying."

Brooker's face pinched with panic. "Sorry," he said. "I didn't mean—"

"Paul, forget it. I was joking. You know, *someone will end up crying*. It's a thing mothers say."

"Oh, right." The boy's face softened.

Pringle made a mental note to be more careful: Brooker had seen Barnes murder Lewis. Add in his injury and being stuck smack in the middle of an emergency zone, and the boy had to be half out of his mind with pain and fear.

Draping Brooker's arm around his neck, Pringle shouldered his weight again, his own body groaning in protest. When Brooker was installed on the lounge sofa, his injured leg elevated on an armrest, Pringle took a look around the house.

Barnes' lot had definitely been here. Drawers had been yanked out in the kitchen and someone had done a job on the bedroom cupboards, half their contents spewed on the floor in a mess of shoes, belts, books, and old photographs. Unlike Pringle and Brooker, they'd come in through the back door: smashing through the pane insert, 1970s amber glass littering the hall. It didn't seem as though they'd been looking for supplies, otherwise they might have uncovered the first aid kit tucked tidily on a shelf in the laundry and the box of Codeine, labelled Mr RJ Smith, in a bedside table in the master bedroom.

While Pringle checked the kitchen, he tried to piece together what might have happened. With transport Barnes' most pressing need, he would have had his boys search the outbuildings first for vehicles. Perhaps there had been a spare farm vehicle here, so they'd broken into the house to hunt for the keys.

Or for firearms and ammunition. Pringle's heart lurched at the thought, but thankfully, he hadn't seen a gun cabinet anywhere.

"Any chance of an order of pancakes?" Brooker called from the lounge.

"Sorry, pancakes are off the menu," Pringle replied. "Power's down." No power meant the landline was useless; nor would there be any steaming hot cup of restorative coffee. But in the pantry, in amongst an assortment of tinned beans and beetroot, was a carton of long-life UHT milk and a family-sized box of Weetbix. The mountain might pulverise them; at least they wouldn't starve.

Carrying the first aid kit into the lounge, Pringle perched on the coffee table, undid Brooker's splint and his boot and examined his lower leg. A pale-yellow blister had appeared where the makeshift splint had rubbed against Brooker's ankle and there was a bruise on his knee that hadn't been there before, no doubt caused by the tumble they'd taken in the forest.

Pringle's heart had almost exploded in terror; Brooker's shout of pain had been loud enough to wake the dead or, worse, bring Barnes down on them. Sprawled on the ground, they'd waited, frozen, like a couple of bunnies, expecting the worst. Thankfully, the forest had stayed quiet.

Gently, Pringle touched the skin around the boy's ankle. "How does that feel?"

"It fucking hurts, that's how it feels," Brooker said.

"The skin isn't hot, so that's a good sign," Pringle said. His ankle was definitely tight and swollen though, Brooker wincing at even that light touch. Pringle put a pad on the blister and re-splinted the injury, then opened the box of Codeine. There were only two tablets left. Brooker took them gratefully.

Pringle went to the kitchen and came back with a bowl of Weetbix and a spoon. "Eat up. I'll be back soon."

"Where are you going?"

"To check the sheds. See if I can find anything useful."

Beyond the house were three outbuildings. There would be no vehicle in any of them, Barnes would have seen to that – but perhaps there was something else they could use.

What like a Segway, or a drone? Maybe the farmer keeps a spare helicopter?

Pringle scoffed. They'd have more chance of finding a pumpkin and a fairy godmother. Still, there might be something. Shrugging off a wave of hopelessness, he trudged across the yard to the first shed. Smaller than the others, the outside of the ancient wood hut was covered with green-grey old man's beard lichen, while inside, it was full of tools, poisons, and an old-fashioned circular saw. Nothing of any use to him. One corner of the shed was stacked with spare fenceposts and rolls of wire netting. There was also a smoker for curing meat, shaped like a filing cabinet, the handle broken off, the door secured with a screwdriver through the latch. Unlocking it, Pringle slipped the screwdriver in his pocket while he checked inside. The shelves were empty; just the scent of smoked mānuka lingered and Pringle inhaled deeply, breathing in the pungent freshness of the wood, a small pleasure in what could be his last day on earth.

The second shed was barn-sized and empty, and judging from the tracks and the spare parts pushed against the walls, it had once held a tractor, possibly a couple of farm bikes. Had they been taken by the farm crew, or by Barnes? He had no way of knowing.

Leaving the barn, he approached the final shed. Clearly a more recent addition to the farm, it was set on a concrete pad and made of powder-coated steel. Inside, the reason for the posh accommodation was revealed: a shiny six metre Ramco boat with twin Honda 90 outboards, still on its boat trailer.

Oh, imagine how that must have hurt, leaving this beauty behind.

Standing on the trailer wheels, Pringle swung his leg over the side of the boat and climbed in. The owner had all the gear, too. Pringle rummaged through the storage compartments, pulling out life jackets, ropes, floats, a winch…He grinned. At last. Something useful. Snatching up the object, he hurried back into the house, jumping over the broken glass on his way through.

"Any vehicles?" Brooker called before Pringle had emerged from the hallway.

"No."

"Fuck."

"But I found this." Pringle opened his hands and showed Brooker the cylindrical parachute flare. Flying three hundred metres into the air, even in daytime, a flare like this could be seen up to sixteen kilometres away. Forty at night, although they couldn't afford to wait that long. "As soon as I've got you out of the house and safely out of sight, I'll set it off," Pringle said. "And then all we have to do is wait to see who comes up the drive."

CHAPTER EIGHT

Desert Road, Central Plateau

Taine was crouched beside the dead guard when a red plume appeared in the sky to the northwest.

"That looks like a boat flare," said Harris. "What the hell? Someone should tell them today isn't the best choice for a little jaunt on the lake."

Getting to his feet, Taine traced the flare's trajectory, trying to pinpoint its origin. "There are a few lakes in the area, but I'm not convinced that one's been fired from a boat."

Harris shielded his eyes with his palm as he too scanned the sky. "I reckon it's in our zone."

Taine nodded. "Even if it's not, with all this ash, we might be the only ones who've seen it."

"I guess that makes it our responsibility, then," Harris replied.

"It does." Taine turned to where the men were bagging up the bodies and making a note of any identifying features. "Read," he called.

"Yes, Boss?" said Read, jogging over.

"We need to wind this up. Get everyone rounded up and back on the trucks ASAP."

Read turned on his heel. "On it."

"Harris, check the maps, will you? See if you can work out where that flare came from. Use a set square or something. As soon as the men are loaded up, we'll check it out."

Harris nodded. "And all this?" His gesture took in the prison bus, the bodies, the carnage.

"We've done what we can for the dead. Right now, we need to focus on saving the living, and that includes any prisoners who survived the accident."

Harris raised a brow. "You're sure it was an accident?"

Taine lifted his chin towards the fissure in the road. "I think the crash was. Looks like the bus rolled while the driver was attempting to avoid the crack in the road. Or he saw the crack, but was surprised by a quake."

"And in the aftermath, when the survivors had crawled out of the wreckage, they took off?"

"They'd want to get clear of the mountains as much as the next person."

Stepping back to allow Read and Lefty to bag up the dead guard, Harris said, "You're forgetting this guy. Someone shot him, and not in a nice way." He shielded his groin with his hands. "It's not a death I'd wish on anyone."

Taine hadn't forgotten. And there were the three men just down the road, all of them shot in the back. It was as if they were dealing with the mafia, or some vendetta.

"Why only one guard? It doesn't seem enough to oversee a busload of prisoners," he said. "Don't they have quotas?"

Lifting the flap of his breast pocket, Harris hesitated. "Good point," he said, pulling an area map from his pocket. "Maybe the prison was short-staffed. It's not like Mother's Day; you don't always know when there's going to be a state of emergency. Or there might have been more guards, only we haven't found them. They could've been thrown under the bus in the crash."

"Or held hostage by whoever shot the guard," Taine said.

Harris' eyes widened. "Or in *cahoots* with whoever shot the guard? Hey, maybe that's how they got hold of the gun. I don't know about here, but, in Australia, prison guards aren't trained police; they don't get to carry firearms, just tear gas, and maybe tasers."

Taine frowned. In New Zealand, it wasn't just prison guards, even the police didn't carry firearms. Not routinely.

"ETD in five, Boss," Read called to them.

"Shit. I'd better go and work out where we're heading," Harris said. He strode away, the map rolled in his hand.

Taine swung into his seat in the Pinzgauer. Harris was right; there were any number of reasons for finding only one guard, and most of them were far from innocent.

Lake Rotoaira township

The girl had been in the bathroom too long. It was making him suspicious. Barnes knocked on the door. "You okay in there, honey?" he said.

"Oui. Yes," the girl replied in her French accent. "Thank you. I am in here."

Barnes' nostrils flared. He kept his voice steady, sweet even. "Are you going to be long? It's just that there are other people out here."

No one was waiting, but the boyfriend might get the tractor going soon and, seeing as the universe had elected to send him this little bonus, why waste time?

"Yes, one moment."

She was stalling. Barnes tried the door. The bitch had locked it. He gave it a rattle to put the wind up her, and was stalking back to the lounge when Climo burst through the front doors, his face red from running the length of the settlement. "Barnes! There's a girl. Out on the highway," he panted.

Still holding their drinks, the other inmates gathered around, like this was a BBQ and Climo was about to tell a ghost story. The man was taking his time getting to the punchline. Barnes wanted to throttle him. "Get it out, man."

"She has a vehicle," he huffed.

"Yeah? How big?"

"Pretty big. It's a Conservation Department twin cab. Has a flat bed, too," Climo said.

Excellent. Barnes could finally fuck off out of here. His mind raced. He'd travel light: taking the women – the French chick in the bathroom and the one out on the road – and the guns, for insurance, and Taliava for added muscle. He'd leave the rest of these losers here. Only he'd need to play it carefully, so the others didn't cotton on. At least, not until it was too late. When he was halfway to Christchurch.

"What did you tell the girl? Howdya make her stay?" he asked.

"Appealed to her better nature, didn't I?" Climo crowed. "The silly cow thinks we're Civil Defence. I told her that you were our controller."

Barnes smiled. The French couple had made the same mistake. He clapped a hand on Climo's shoulder. "Fucking genius. Let's get rolling, then." He scanned the group, making eye contact with as many as he could. "You lot take Climo over to the tractor and see how they're getting on with the repairs. Maybe see if you can find a trailer. I'll get the Frenchie and wait for you out at the main road." Barnes was confident Taliava would find a way to join him; the man had a particular interest in ensuring Barnes' good health.

Pope didn't like the suggestion, because his eyes narrowed. "Why not come with us, Barnesy?"

"Yeah, why not come with us, Barnesy?" Ants parroted.

Barnes picked up the rifle. "You heard what Climo said: the conservation chick thinks I'm the Civil Defence controller. It'll make it easier for everyone if we keep it that way."

Climo giggled. "It's okay. She's not going anywhere. Pete's standing in the middle of the road."

The door of the bathroom clicked open, the French girl finally deciding to make an appearance. Barnes breathed deep. He could shoot Ants and grab the girl, but without Taliava here on hand to back him up, he'd be risking a face off with a dozen disgruntled crims. Better to play along for now.

"Sure," he said, cheerily, taking the French chick by the arm. "Why not? Let's all go and see if Alain has got that tractor running."

A few of the boys stopped to get in a last round or three before they left the beach house, carrying their bottles with them over to the tractor shed. That's if you could even call it a shed. Barnes had seen dunnies in better shape. The miserable structure was missing the lower half of its boards, more than half its paintwork, and both doors.

Only the Frenchman was working on the engine. Leaning against the empty doorframe, Knife was picking his fingernails with a stick, Smithy was perched on the driver's seat conducting an imaginary orchestra with his fingers, while Monobrow, Grant, and Pope had their heads together in the gloom at the rear of the shed, talking about something. Barnes didn't like the look of that. Taliava stood outside, the rifle cradled in his arms, like the good guard dog that he was. They all lifted their heads at the group's approach.

"How's it going? Any closer to getting it started?" Barnes asked. He tightened his grip on the girl's arm.

Pope emerged from the back of the shed and gave the tractor's front tyre a kick. "Nah, nothing doing. Alain here says it's foutu. I don't know much, but I reckon that's French for fucked."

"It is an old tractor," Alain said, stepping back from the engine and wiping his hands on a greasy scrap of towel. "A lot of rust. I think maybe there is too much salt in the air."

"Well?" Pope said. "Any bright ideas?" He looked at Barnes. "How are we going to get out of here without a vehicle?" Barnes didn't appreciate the threat in his voice; the weasel was getting above himself. He lifted his eyes to Taliava, who took the hint and moved closer, making sure the men could all see the rifle, reminding them all exactly who was boss.

"There's a girl with a twin cab out on the main road," Climo piped up.

"One twin cab isn't going to cut it," Pope said. "There are sixteen of us."

"Hey look!" someone shouted.

Barnes turned, his heart thumping. *What?* Several of the men had their heads tipped back and were gazing at the sky, shading their eyes against the glare with their hands.

Barnes stepped away from the shed, and saw the trail of red smoke.

"It's a flare," someone said, as if it wasn't obvious.

"Whoever set that off wasn't far away," said Pope.

Knife flung his manicure stick into the grass. "There's a lot of ash. You reckon anyone saw it?"

"We saw it, didn't we?" Ants said.

"Maybe some goody-two-shoes, will swoop in to rescue them," said Smithy, jumping down from the tractor.

Barnes grinned. "I think you're right, Smithy We should get ourselves to that pickup point. That way, if some goody-two-shoes does swoop in, we can persuade them to rescue us instead."

Climo giggled. "Wouldn't that be rich? If the real Civil Defence turned up and we stole their fucking transport."

There was a hushed silence, and Alain's eyes widened.

Climo, you fucking idiot.

"Wait. You are the authorities, no?" the Frenchman said slowly. He stumbled.

The ground had shunted suddenly, the mountain choosing that moment to turn over in its sleep, rolling and pitching beneath their feet. They waited to see if it would wake up, but after a while the tremors subsided.

Still giggling, Climo clapped his hand over his mouth. "Whoops."

But now the boy had caught on; he rushed forward, yabbering away in French, grabbing his girlfriend by her other arm and trying to pull her away.

Barnes sighed and tightened his grasp on the girl's upper arm. He was going to have to off the boy. Unless there was a way this could be turned to his advantage... "It's unfortunate," he said, feigning disappointment, "that we've got to leave our French friends here."

Taliava straightened. "Barnes, you sure about this?" he said quietly.

"Barnes is right. We have to leave them," Knife said. "They'll rat on us."

"No!" Alain shouted. "You can't leave us." He lunged for Barnes, but Smithy reached forward and pulled him back.

"Don't take it so hard," Barnes said. "It'll be like it was an hour ago, before we arrived, when you and your girlfriend were cowering in the campervan."

"Please, don't leave us," Alain begged. "The mountain will explode. *Please.*"

Barnes waited for the boy to stop his blathering. "Okay, just to show I'm not entirely heartless, here's what I propose. We'll take your girlfriend with us. I promise we'll take good care of her. In fact, I'll make it my personal responsibility. If she stays quiet and doesn't mention a word to the authorities, I'll see to it that someone comes back for you. Now I can't say fairer than that, can I?"

Alain looked at his girlfriend, then his eyes tracked to the tractor. It was the tiniest movement, barely noticeable. Laughable really. Barnes could practically hear the fucker's brain working. He was thinking he'd fix the tractor and run to the authorities, wasn't he?

The girl clearly thought so, because she whined, "I want to stay with Alain."

Barnes patted her hand and played the benevolent uncle. "No, no. Alain would want you to be safe. It's best you come with us." He turned to Pope. "You and Taliava take Alain into the house, get him comfortable with some water, something to eat. If his girlfriend behaves, he shouldn't have too long to wait."

"Alain!" the girl whimpered. She started to cry. It was so sweet. Like a movie.

Barnes dragged her towards the main road.

"Come on," Pope said, nudging the boy towards the house. The kid didn't even try to resist. What was the point? He must have realised it would only make things worse.

As Pope passed, Barnes turned away from the girl. "Fix this, and you can have his passport," he said under his breath.

Maungapōhatu, Te Urewera Forest

Temera put the mower back in the shed, giving it a shove with his foot to push it all the way in. Then he sat on the porch, shucked off his grassy gumboots, and surveyed his handiwork. Crap. It was pitiful. All afternoon, and what had he achieved? Barely half the job. Back in the day, when Temera was a boy, he used to knock off this lawn in an hour and still have energy left over to go fishing. Chuckling, he rubbed the back of his neck with his palm. Yeah, well, back in the day, he wouldn't have got away with letting the lawn get this long, either.

He leaned back against the veranda post and looked through the trees to Te Maunga, a flake of ash fluttering from the sky to land on his sock. Temera had no sooner brushed it away when another one landed, a grey-white flake vibrant against the black wool. He looked up. The sky was raining white.

The girl on the radio yesterday had said things on the plateau were getting worse. She'd had a volcanologist in the studio, a guest speaker, who was telling everyone how many cubic metres of ash had been belched into the air and going on about earthquake swarms being the first clue to volcanic activity.

Temera snorted. He didn't need a fancy title or a PhD to know what was going on. Any kaumātua could tell you that the mountains were bickering again. But over what? And what did Te Hoata and Te Pūpū have to do with it?

Well, if he was going to worry about it, may as well get a cup of tea and sit on a comfy couch. These wooden planks were hard on an old bum. Grabbing hold of the veranda post, Temera hauled himself to his feet. Already his body was aching from pushing the mower, and it would be worse tomorrow. This getting old sucked. More than ever, he missed his little jaunts into the forests in his nine-year-old wairua-spirit form.

He switched the jug on, then sank into the sofa while he waited for it to boil. The hum of the appliance filled the room. He closed his eyes...

Temera had been twelve. It was autumn and a bit cold, so there was no one else at the foot pool. Temera's teacher, Mātua Rata, said that was why autumn was the best time to come, so they could have it all to themselves.

Rolling up his trousers to the knees, the old man sat on the edge of the pool and eased his wrinkly feet into the hot water. Then, his palms braced on the ground behind him, he put his head back and breathed in the steam.

Temera could never understand why anyone would want to sniff in the pongy air. It smelled like rotten eggs. Mātua didn't seem to mind.

"Ah that feels good," Mātua said. "Come on, Temera. Get in." He waved a skinny arm at the water.

"What if someone peed in it?"

"Don't be ridiculous."

"Well, it looks like someone peed in it," Temera grumbled, but he stepped into the brown water and immediately leaped back onto the bank, jumping up and down on the spot. "Ow, ow, ow, that's hot," he wailed.

Mātua chuckled. "You have to ease your feet in slowly, get used to it. Have another try."

"I don't want to."

"Suit yourself," Mātua said.

"Why are we here, anyway?" Temera asked. With Mātua, there was usually a lesson involved.

Mātua folded his arms across his chest, closed his eyes, and took another deep breath. "To soak our feet."

Temera rolled his eyes. Mātua always did this; made him wait for the lesson. Although Temera didn't mind the stories. Some of them had epic battles: a great chief fighting a taniwha-serpent, or two rivers racing one another to reach the ocean. Sometimes it would be about a journey, or how the Māori people had learned to make nets. Temera especially liked the ones about Māui – the demi-god who fished up the land with a fish hook made from his grandmother's jawbone. The problem was, he was supposed to learn things from the stories, and that was the hard bit.

Sitting down with his wet feet not quite touching the water, Temera plucked at a hebe bush, shredding the tiny leaves with his fingers and letting them drop onto the ground between his legs. "I don't see what's so great about soaking our feet. It's just a hot pool," he said.

Mātua's eyes flew open. "Not just a hot pool. A special gift."

"Is there a story?"

"What do you think?"

"I think there is."

"Well, are you going to listen?"

"I guess so."

"Put your feet in the water, then."

Temera dipped his toes in the pool as Mātua began his tale.

"The tohunga-priest Ngātoro-i-rangi came to Aotearoa on the mighty Te Arawa waka-canoe. It was a long trip from our ancestral lands in Hawaiki. Even before his people left there'd been a famine and some family squabbles, and then the entire waka nearly got eaten by a big shark, so they were pretty pleased to get here."

Temera slipped his feet deeper into the hot water.

"After blessing the new land, Ngātoro-i-rangi set off to explore, leading his people inland to—"

"Here?" Temera interrupted.

"Not quite. Close, though. He came to Lake Taupō—"

"The eye of Māui's fish!"

"Exactly." Mātua put his hands into the water, his fingers spread wide, warming them. "While Ngātoro-i-rangi was at the lake, he climbed the nearest mountain, Mount Tauhara, and stood at the summit, where he looked to the south, taking in the view. Imagine how he must have felt, way up there, gazing over the lake and the mountains."

"Tired."

Temera's mentor chuckled at his joke, sending ripples across the surface of the pool. "Probably," he said. "It's a long way up Mount Tauhara. But Ngātoro-i-rangi was determined to visit the mountains in the distance. So, the next day he and his people set off, skirting the edge of the lake until they came to the biggest mountain, which Ngātoro-i-rangi named Tongariro. They'd almost made it to the top of the mountain, when a huge storm blew in from the south."

His feet fully submerged now, Temera curled his toes in the water.

"*The travellers were hounded by bitter winds carrying snow and ice. Soon, Ngātoro-i-rangi and his people were dying: freezing to death. He had to do something. So he called to his sisters Kuiwai and Haungaroa, who were waiting nearby on an island called Whakaari.*"

"*Wait! He called across the ocean to them. So Ngātoro-i-rangi was a matakite then? A seer like us?*"

"*He was.*"

Temera stood up in the pool. "*Did Ngātoro-i-rangi get his spirit guide to carry the message to his sisters? Or did he use a pūrerehua?*"

Mātua sighed. "*I don't know. I've told you before; it's not the same for all seers, Temera. Now do you want to hear the rest of the story or not?*"

Temera sat down again. He wrapped his arms around his knees, his calves still in the water.

Mātua went on, "*Almost dead, Ngātoro-i-rangi begged his sisters to send him fire to keep his people warm. 'Kuiwai e!, Haungaroa e!, ka riro au i te Tonga. Tukuna mai te ahi!' he called. Sisters, the south winds have me pinned down. Send me fire!*"

"*What did they do?*"

Mātua dropped his voice to a whisper. "*Well, there was a problem. While the sisters were able to get the sacred fire from the god Rūaumoko, there was no way they could bring it to their brother themselves. There wasn't enough time. Ngātoro-i-rangi's people would die before they got there. So instead, the sisters sent the fire spirits, Te Hoata and Te Pūpū, who carried six baskets of sacred embers to Ngātoro-i-rangi through secret tunnels beneath the earth.*"

Despite the stinky steam, Temera sucked in his breath. This story was so cool.

"*Only, there was another problem. Travelling under the ground, the fire spirits couldn't see where they were going, so they were forced to raise their heads...*" Mātua lifted his toes out of the water. "*...and each time they did, they lost a basket of the sacred fire, which spewed from the earth's crust in a burst of sparks and embers. By the time the fire spirits emerged from the tunnel at the top of Tongariro, only one basket was left, and Ngātoro-i-rangi's companion Ngāuruhoe was dead.*"

"*Hey, Ngāuruhoe,*" Temera said. "*There's a mountain called Ngāuruhoe.*"

"*Named after Ngātoro-i-rangi's companion, yes.*"

"*Ngātoro-i-rangi must have been pretty sad.*"

"*Actually, he was furious; only one basket had arrived, and too late to save his companion. He was so angry, he kicked up a stink, stomping his feet and slamming his paddle into the earth.*"

"Wow. He had a bit of a temper, then?"

"More than a bit. In his rage, Ngātoro-i-rangi knocked over the precious basket of fire and the embers caught, filling the mountains, and the underground tunnels with Rūaumoko's volcanic power." Mātua lifted his feet out of the pool and began to dry them on an old rag. *"Quite the story, isn't it?"*

Temera sat up. He frowned. *Hang on, that couldn't be it.* Mātua never let him off that easily. *"So, what's the lesson?"* he demanded. *"I'm a matakite so I can get fire from Ngātoro-i-rangi's sisters?"* He stepped up on to the bank and, one foot at a time, shook the droplets off his feet.

"No."

"Don't have a temper?"

Mātua smiled. *"No – well yes, you need to control your temper – but there's no lesson, Temera. I just thought it would be nice to soak our feet."* Mātua threw him the rag. *"And since this is one of the places Te Hoata and Te Pūpū popped their heads above the ground, we have this lovely hot pool."*

Temera pushed himself up from the sofa. Even that small action made every muscle in his body groan. He scratched the back of his neck where a piece of grass had worked its way inside his jersey, fishing it out and throwing it in the sink. Then, switching the jug on again, he leaned against the kitchen bench and looked through the open door at the veranda post. The tiny blackened print where the fire demon's talon had scorched the wood stared back at him, demanding his attention, like the dot on an exclamation point. Mātua had said there was no lesson, just a chance for an old man and his student to enjoy the thermal waters, but as a swirl of ash drifted across the open door, Temera understood. It might not have been important back then, yet it was significant *now*. Te Hoata and Te Pūpū had carried a message for Ngātoro-i-rangi from his sisters when the tohunga-priest was in mortal peril. The fire spirits were *messengers*. When the pair had visited him many years ago in Rotorua, they had carried a message from Rūaumoko, a warning which had prevented his grand-nephew's death.

What message were they carrying, this time? And for whom?

And why would they stop to visit him?

CHAPTER NINE

Lake Rotoaira, Central Plateau

When she spied the trail of red smoke in the sky, Jules climbed out of the cab. "Someone's in trouble," she said to Pete.

Pete didn't move from his spot in the middle of the road. "Looks like it," he said, and he gave her that stare again.

Jules moved closer to the vehicle. Put a hand on the door handle.

Moments later, a group of men appeared on the road leading from the hamlet. Fourteen men in Civil Defence orange accompanied by a single civilian.

The man clutching the civilian gave Jules a wide smile. Slinging his firearm to the back, he held out his free hand. "Thank you for waiting. Name's Barnes. This is Brigitte."

Jules shook his hand. "You're very welcome. Jules Asher, Conservation."

Brigitte had been crying. The girl's nose was red, and her pale cheeks were wet with tears that she'd attempted to scrub away.

Jules put a hand on her shoulder. "Are you okay?"

"Brigitte is French," Barnes replied for her. "She came to New Zealand for one of those farm exchanges. Sad thing: her friends let her down, abandoned her when the earthquakes started. Naturally, being left like that has upset her. You wouldn't believe how relieved she was when we turned up. Isn't that right, Brigitte?" Opening the Toyota's rear door, he tightened his grip on her arm. "Brigitte?"

Clearly traumatised, the girl dropped her eyes, mousy brown hair falling over her face, and gave a small nod. Barnes nudged her towards the back seat. The poor kid was in such a state, she was reluctant to get in.

Leaving Barnes to it, Jules dropped the tailgate, pushed back the roll top and climbed onto the Toyota's flatbed. She shunted the plastic tubs containing her equipment towards the rear of the bed. "We're going to need to ditch these to make room," she said. In her head she divvied up the space: with five in the cab, and maybe two on the running boards, could they get nine men on the bed? Even with the tailgate down, it would be tight.

"Pass those here," said one of the men. He reached forward and dragged the tubs to the edge of the flatbed, and lifted them off. Another man took the boxes from him, setting them against the posts of the weather-beaten sign announcing the turnoff to Lake Rotoaira.

The truck empty, Jules was about to jump down when two men, a big islander and a redhead, came running down the road from the hamlet.

"Are you the last?" she called.

"Yep, that's everyone," Barnes said, and Brigitte whimpered.

"There's not going to be enough room," Jules murmured.

Several of the men had already come to that conclusion. As soon as she got down, they clambered onto the back of the Toyota, using their elbows to push ahead of the others. The wheel arches sunk under their weight.

"Stop!" Barnes said quietly, and the men froze. His command of them was impressive: especially since Civil Defence teams were largely volunteers.

"No more than six on the back of the truck," Barnes barked. "Grant, get down. Knife, you take the wheel. Pope, you get in the back with the women." The men destined for the cab didn't waste any time, opening the doors and climbing in.

"What about you, Barnes?" one of the men shouted. "Where are you going to be?"

Barnes glared at the speaker. "I'll be riding shotgun, won't I?" he said, lingering on the word shotgun.

"You can't leave us behind," Climo said, his voice high.

Smiling, Barnes shook his head. "No one said anything about leaving you behind, but we're under the hammer here. Whoever responds to that flare won't be keen to stick around. If we want to take advantage of them for a ride out, we're going to have to hurry."

The group on the ground moved closer, their menace like a gathering thunderstorm.

"If anyone stays, it should be you," someone muttered.

Swinging his rifle to the front, Barnes coughed. "Look, we can't afford to stand here yabbering."

"So give someone else your seat."

Jules shivered. Barnes might command their obedience, but he didn't have their respect. Unlike Taine, whose men would follow him into the pits of hell. Of course, Taine would never accept a seat if there were people still to be rescued. He would always put his own safety last. Be the last to leave. Hell, she'd seen him carry a man out of a forest on his back. She wasn't being fair. Barnes wasn't Taine. He wasn't even a soldier; just a civilian trying to help in an emergency.

The big islander who'd arrived late, pushed his way to the front, his forehead still shiny from his run across the hamlet. "I'll stay with the others," he said. 'We'll follow on foot."

Barnes grinned. "Good man. Well, that's sorted then."

"You'll owe me, though," the islander said. He gave the controller a hard stare.

"And I won't forget, "Barnes replied.

*

In the driver's seat, Knife slammed the vehicle into drive and gunned the engine. The motor protested, sluggish under the men's weight, but slowly the twin cab gained momentum. They rounded the first corner. Knife picked up speed with little mind for the men in the back.

"Be careful," Jules said. "We don't know what—"

"I don't need a Doris telling me how to drive," Knife snapped.

"I wasn't trying to tell you how to drive, only you might want to keep an eye out for lahars."

"For what?"

"Rivers of mud and ash. The road up ahead could be washed out."

Barnes smirked. "Yeah Knife. Look out for lahars."

"I fucking know how to drive," Knife said.

"It's just, they could be deep," Jules said quietly. "I came across one before. It was—"

"Don't worry. I see one, I'll put my foot down and we'll plough right through."

"No!" Jules said. "Please, don't do that. The men on the back will drown."

Knife looked at Barnes. "You expect me to drive when that bitch is rabbiting in my ear?"

"Shut it, both of you," said Barnes. "Knife, get us the hell out of here. We've hung around long enough. There's a fucking shitstorm coming."

Brigitte gave a little moan.

Poor kid. She must be terrified. Jules felt a pang of remorse. Her argument with the driver had probably contributed to the girl's anxiety. Not to mention Barnes' lack of professionalism.

Jules gave her hand a reassuring pat. "*Ça y ira,*" she said; one of the few French phrases she'd picked up on her trip to France with Taine. "Everything's going to be fine. I promise. Another hour or two and we'll all be safe."

The girl's lip trembled, and her head dropped even further.

"So where do you reckon that flare came from?" Pope said. "One of these driveways?"

"About that," said Barnes, and Jules saw his lip curl. "I'm thinking we forget about looking for the flare and drive the hell out."

Pope sat forward. "No way, Barnes. What about the others? The guys back there on the road?"

Barnes shrugged. "It's in their best interests. We could waste hours pissing around looking for whoever sent that flare."

"But—"

"I reckon we were the only ones to see it."

"All the more reason to find them," Jules muttered.

Barnes' head whipped around, his eyes fixed on her.

All at once the truck lurched sideways, the smell of burning rubber hitting her as they were shunted sideways, the vehicle skewing, then graunching across the road and onto the shoulder.

Jules' stomach clenched. They were still moving.

Sliding.

The men on the flatbed screamed.

Jules gripped the door handle with one hand, and Brigitte's arm with the other. For what seemed like hours, the twin cab ground through the gravel, finally jolting to a halt in long grass. Brigitte and Pope slid into Jules, their weight crushing her from the side. Her head banged the side of the cab. She gasped. Then they were hurled back the other way.

"Shit a brick!" Barnes threw open the door. "Pope, watch the women."

Stars arcing across her eyes, Jules lifted the door handle and promptly fell out of the truck. She wasn't hurt, but it took her a minute to get to her feet, dragging herself up on the door. She looked back the way they'd come. Loosened by the earthquake swarm, a boulder the size of a filing cabinet had rolled down the hill, hitting the back of the truck. The rock had pushed the truck sideways, smashing into the back corner and crumpling it like a beer can. Its momentum dulled in the collision, still the boulder had carried on, tumbling for several metres before coming to a stop, wedged between two pines.

"Crap. Smithy's dead," one of the men said, his face pale against the bright orange of the overalls.

Jules couldn't help but look. Flung from the truck, the man had been crushed by the runaway rock. His body lay on the tar seal like a damp towel, ash already settling on him. Fifteen metres away, two men huddled beside a second man, also catapulted from the flatbed.

Perhaps that one would be okay?

On shaky legs, she inched forward.

She let out a breath. It was okay. There were no visible injuries. No blood. He'd been knocked out from the fall, that's all...Then the men turned him over. The back of his head had caved in, hit by road, or maybe a tree. The hair around the gaping cavern was matted with blood and grey matter.

He'll need a hat to cover that, Jules thought.

Her legs wobbled. She put out a hand to steady herself and, finding nothing, sunk to her knees.

"Gao didn't make it either." The man who'd turned him stepped away from Gao's body and trudged back to the flatbed, while another promptly vomited on the side of the road. The stench pricked Jules' eyes and made her heave. Saliva welled. Her hand over her mouth, Jules staggered to her feet and backed away. Two men dead. What had they felt in that moment? Confusion followed by oblivion? Or had they not seen it coming? Perhaps their quick deaths had been a mercy, given the lack of medical help.

While a couple of the men dragged their colleague off the road, Jules leaned against a tree and breathed deep. She looked south, up the hillside towards Tongariro. Where had that boulder come from? It was as if the mountain had spat it at them, like an unwanted apple pip. When mountains started throwing boulders around, it was time to get out. Only, the rear tyre of the twin cab had been shredded in the accident, the rim showing through where the rubber had been gouged and pitted.

"You fucking idiot, Knife," Barnes was yelling at the driver. "Look what you've done!"

The controller's panic was getting the better of him.

"It wasn't his fault," Jules interrupted. "And laying blame isn't going to help. It doesn't bring the dead men back and it doesn't get us out of danger. We need to get back on the road."

Barnes rounded on her, nostrils flaring, then hesitated. "Pope, I thought I told you to look after the women," he drawled.

Pope didn't get a chance to respond because an avalanche of rocks crashed on to the road behind them. Someone shouted, "Come on, Barnes. Let's just go before the mountain comes down on our heads."

"What about the guys back up the road?" another said.

"What about them? We can't go back now," the first replied. "They won't fit, anyway."

Knife scuffed his boot on the ground, kicking up stones. "Even if we had the space, we'll never make it out on this tyre."

Barnes grinned. "We don't have to make it out, do we? Just far enough to find that flare." Skirting the twin cab, he thumped the bonnet with his palm. "Load up," he shouted. "We're getting out of here."

Remote Farmhouse, Central Plateau

Up ahead, the Unimog took a left turn, snaking up a narrow gravel driveway into the foothills. Taine signalled, and followed suit.

For decades, the army had housed its training grounds on the central plateau, the area providing plenty to challenge a soldier's skills and resilience. As fickle as a teenager on the eve of Valentine's Day, the terrain could be starkly beautiful and uplifting, while at other times it was windswept and desolate. Before now, Taine had always revelled in the adventure of the place, the majesty of its sacred mountain backdrop. Not today. Today, under the cloud of drifting ash, the dark countenance of the mountains filled Taine with unease.

"Is this where the shooting star started?" Hine asked from the rear.

Read twisted to look back at her. "Hairy must think so."

"Reckon it's a good bet," Eriksen said. "There was no Civil Defence paint at the end of the driveway."

"And it's off the beaten track," Taine said. "Which means it would have been easy for the authorities to miss."

Pulling forward to allow the second Unimog space to park, he stopped the truck in the yard and swung out of the vehicle, his boots crunching on the gravel.

Meanwhile, Harris got out of the Unimog in front. Taking a couple of the men with him, he went to check inside the house, bounding up the steps two at a time.

Taine turned to Lefty and Eriksen. "You boys check the outbuildings."

The two men peeled off.

Moments later, Harris emerged. He trotted down the steps to join Taine, the men who'd been with him re-joining the Unimog.

"Anything?" Taine asked.

"No one in the house, Boss, but—"

Her eyes closed, Hine sniffed the air. "A shark is coming," she said, matter-of-fact. "I can feel it."

Hidden for over a century in a southland cove, Hine's people had become attuned to danger. What had Hine meant by *a shark*? Was it a metaphor for danger, or something more specific? Something to do with whoever set off the flare? Taine put his hand to his heart, feeling for the comfort of the pūrerehua, because he felt something too: the sensation that someone was watching them...

"The house has been trashed," Harris said out of the corner of his mouth. "We found a couple of gauze bandages with blood on them in the lounge."

Taine nodded. People who were injured and afraid often hid, making it hard for rescuers to find them. It was common in housefires, sometimes with tragic results.

"Hello!" Taine shouted. "I'm Sergeant Taine McKenna of the NZDF. We saw your flare. We're here to help."

There was a moment of silence, then someone said, "McKenna?" The voice was familiar. "I can't believe it!" Karl Pringle stepped from beneath a stand of gnarly pines and waded through the long grass to stand at the edge of the drive.

Never one to weigh up risks, Read ran over to meet him. The two men clasped hands.

"Pringle! What on earth are you doing out here?" Read clapped him on the back. "Look, Hine, you remember Pringle?"

Smiling, Hine stayed where she was.

Pringle raised a hand. "Hine, wow, you look great. I can't tell you how pleased I am to see you."

Taine and Read had met Karl Pringle last year, while on a deer culling excursion with the Department of Conservation. Turned out, they'd found more than deer. On that occasion, Pringle had been an ally, but a lot had happened since then.

"Did you set off the flare?" Taine asked.

"Found it in one of the sheds. I didn't fancy walking out of here, I can tell you." Pringle didn't move from his spot at the edge of the driveway.

Taine lifted his gun. "Read, step away." To his credit, Read didn't argue.

Out of the line of Pringle's vision, Eriksen and Lefty were returning from the sheds. Seeing Taine's gun go up, they stayed out of sight.

"Come forward, Karl," Taine said.

"I can't," replied Pringle. "There's an injured boy back here in the trees. One of the Rangipō boys. An inmate. I think his lower leg could be broken. We walked cross-country from the Desert Road after the prison bus overturned."

"We saw the bus," Taine said quietly.

Pringle's face fell. He took a step forward. "Then you'll know what happened. The bus flipped, killing the driver and about ten others. A bunch of the inmates decided they'd use the commotion to take off."

"And murdered a guard," Harris said.

"That was Barnes. And it wasn't only the guard; there were four others."

"How did the prisoners get the guns?" said Taine.

Pringle launched into an explanation, something about talking with Civil Defence and him and Lewis being the only ones left on the ground when the evacuation order came. McKenna didn't need to know any of it; he just needed to keep Pringle talking long enough for Eriksen and Lefty to double around to see if the rest of the inmates were waiting in the trees.

"Harris?" Taine murmured.

"I don't know, Boss," the corporal said under his breath. "If he's lying, he's telling a good story. How well do you know this guy?"

"Spent a few days down south with him once."

Harris arched a brow.

"It was a camping-fishing trip for the Conversation Department. Read was with us, obviously. And Hine," he added.

"Catch anything?"

"My biggest catch ever. Had to let it go. Catch and Release."

"No photos, then it didn't happen," Harris murmured.

Exactly. A lot of people counted on the details of that trip remaining a secret. Pringle was one of only a handful who knew the truth about Hine. As far as Taine knew, he'd held his tongue.

"It's okay, Boss," Eriksen called from beyond the pines. "Brooker here told us the same story." The two soldiers appeared behind Pringle, each of them supporting a youth wearing a temporary splint. "Seems Brooker was stranded in the tussock and instead of saving his own neck, Pringle stuck around to help him. Now Brooker owes him his first-born son and any money he wins on the Lotto on Saturday."

Using his free arm, Lefty pointed to the Unimog. "Let's get you set up in the Beast over there. What do you say we check out your mate's First Aid skills?" he said to the youth. The trio hobbled off.

Lowering his rifle, Taine strode across the gravel to shake Pringle's hand. "Karl. Good to see you. Apologies."

"No, no, you were right to be careful. These are strange times."

Taine signalled to the others, letting them know they'd be pulling out shortly and to get back into the vehicles, and turned back to Pringle. "What can you tell us about the inmates? How many of them are there?"

"When Brooker and I last saw them, there were a dozen or more, travelling north-west on foot." Pringle pulled a sheet of paper out of his pocket, turning briefly as Read gave him a farewell pat on the shoulder. "I have the manifest. I made a note of the men I saw leaving. Put a line through the ones I know are dead. Some of the others might be under the bus or flung further afield; I didn't see them. I don't know. I don't even know why I kept a list. Something to keep my mind busy, I guess." He trailed off, then thought again, adding, "You know, most of these Rangipō blokes are just kids who got dealt a crap hand; boys from troubled families who got in with bad crowds, and went to seed. All they need is a second chance to turn their lives around. I completely misjudged Barnes, though. If my intuition had been better, Lewis and the others might still be alive."

Taine's jaw twitched as he recalled the murdered guard. "No one's blaming you."

"Even so."

Taine understood how he felt. Friends had lost their lives and their limbs as the result of his decisions. People could tell you it wasn't your fault, still you carried it with you. He cleared his throat. "Right, well, we have a big area to cover, and no idea what the mountains have planned, so we should move our arses."

"I'd like to travel with Brooker if that's okay? The kid's pretty shaken up."

"Of course." Taine watched Pringle go, then pivoted in the gravel about to make for the Pinzgauer.

Damn. They weren't going anywhere yet. A battered vehicle was limping up the driveway. A white Toyota twin cab with Conservation Department branding, it was loaded with people: in the cab and on the flatbed.

And all but two wearing orange jumpsuits.

The newcomers got out of the cab. Taine drew in a breath. That woman looked like... Taine clenched his jaw.

Behind the Pinzgauer, Pringle hissed, "McKenna, the scrawny guy at the back is Barnes. Oh Jesus, that's Jules, isn't it?"

It was all Taine could do to keep his voice even. "Does Barnes know you're alive?"

"No, or he would have taken me out, same as Lewis. He thinks I was squished under the bus."

"Let's keep it that way, shall we?" Out loud, he said, "Harris, with me."

*

It was Taine. Striding down the driveway towards her in the middle of a volcanic hell-storm. Jules wasn't surprised to see him; the army often got called in to help in national emergencies. What surprised her was the way her heart had done a backflip the moment she laid eyes on him. Like a one-thousand-volt kick from a defibrillator. All this time pretending she'd moved on, only to find out her feelings hadn't changed. Well, her reasons for leaving him hadn't changed either.

"Sergeant Taine McKenna, NZDF," he said to Barnes. "And this is my corporal, Shane Harris. How can we help?"

Jules waited for him to acknowledge her, for that familiar twitch of his jaw, but he didn't even make eye contact. Had it really come to that?

"Barnes. Civil Defence, Taupō. As you can see we're a little short on transport. Wondered if you could lend us a vehicle?"

"We can certainly give a lift to anyone who needs it," Taine said. There was a thud as a couple of the men jumped down from the flatbed.

Barnes turned. "And where the hell do you think you're going?"

The men shuffled back.

What was going on? Jules' spine tingled. How could she have been so stupid? She was a scientist and yet she'd ignored all the outlying observations. The fact that Barnes knew everyone's name. Their lack of transport. The guns. The way Pete had looked at her...

"We have a Unimog heading out of the area in a few minutes," Taine stepped forward. "Maybe the ladies would like a ride out?"

This time his eyes met hers, and Jules knew something was wrong.

She took Brigitte's hand, bustling the girl away from Barnes. "Yes, come on, Brigitte, let's get on the truck," she said.

Gunfire exploded behind her.

"No one is going anywhere," Barnes said.

*

Taine's blood pounded. Idiot! Pringle had warned him and still he'd underestimated Barnes. Worse, he'd put Jules in harm's way. Now a man who'd killed four men in cold blood was using her as a human shield.

Taine tightened his grip on the MARS-L, keeping his voice even. "Don't make things worse, Barnes. Let the women go." Taine should have put a bullet through Barnes' brain when he had the chance. There'd been a moment when he'd had a clear shot. *Would have, could have, should have...*

Barnes pushed the barrel of the M4 into Jules' back. "I don't think so." He smiled.

"What do you want?"

Barnes snickered. "Same as everyone else. To piss off out of here. But as you can see, our transport is somewhat fucked. Blindsided in an unfortunate accident. Luckily, the army is here to save us. I reckon one of your Unimogs should do the trick nicely."

"What if we can't give you one?"

"What if I blow this little lady's head off?"

Barnes' grin made Taine's blood run cold. He'd faced some monsters in his time but nothing as evil as this.

"Boss?" Harris prompted.

Taine ran over the risks. Barnes had the best hand. Trying to rescue Jules and Brigitte was out of the question. Not while Barnes had his M4 trained on Jules. That way could only end in a bloodbath. Because if she died, Taine would kill Barnes and every man with him. On the other hand, if Taine let Barnes take her, then as long as she was useful to him as a hostage, Barnes might keep her alive. She'd have a chance.

Their best option was to reshuffle the deck. Regroup. Then he'd go after Barnes.

Providing the mountains didn't kill them all first.

"Stand down, Harris," Taine said.

"Boss—"

"I said stand down."

Barnes chuckled. "Smart decision. Throw the guns on the ground in front of you. Slowly." Taine lifted his MARS-L over his head and dropped it on the driveway. Harris did the same with his. "Now step back. A little more. Pope, Ants, take the guns."

Taine avoided Jules' eyes. He had to trust that she'd know he'd come after her. That she'd understand.

When Pope and Ants had Taine and Harris' own rifles trained on them, Taine said, "Why don't you take that Unimog?" He waved a hand towards the Unimog that Lefty and Eriksen had taken Brooker to, diverting their attention and praying Pringle would have the sense to make himself scarce.

Barnes eyes narrowed. "I don't think so. Not that one. We'll take this one, at the back."

Taine didn't blink. Barnes could still change his mind.

Pope fired into the sky. "Right, you lot," he shouted to Taine's men. "All of you, out of the vehicles. Put your guns in a pile here. The headsets, too."

One by one, his soldiers descended the vehicles and laid their weapons on the pile. None of them were too happy about it. Taine prayed those who knew her wouldn't give Jules away.

Miller was the first to lay down his MARS-L. "Wankers," he said, none too quietly under his breath.

Read's glare could strip paint.

Lefty wasn't having a bar of it. He held his gun across his chest like a toddler with a lollipop.

"Private Wright," Taine said quietly.

Barnes shoved Jules in the back, pushing her forward, the barrel never breaking contact. "NOW!"

Lefty added his rifle and a Glock17 to the pile.

"And the headset."

Lefty ripped it off. Tossed it over.

"Knife. Collect them up," Barnes said. He dug in his pocket, pulled out a plastic Bic lighter, and lobbed it to one of his men. "Ants. Make a fire."

"What?" Ants giggled. "I don't think that's going to work. You can't burn guns, Barnes."

"No, but we can burn the radios and the sat phones, can't we?"

Ants chuckled. "Awesome. I think I saw some firewood in one of the back sheds when we were here earlier. Farm like this, there's probably some kerosene, too. We'll throw them on the BBQ – they'll cook up a treat." He turned and scampered around the side of the house. By the time, Barnes' men had loaded up the weapons, Ants was back, throwing firewood into the kettle BBQ on the deck. It took only minutes to incinerate the section's communication equipment, the black cloud of burning plastic mingling with white volcanic ash. Ants poked at the melting casings with a kitchen spatula.

"Right, you've got what you want, so go," Taine said.

"Not quite yet," Barnes said slowly, and suddenly Taine wanted to take it all back. Go back in time. Shoot the bastard's head off. How could he abandon Jules to this monster? Who knew what Barnes was capable of?

"Barnes, come on. Don't push your luck. Let's just go," Pope said.

"Shoot out all the tyres first," Barnes said. "I don't want any of these heroes following us."

Pope wiped his mouth with the back of his hand. "Okay, yeah. Good call." He lifted Harris' rifle and ripped into the Unimog's rear tyre...barely making a dent. Something Trigger Grierson had said once about their rifle penetration being weaker than weasel piss flitted through Taine's mind. Those Michelin tyres would take a few rounds to disable and Barnes didn't seem the patient sort. There was a chance the remaining trucks would still be functional.

"Pope, knock it off," a man shouted over the racket. "I already sorted it." He held up a greasy orange-sleeved arm and dangled some black cables. Taine swallowed. Damn. He'd ripped out the spark plugs.

Barnes' cackle made Taine's skin crawl. "Gotta love it when the government goody-goods insist on teaching us helpful new skills, don't ya? Bring those with you, Rutledge," he said, flicking his head at the man. "Let's get the ladies on the truck, shall we?" He shoved Jules in the back.

Taine clenched his teeth.

Twisting, Jules glared at Barnes a moment before speaking softly to the girl, "Come on, Brigitte. It's okay." Jules took her hand, helped her onto the truck, then climbed in after her.

"Hey, Barnes," Harris called, just as Barnes was about to get on himself. "What about you leave the women and take me instead?"

"Harris—" Taine said.

Ants grinned. "I reckon he's trying to save his own skin."

Harris held up his hands. "Yeah, yeah, okay, so maybe that's true. I can't deny that I'd prefer to have my boots on solid ground. Think about it: the women are a liability, whereas me, I'm army. I can use a sat phone, drive the truck, navigate." He took a step closer. "The army does all its training in this region, so I know it like the back of my hand. Plus, let's say the truck rolls; how useful are two women going to be?"

"God loves a trier, aye, Barnesy?" Shaking his head, Ants turned on his heel.

"You're making a mistake," Harris went on. "How do you think you're going to get through the check points? You think the army haven't heard about you lot? That McKenna didn't call it in already? Take me with you. I can get you wherever you want to go."

What was Harris playing at?

"Anywhere we want to go, aye?" Ants turned back. He put his face up to Harris', the MARS-L pointed at his boot. "Can you get us out of the country?"

Harris paused, then shrugged. "Dunno. Maybe. I used to be with the Aussie police."

Taine felt the muscle at his jaw twitch. A man on the inside. Would Barnes go for it?

Sauntering over to Harris, Barnes folded his arms. Sniffed.

Taine waited, his stomach in knots.

Finally, Barnes said, "Okay, get in the cab, arsehole. Any trouble, I'll fucking shoot you, you got that?"

"You said you'd let the women go," Taine said.

Barnes' smile didn't reach his eyes. "I never said that."

Harris scrambled for the truck.

"Harris," Taine called after him, "when this is over, I'll have you court martialled."

At the top of the step, Harris turned and looked Taine hard in the eye. "I'll look forward to it, McKenna," he said.

Barnes laughed. He leapt into the Unimog after Harris, calling, "Move out."

CHAPTER TEN

Central plateau, remote farmhouse

"Harris, take the wheel," Barnes said. "Pope, you watch him. I don't want any funny business."

Harris slipped into the driver's seat, and reversed the vehicle. Barnes stood in the aisle, his legs wide to brace himself as they turned.

At the rear of the vehicle, Jules glanced back at her friends assembled on the driveway: Hine, Read, Eriksen, Lefty.

Taine.

When he'd disappeared from view, Jules turned to the man nearest her. "Who are you?" she demanded. "You're not Civil Defence."

"Took you long enough, sweetheart. We're from Rangipō."

The prison? That explained the orange jumpsuits. But Rangipō was a low security facility. They didn't hold hardened criminals there. Not typically.

"I don't understand. Why are you boys doing this? You can't abandon those people while the area is under a state of emergency. They have no way of getting out. The crater lake could erupt. You're leaving them to die."

Whining softly, Brigitte dropped her head onto Jules' shoulder.

"It's what they did to us, isn't it?" the man said, his face grim. "Left us to die."

"I'm sure that's not—"

"You don't know fucking shit, lady. Everyone left us. *Everyone.* There was no one coming. Wouldn't even send us a vehicle. Why bother to risk your neck for a bunch of lowlife crims, hey?"

"Not *those* people back there. Not the army. They'll help. It's their job to save lives."

The man shook his head. "Not ours."

"Yes, even yours. You're New Zealand citizens, aren't you?"

Brigitte groaned. Jules put her arm around Brigitte's shoulders and pulled the girl to her. She buried her face in Jules' chest.

The man stood up, placed his hand on the roof to steady himself. "It's too late now."

Jules reached out, touching his hand. "What's your name?"

He paused, then mumbled, "Eaton."

"Look Eaton, please, it's not too late. You could still save them. Just convince Barnes to turn back."

Eaton's laugh was harsh. He leaned close, his breath on Jules' forehead. "You know what happened to the last four people who stood up to Barnes? They're dead. Shot in the back. In the face. Worse. Their bodies are lying on the Desert Road where the birds are probably pecking out their organs. No way I'm going to end up like that, so you can sit down and shut up."

Jules' pulse hammered. "But—"

Eaton pointed an index finger at her. "Another word and I'll tell Barnes."

In Jules' arms, Brigitte's body trembled with terror. Jules closed her mouth. She swallowed.

Turning on his heel, Eaton stalked forward and took a seat near the front.

Something was going on up there. Jules strained to hear over the rumble of the truck.

"Why the fuck did you let Harris drive this way?" Barnes barked. "You saw the rocks. And what about the lahar-thing the Conservation chick was talking about? We have to turn around."

"Not yet," said Pope. Through the crowd of men, Jules saw him poke Harris in the ribs with the soldier's own rifle. "We're going to pick up the others: Climo, Pete, Grant, Taliava. Remember them?"

Barnes grunted. "I'm trying to look after your best interests here. We should get out while we can," he said. "Is this really how you planned to die? Under an avalanche of rocks and mud?"

"It'll take a few minutes," Pope said. "If we don't see them by the time we get to the rockfall, we'll turn around."

"For all you know, they could already be dead."

"We'll take that chance."

Barnes gave it one more shot. "What about McKenna and his men?"

"Those army guys aren't going anywhere," Eaton said, his eyes flicking back towards Jules.

"Yeah-nah, they're not going anywhere," Ants echoed.

Jules wished she could see Barnes' face. The douchebag clearly didn't care who he fucked over. Friend or foe, it was all the same to him. She wouldn't mind a look at Harris' face either. Another piece of shit. Turning on his mates like that. Jules thought of Taine's former corporal, a quietly spoken Chinese-New Zealander with the stealth of a cat. Jules had barely known Coolie, just a matter of days, but he'd never have betrayed the soldiers in his section. Whatever the circumstances.

They rounded the corner to a sea of orange. The men from Lake Rotoaira were all there, clustered around the bodies at the side of the road.

At the front of the pack, Climo waved the truck down. He opened the cab door, and swung up on the running board. "Nice wheels," he said.

"Yeah." Barnes tilted his head towards Harris. "Came with a chauffeur, too."

"And fucking guns," Ants said.

Barnes leaned out the window, shouting, "Taliava! Tell those guys to move their arses. We're out of here."

"What about the bodies?"

"What about them? You expecting an invite to the funerals?"

Taliava gave Barnes a long look, then jogged to the back of the truck, and clambered onboard. Sitting opposite Jules and Brigitte, Pete picked up where he'd left off earlier, staring at the pair of them like they were steak.

Only now, Jules understood why.

Brigitte huddled closer.

Harris turned the truck around, heading east on Lake Rotoaira Road towards the main highway. The old Mercedes truck bounced and jolted along the road, the rumble of its engine numbing nerves stretched as thin as tin foil. Ignoring Pete's stare, she looked over his head at the swirling ash. Eventually, they emerged from the pines into the raw beauty of the tussock.

Jules' shoulder had gone to sleep. She patted Brigitte on the arm. "Hey, where are you from, honey?" she murmured.

Brigitte stopped sobbing. She sat up and scrubbed at her eyes. "France. Saint-Rémy-de-Provence."

Jules rolled her shoulder, stretching out the aching muscles. This was good. Talking might bring Brigitte out of herself. If there was a chance of escaping Barnes, Jules would need her to not fall apart. "Saint-Rémy? It's in Provence? Is it near the ocean, then?"

"Yes, it is in Provence. However, it is not on the coast. It's near Les Baux."

Jules nodded. "I don't know the town, but I've visited Les Baux."

Brigitte gave a weak smile. Even with her cheeks streaked with tears, she was pretty. "There are a lot of tourists who go to this place."

"I know, right? And they drive buses up there on those skinny windy roads. We stopped to see the Van Gogh exhibition in the quarry before going up to the citadel. We loved the catapults." Jules traced a parabola with her hand, punctuated it with a cheery doink when her imaginary boulder landed.

"Les trébuchets. Yes, yes."

"It's a fabulous spot. Wonderful views of the countryside, too. Olives and vineyards. I was there with my boyfriend a couple of years ago."

The man we left on the driveway.

Brigitte's face crumpled again, her lower lip trembling.

"Brigitte?" The girl shook her head. She glanced towards Barnes at the front of the truck. "Can't," she whispered.

She was too frightened. Understandable. If what Eaton said was true, even his own men were too scared to cross him. Jules needed to give her some hope. Dropping her head close to Brigitte's, she lowered her voice until it was barely a sigh, "The sergeant back at the house. Taine McKenna. That was him."

Brigitte's eyes grew wide.

"We're not together now, but Taine will find a way to come for us. I know it."

There was no question that he would come, and it had nothing to do with the history between them. Taine was a pathological hero. For the briefest moment Jules was back in Te Anau looking over the lake, the day she'd told him it was over.

"You're a soldier first, Taine. It's etched on your being. You think it's your job to save everyone."

Brigitte's face softened. She took Jules' hands in hers as if Jules were a little girl who'd told her she was going to grow up to be a fairy. And to be fair, with no vehicles, no weapons, and the entire region about to blow, it was an impossible mission.

Jules smiled inwardly.

Since when had that ever stopped Taine?

*

Pringle rolled out from under the Pinzgauer. McKenna put out a hand to pull him to his feet.

He dusted off his pants. "Jeez, that was close. I thought Pope was going to kill me when he was shooting out the tyres."

McKenna's eyes swept over him. "You're okay? He didn't hit you?"

"Nah, nah, I'm good. A bit shaken up, that's all. Nice bit of reverse psychology earlier, steering Barnes away from Brooker. Although, the poor kid's in for a hell of a time now we have to get him out on foot."

"I didn't see them take the stretcher," Read said. "It should still be on the Unimog."

Eriksen rolled his eyes. "Please no. Where are the Zambucks when you need one, aye? I hate doing stretcher duty. Remember that time me and Lefty carried Jug out of the Ureweras? It bloody near killed us. Gave me calluses the size of golf balls. I reckon Jug was in better shape at the end of it than we were."

"Tell me about it," Read said. Glancing at Pringle, he arched an eyebrow, then checked out some imaginary calluses of his own. Pringle grinned. He and Read had done their turn on either end of a stretcher during that trip to the Fiordland sounds.

"We're not there yet," said McKenna, cocking his head back toward the road. "Barnes forgot about the twin cab."

They all turned. He was right. The twin cab was still sitting where Barnes had left it on the driveway. Granted, when they'd arrived, the vehicle had been so weighed down the chassis was dragging on the ground, nevertheless they'd been able to drive it. Which meant the engine was fine.

"It'll be a slow trip," McKenna went on, "and it'll shred the rims, so the truck'll be a write-off, but it should get him out."

"Pity we can't swap out one of the Unimog tyres," said Lefty.

"You mean, the ones that aren't munted," replied Eriksen.

Lefty's comment set off a sparkler in Pringle's head. "Hang on. There's a Ramco boat on its trailer in one of the back sheds! What if we swap out a trailer wheel?"

"Eriksen?" McKenna asked.

"Yeah, that'll work."

"I'll give you a hand," Pringle said.

*

When they'd gone, Hamish Miller scuffed the gravel with the toe of his boot. "One twin cab isn't going to carry everyone," he said quietly.

"Doesn't have to," Read said. "Because some of us are going after Barnes."

"That *was* the doc with Barnes, then," Miller said, which made Taine look up. He'd forgotten his men had taken to calling Jules doc.

"Hairy will look after her," Lefty said quickly.

"So all that stuff Hairy said before. That wasn't for real? He wasn't trying to save his own skin?"

"No!" Read frowned. "Of course not."

Lefty cuffed Miller on the shoulder. "Geez, Miller. Why would you even say that? No way Hairy would sell us out to save his own arse. He's good people."

"I'm just saying, is all. I mean, he wouldn't be the only one wishing he was somewhere else right now, would he?"

Taine clenched his jaw. Miller had a point. Right now, all Taine wanted was to get Brooker on that twin cab and on his way south, so he could go after Barnes, but not everyone would feel that way.

"Shut the fuck up, Miller," Lefty took a step toward the private. "My nephew has more balls than you, and he isn't even two yet. Why did you even join up, anyway?"

Taine stepped between the two men. "Stand down, Wright." He turned. "Miller, as soon as we get the twin cab sorted, you'll be taking Brooker back to Waiouru. Alert Major Arnold about what's happened. And if the army has already pulled out, then it's your responsibility to get Brooker to safety. Understood?"

Miller nodded.

"Anyone else who wants to go should take the opportunity now," Taine said. "The rest of us will go after Barnes."

"Hine should go with Miller," Read said.

Hine shook her head. "I'll stay."

"Hine—"

"Matt, Jules is my friend, too. I want to help."

Read wasn't keen: his face said it all, pleading Taine to order her back to base.

"Besides, how many men were on that truck?" Hine continued. "If he's going to save those people, McKenna is going to need us."

At that moment, Pringle and Eriksen appeared from behind the house, Eriksen rolling the wheel in front of him.

"Some of us are going after Jules," Hine called.

"Yep, I'm in," Eriksen yelled back as he manoeuvred the wayward wheel towards the twin cab.

"I'll go, too," Pringle said, slipping in beside them.

McKenna turned to him. "Karl, no. You don't have to do this. This isn't your responsibility: we're soldiers, it's our job to protect."

"And I know those men. They're not all like Barnes. I might be able to help."

Taine frowned. Did he understand the stakes? "You're sure about this? Because given the chance, Barnes will kill you. You witnessed what he did to your colleague. And those others on the road."

Eriksen interrupted them. "I hate to break it up, guys," he called, "but I don't have a jack, and if we're going to get Brooker out of here, I'll need some muscle to lift the truck."

*

Good one. Just jump on a truck with a bunch of armed fugitives. Not to mention their murderous leader. Shane tightened his grip on the wheel. Well, it had made sense at the time. Although, he probably should have paid more attention to Pringle's comment that a dozen or more prisoners had survived the crash, or at least asked for a gander at the sheet of paper he'd been waving about. That way Shane would have been prepared for these others waiting around the corner. How many of them were there in the back of the Unimog, now? Fourteen, fifteen? Made the odds of him getting out of this and home to Wendy even slimmer. Would it have changed things? Probably not.

He'd seen an opportunity to help the women, so he'd taken it. It was a spur of the moment thing. And one of the women was McKenna's ex, Jules. Shane had heard the others talking about her. Maybe knowing she meant something to McKenna had spurred his decision. If it had been Wendy or the kids herded onto the truck with Barnes, he hoped someone would have done the same. A niggle wormed its way into his thoughts: what if McKenna's court-martial comment back at the farmhouse had been for real and not just for Barnes' benefit? What if he'd really taken Shane for a deserter? It was no secret that the sergeant hadn't warmed to him.

Shane shook off the thought and concentrated on the road. When McKenna and the others caught up, Shane would find out exactly what they were thinking. Until they did, he'd do whatever he could to keep the women safe. And from what he remembered of his hostage training with the police, to do that he would need to gain Barnes' confidence.

They were coming up to the state highway intersection. Shane slowed the Unimog. "Okay guys, which way?" he said, keeping his tone light-hearted. "North or south?"

"Barnes?" Pope asked.

Barnes hesitated.

"What about south?" Shane said, turning the wheel and rolling the vehicle forward.

"Stop."

The command was so quiet the hair rose on the back of Shane's neck. He stopped the Unimog in the middle of the road. There wasn't much chance of a collision. Apart from McKenna and the guys back at the farmhouse, there was no one else for miles.

"Why the fuck are we stopping?" someone shouted.

Barnes turned and pointed the gun down the length of the vehicle. The men pulled back as if he were Moses parting the Red Sea. "Because I don't rate our chances of getting past an army roadblock at Waiouru, that's why."

Pope sniffed. "Yeah, well that's why we have this guy, isn't it?" The safety off, he jabbed Shane in the ribs with the rifle again. The wanker had done it a few times now and it was starting to piss him off royally. Shane grinned anyway. If Barnes decided on going south to Waiouru, Shane might be able to signal to the soldiers on the roadblock...

"I don't know," said Knife. "You really want to go north? The road around Lake Taupō is already pretty hairy, and that's *without* an earthquake shaking the shit out of you every five minutes."

"My missus is always complaining about that road," said another. "She hates driving it. Thin as a wafer, with the cliff on one side and the lake on the other."

"Barnes is right. We can't go south," said a big Samoan near the front. "You're forgetting about the prison bus. It's lying across the road."

"The army might have cleared it away by now." Shane recognised Ants' nervous giggle.

"What if they haven't?" the Samoan said. "If it's still there, we'll have to turn around and come back. Things could be worse by then."

Shane glanced in the side mirrors, hoping for a glimpse of the twin cab.

Come on, McKenna.

"What are you gawping at, Harris?" Barnes said.

"Nothing."

"Pining for your sergeant?"

"No."

"Then how about you turn this truck around? We're going north to Taupō."

Shane took his time backing up the Unimog, making a three-point turn, before heading north. How long would it take McKenna to work out that the twin cab was still functional? The sergeant had better hurry. Already Shane had had to swerve for boulders, cracks, even a fallen tree, obstacles that hadn't been there when they'd been looking for the flare. The Unimog was built for unpredictable terrain, but an overloaded, damaged twin cab?

A vehicle's headlights shone through the ash. It was still a way off, maybe a minute out.

"Shit, that's an army truck!" Knife said.

Shane's heart leapt. An army LOV.

"Drive right past," Barnes replied.

Shane shook his head. "That's not how it works, Barnes. It's a national emergency. The army's evacuating civilians from this area. They'll expect me to stop for a quick sit-rep."

Barnes sucked air over his teeth. "Okay, so you stop, say howdy, and move on."

"Except that's not how it'll play, is it? They'll be expecting soldiers in uniform, and maybe some civilians. You guys are all wearing orange jumps suits."

Out of the corner of his eye, Shane caught Barnes' smirk. "Of course, that's because we're Civil Defence, aren't we?"

"It won't work. Not this time. I wasn't kidding when I said McKenna reported your bus earlier. Even without clearing the bus off the road, the army will be looking for you."

"Not in one of their own trucks, they won't," Barnes said. He thrust the gun in Shane's ribs, digging it into his skin. "Send them on their way."

"Is this really necessary? I already said I'll help."

Barnes bent and put his lips to Shane's ear. "You will indeed, because otherwise I'll blow your insides all the way to Auckland. Same goes for anyone on that truck."

Shane's stomach lurched. "Hey, take it easy. I'm only trying to—"

"Shut up," Barnes hissed. "Everyone get down out of sight. Pope, you too. And keep those women quiet."

Flashing his lights, Shane slowed the Unimog, pulling up to the MV-GS until the two driver doors were adjacent.

Maybe it would be someone he knew? Someone who he could send a message to without Barnes knowing. The window of the truck lowered. Damn – Shane didn't know the driver, so a cryptic message wouldn't help. He needed something else.

Rolling down his window, he lay his forearm on the sill. "Hey," he said, letting his hand curl over the sill. "Where are you headed?" On the outside of the door, out of sight of Barnes, Shane's fingers tapped out a silent message. Shane hoped the soldier would notice, and that he was half-way proficient in Morse.

"On my way back to base," the soldier said. "Got some civilians in the back. My last trip. You?"

"Farmhouse a bit further north," Shane replied.

"Someone change their mind at the last minute?"

Shane laughed. 'Something like that."

"You might want to keep your eyes peeled," the driver said. "Some Rangipō prisoners made a run for it."

Coincidence? Or had he understood the message? Shane couldn't tell.

"No kidding."

"They reckon they killed a guard. Didn't you see the bus?"

"Must have missed it. Too busy looking out for cracks and rocks, I guess. Does that mean the Turangi road block is still in place?"

"It was still there when we came through, but things are hotting up all over, so everyone's waiting on the call to get out. I don't reckon they'll be there much longer. A few hours maybe."

The barrel of the rifle jabbed deeper into Shane's side. "I'd better get cracking, then."

"Good luck, mate."

"Yeah, you too."

The LOV pulled away.

Behind him, the men sat up.

"What do we do now?" asked Ants. "You heard what that soldier said. The army are looking for us."

Barnes clucked his tongue. "You want to listen a bit harder, Antony. He also said they'll be pulling out soon. Which means all we have to do is hole up somewhere for a couple of hours until everyone clears out."

"Yeah," Ants said. "Good call, Barnesy."

Shane watched the mirrors until the red points disappeared in a cloud of ash.

CHAPTER ELEVEN

Maungapōhatu, Te Urewera Forest

Wayne's truck crunched through the gravel, throwing up dust and adding to the film of ash on the windshield. He turned on the wipers, the dry blades scraping against the glass like fingernails on a blackboard. There was nothing else for it; spraying the window would just make it worse. He opened the side window and promptly closed it. Too dusty. He'd choke to death before he got there. It wasn't far now; just a couple of kilometres outside Maungapōhatu, for all that it felt like another planet.

As a boy, he'd always loved to come out here to the family homestead, their kāinga tipu. Even now, as he turned the truck off the gravel road onto the narrow dirt track, he could feel his excitement rising. There was something about the air out here. Not this dust and ash but the way the air seeped up from the ground and draped itself about the trees in misty shrouds. Air that was centuries old, yet so fresh it made your nostrils sting. So, when you breathed in, it was like you were being reborn, like you could start your life over and anything would be possible. He chuckled. That sounded like a poem. Or a song. He should try and remember that. Impress Pania.

He wasn't even a kilometre from the house when the truck stalled. It had happened last week too. Pania had been on at him to get the battery looked at. He tried restarting the truck a couple of times and ended up flooding the engine. He'd have to wait a few minutes before he tried again.

Wayne lowered the window and took a deep breath.

Actually, maybe that isn't such a good idea today.

Instead, he closed his eyes and listened. He'd scared away the birds with his truck, and the patu-paiarehe-fairies only played their flutes at night, so the forest was quiet. Maybe that explained why he loved it here so much. Life was simpler. Less hectic. Every return was like a spiritual homecoming.

Let's be honest, it's because Uncle Rawiri let you get away with shit Mum and Dad would have skinned you for.

It was a pity there were no jobs out here. Then again, if there were, the place might lose its magic.

Wayne tried the ignition again. The engine started. He chugged the last few hundred metres to the homestead, the house coming into view through the trees. It looked like Uncle had been busy mowing the lawns. He'd done a pretty good job too, given that the mower was about the same age as he was, and the blades hadn't been sharpened in god-knows-how-long.

Wayne parked at the end of the track. He didn't bother to lock the truck, just left the keys on the dash. "Uncle Rawiri!" he called.

"Wayne?" Uncle stepped out onto the porch. "What are you doing here? I thought you weren't coming until next week."

Wayne stepped up onto the porch and they shared their breath in a hongi. When Wayne stepped back, he said, "Pania sent me."

Looking skyward, Uncle shook his head. "Well, don't tell me she's sent *more* groceries? It's going to take me until Christmas to get through all the food she left last time."

Wayne laughed. "Nah, it's not that." He grabbed at the air and caught a flake of ash. "It's this national emergency. They're evacuating people from around Lake Taupō."

Uncle's face clouded. He was going to dig his toes in. When he made his mind up about something, the old man was as tenacious as a tapeworm.

"You'd better come in," Uncle said. "I'll put the kettle on."

Wayne followed him inside, waiting while his uncle brewed up, the old matakite eventually handing him a cup of tea and one of Pania's home-baked Anzac biscuits from a Tupperware container.

Wayne took a swig of the tea. "Pania sent me to bring you back to Rotorua. At least, until this blows over."

"The earthquakes. Yeah, I was listening to the girl on the radio. They never said anything about evacuating this far out."

Wayne brushed a biscuit crumb off his jersey. "They didn't. Not yet. Still, if things get worse and they close the roads, you could be stuck out here on your own."

"I'll be fine. Like I said, I've got groceries to last until Christmas."

"This isn't about groceries."

Uncle rolled his tongue inside his mouth. "This is my home, Wayne. I've only just got back."

"Tell that to Pania. Girl's giving me a headache going on about how much she misses you."

Uncle Rawiri snorted. "That's because you're crap at fixing stuff."

"Yeah? Well, you hog the bathroom." Wayne grinned.

Uncle Rawiri sat down at the kitchen table, the same one Wayne used to eat his breakfast at during the school holidays. He clasped his mug in his hands. "I can't go, Wayne."

"C'mon. I'm not asking for you to come back for good. Just for a few days, until the danger's passed. Pania's already made your old bed up. When I left, she was baking that slice you like."

"I can't."

"Look, I get that being in town stifled your visions, but what's the use of a gift if you're dead?"

"Wayne, I'm old."

"And because you're old, you're not important? That's bullshit."

Uncle Rawiri looked up. "The sisters appeared to me again."

Wayne gaped. He dragged out a chair and sat down. "What?"

Uncle shrugged. "They popped in for a visit. I was sitting on the porch, dozing. The morepork didn't come – well, how could she? – but I saw them."

"It's been decades. Why now?"

Uncle threw up his hands. "I don't know. When do I ever really know? I think they came to give me a message."

"What message?"

Uncle Rawiri stared at him.

"Sorry." Wayne sipped his tea. He should know by now that deciphering uncle's visions was like figuring out the answers to the entire crossword from a single clue.

"Could it be another taniwha?" Wayne said, his heart skipping a beat.

A flake of ash blew in and settled on the table.

"It might be about the volcanoes," Uncle said eventually. "The last time the sisters came, they warned me about the geyser… I was thinking, if the mountains or the crater lake erupted it would be the same thing, wouldn't it? Just on a bigger scale."

"If that's the message, if Lake Taupō is going to erupt, then you have to get out with me. They're saying the last time it happened, two thousand years ago, people knew about it as far away as Rome and China. I reckon that puts Maungapōhatu in the danger zone." He swallowed the last of his tea. It was cold.

"I can't leave, Wayne. The fire demons might come again."

"And what if they do? What if they come with a message from Rūaumoko, earthquake-maker and god of volcanoes himself? If they say Rūaumoko plans to light the bonfire to end all bonfires beneath the earth to keep his mother warm, what then? Who will you tell? Your soldier-friend Taine McKenna? The entire army couldn't hold this back. The supervolcano is *already* erupting and no one has the power to stop it."

The old man looked up. "Could you call Taine for me? When you get back to town? Tell him what I said."

"Come back with me, Uncle. Please."

Getting up from the table, his uncle tipped the remains of his tea in the sink. He placed a hand on Wayne's shoulder and gave it a quick squeeze. "You give that girl of yours a hug for me, won't you? Tell her, thank you for all the baking."

CHAPTER TWELVE

Remote Farmhouse, Central Plateau

With his shoulders touching Miller's on one side and Pringle's on the other, Taine hooked his fingers under the chassis, bent his knees, and took a breath. "Lift!"

They all heaved, raising the twin cab so Eriksen could change the wheel.

"Bugger," Eriksen said. "There's some damage beneath the wheel arch. Crumpled metal. It's going to take me a bit to get the old one off."

"Make it quick, Adrian," Lefty wheezed. "This fucker is heavy."

"Okay, okay."

All at once there was a roar, louder than the blast from a Carl Gustav M3. The ground shook and the slope behind the farmhouse erupted in an explosion of red-black lava. Boulders flew from a fissure in the earth, some of them the size of footballs. Thrust metres into the air, they rained on the sheds, or hit the ground, spitting up dirt like a volley of mortar fire.

A wave of heat hit them. It was all Taine could do not to release his grip on the chassis. Eriksen was still under the truck. "Nobody move," Taine shouted.

"What's happening?" Read called. On the other side of the twin cab, their hands hooked under the chassis, Read and Parata twisted their torsos this way and that, turning themselves inside out to see. "What's going on?"

"Eruption," yelled Miller.

"Jesus," said Parata, his face creased in panic.

"It's coming straight for us," said Miller, his eyes on the hillside where the mountain's lifeblood pumped from the wound, the torrent surging towards them.

"Eriksen!" Taine called.

"I can do it, boss. All I need is one minute."

The river of lava had reached the sheds, the first structure exploding in flames, its gnarled timbers cracking and firing red-gold embers into the air.

"We've got to help Brooker," Pringle screamed in Taine's ear. 'He's still on the Unimog."

Hine was the closest.

"Hine!" Taine yelled.

"No!" Read said.

"I'll get him." Hine let go of the truck, Private Bahr groaning as the load increased.

Spending most of her life on the run had made Hine fleet-footed; she'd already covered half the distance to the Unimog.

"The rest of you, hold your ground," Taine said as Eriksen wrestled the mangled wheel off the axle. Metal clanked and the wheel ground loose. Eriksen thrust it behind him, the mutilated doughnut running in a wild half circle before collapsing. With pit stop speed, Eriksen deadlifted the replacement trailer wheel upright, ready to roll into place.

Behind the house, the lava snaked forward, its timbers cackling and shrieking as the fire took hold.

Hine leapt into the back of the Unimog.

"Hurry!" Miller screamed.

"This is crap," Bahr said. "Boss, come on, we have to get out of here."

"Not much longer," Taine said. "Unless you want to volunteer to carry Brooker."

Bahr grimaced. "Much longer and you can forget about Brooker," he whispered. "We're all gonna look like a Pompei exhibit."

"That's it. Get ready to take the weight, Parata. I'm going," Read said.

"Read!" He was gone. The twin cab sagged. Taine and the rest of the section battled to support the vehicle's two tonne kerb weight with only their fingertips. Taine's forearms burned. Curled around the metal chassis, his fingers cramped. Lucky for Read, or Taine might have been tempted to strangle him.

Hine was back on the ground, helping Brooker swing his ruined leg off the back of the truck. Read climbed on the Unimog, lifting Brooker by his armpits towards the back of the vehicle.

The hell-tide poured over the front deck.

"Eriksen," Taine shouted over the screech of shattering windowpanes. "You've got twenty seconds."

"Nearly there."

"Jesus," Parata said again.

"Adrian!" Lefty huffed.

"Okay, let it go—" Eriksen leapt clear. The twin cab bounced once, then Eriksen ducked back in with a crescent to tighten the wheel nuts.

"Miller, take the wheel. Get this baby turned around. The rest of you, get clear." Taine didn't wait to hear the private's response. He ran up the drive towards the Unimog.

A deadly wash of lava and rocks, as wide as the Waikato River, surged around the house, taking the line of least resistance. The side of the house exploded in flames. Taine had no time to take it in because the front wheels of the Unimog were lifting in the swell, the air blackening with the smoke and stench of immolating tyres.

"Hine, go!" Read croaked. Grabbing Brooker by his shirt, he dragged him back onto the Unimog.

She jumped clear, landing near Taine as the lava surged around the Unimog. Carried on the broiling wave of lava, it circled in a bizarre ballet, Brooker and Read still inside.

Floating.

Dammit. Taine had to get them off now. That truck was a toaster oven bobbing on a sea of red heat.

"Read!"

"I'm sending Brooker to you. Line-out style. Be ready!"

Taine had to hand it to him: as ideas went, it was gutsy. With the bed of the Unimog still floating above the flow, there was a chance it could work.

"Hine, we're going to have to catch Brooker."

Hurry it up, Read.

Standing as close as they dared, Taine and Hine braced themselves...

The Unimog circled.

Come on!

The vehicle came around. Read bent his knees, grabbing Brooker by the overalls below his hips. When the vehicle neared the lava's leading edge, Read thrust him upwards, Brooker jumping as best he could.

Brooker yelped.

Dammit. He was going to fall short. Taine stepped forward, his boot searing at the edge of the liquid rock. He leaned out and yanked Brooker to him, while, crouched low, Hine caught the boy's trailing leg before it hit the lava.

Taine snatched his own foot back.

"Fuck me! That was close," Brooker panted, his chest heaving.

One down, one to go.

What if Read leapt and missed? Taine glanced at Hine. He could spare her that at least. "Help Brooker to the twin cab," Taine shouted. "I'll get Read on the next pass."

Suddenly, Lefty was there, pushing Hine out of the way. "It's okay. I'll do it. You get clear." The soldier hefted Brooker over his shoulder, carrying him down the driveway, where Miller was backing up the truck, slowing just enough to allow the men to pile on.

The Unimog was like a raft on the rapids, the viscous current pulling it towards the middle of the lava-river.

"Read!" Taine yelled.

"Is Brooker safe?" Read called over the roar of the lava.

Taine glanced back. Lefty and Pringle were lifting Brooker onto the truck while, on the flatbed, Parata dragged him in.

"He's safe. Read—" Taine jumped back as a spray of lava spurted off the surface.

"I know, I know. I'm coming. Just waiting until the…" he trailed off.

"Matt," Hine whispered.

At last, the vehicle turned. Where was he? Taine looked in the back. At the far end of the truck, Read was gathering himself to jump. Taine's heart sank. Even using the aisle as a runway, the distance was too far. Read would have to be an Olympic athlete to make that.

Then the nose of the truck dived, momentarily lifting the rear and Taine knew they were out of options.

The fuel tank…

"Now!" he yelled. "Read, jump!" Taine turned, shielding Hine with his body, as the Unimog exploded.

The shock wave blasted them across the driveway in a wall of sound and hurt. Hurled through the air, Taine landed on the grass, the breath jolted from his lungs and his body pummelled by the impact, Hine's screams penetrating the ringing in his ears. Where was she finding the air to breathe, let alone scream? Taine hurt all over. He had to get up. Had to look for Read. Had to help…

Taine staggered to his feet, ignoring the chronic pounding in his head. He turned.

What?

A warrior woman was running across the lava. Hine? No, Hine was still on her knees beside him.

"Wait!" he shouted.

The warrior paused, turning, her piu piu skirt swishing around muscled legs, and glared at him. She wasn't real. She couldn't be. What about the heat? The gas? And the lava was still flowing, plummeting down the slope towards the road. He shook his head and felt for the carved pūrerehua at his neck. It was the blast playing tricks on him: his bruised brain seeing things that weren't there.

Taine closed his eyes…and opened them again. She was gone, leaving only the pounding in his temples.

"Where's Matt?" Hine snatched blindly at his arm, bringing him back to the present. Taine pulled her to her feet.

Damn it, Read. You better not be dead.

Read had landed in the lava, but only just; Lefty and Eriksen, further from the blast zone when the truck had exploded, were plucking him out of the lava by his feet. Read was screaming. Still alive, then. But his shirt was on fire.

Taine crossed the distance in a split second. Hine matched him stride for stride. Eriksen and Lefty pulled their friend clear. Shucking off his tunic, Taine pushed between the pair, diving on Read and rolling him, smothering the flames with the fabric.

Read grunted.

Still alive.

Taine rolled and rolled, away from the lava into the grass.

"McKenna, stop! The fire's out. He's good," Pringle yelled.

Taine pulled back, his heart in his throat. He pushed himself to his knees and stood up. Read lay face down in the grass.

Hine threw herself down beside him. "We need to get his shirt off," she gasped. "Help me!" Pringle jumped to aid her, but while Hine had gloves, Pringle only had his naked hands. "Here!" Tearing up the scorched remains of Taine's shirt, Hine thrust the fabric at Pringle, who wrapped it around his palms. The two of them set to work, teasing away the smouldering crusted fabric of Read's shirt. Read groaned in agony.

Still alive.

As Hine wiped away the last of the scorching lava, Taine sucked in a breath. Read's upper back and shoulders were raw and blistered. He was going to need medical help.

"Let's get him in the twin cab," Taine said. "Miller will get him back to Waiouru. Jug will look after him."

Nobody moved. The lava flow continued, intent on its journey.

Taine swivelled, his melted sole uneven beneath his heel.

Miller hadn't waited. The twin cab was already gone.

*

The driveway was a river of lava, so they were forced to walk through the pines and across the paddocks to the road. Taine carried Read, who'd passed out.

"Well, the State Highway is out. No way we can cross that," Lefty said, gazing at the lava flow blocking their route east.

"What if we follow it? Maybe the lava will peter out," replied Pringle.

"We'd have to go close country," Eriksen said, his eyes flicking to Read balanced across Taine's shoulders. "Through the forest. And in the middle of a bunch of earthquake swarms. That'd be a tough hike."

"That's assuming we ever get to the end of it," said Lefty.

"Let's stay on the tar seal and head the other way," Taine said, shifting his shoulders to adjust Read's weight. "The road circles Mount Pīhanga, so either way we'll end up in Turangi."

"You never know; we could get picked up by another section," Lefty said hopefully.

"You're forgetting about Barnes," Eriksen said.

"He's got a half an hour start on us," Pringle replied. "He might have already passed through a checkpoint."

Eriksen snorted. "So, we're going to just forget about Jules and the other woman? Let them take their chances?"

"It's not like we have a lot of choices, is it?" Lefty retorted. "Not without a vehicle. Anyway, Hairy's there with them."

"Yeah, him and a dozen armed criminals."

"They're not *all* bad," Pringle insisted. "Some of them—"

Taine cut across their bickering. "Lake Rotoaira is a couple of kilometres west of here. It's got a camp ground and a cluster of beach baches. Let's head there and see what we can do for Read. We can make a plan then."

Hine gave Taine a grateful smile as she led them out.

Away from the lava, the road was peaceful, deserted. Light caught the ashfall that filtered through the bush. Under different circumstances, Taine might have enjoyed the walk. Instead, he put one foot in front of another, breathing hard and sweat rolling down his back as he struggled to carry Read's weight on the shifting earth. He hoped for Read's sake that he stayed unconscious because when the soldier woke up, the pain would be hell on earth.

The quakes shook the ground and Taine trudged on, the conversation from earlier playing over and over in his head…Pringle saying Barnes would be out of the area already, or if he wasn't, he would be soon. Lefty insisting Harris would look out for Jules, despite the crappy odds, and the fact that Barnes had enough explosive ordnance on him to take out a small town.

Taine almost laughed. Barnes didn't know Jules, did he? He had no idea what she was capable of when she put her mind to it. Taine had seen her face down bigger monsters than Barnes.

But for how long?

"Bugger me," Eriksen said.

Taine had been lost in his thoughts. He raised his eyes. An avalanche of rocks and boulders blocked the road.

"Looks like we're stuck between a rock and lava place, huh?" Lefty replied.

Eriksen punched him on the shoulder.

"It's just rocks," Hine said. "There aren't too many." Like a cat, she darted over the pile, picking a route for them to follow.

"Boss?" Lefty said.

"I'm fine. You go." With Read on his back, it was worse than navigating a mine field, and by the time he'd made it over the rockfall, the others had gathered at the side of the road.

"What is it?" As he approached, Taine shifted his shoulders, redistributing Read's weight.

"Orange jumpsuits. Two of them. Both dead," said Eriksen.

Taine stopped cold. "Shot?"

"No," Pringle said, moving aside so Taine could see. "Just hit by the rocks from the looks of it. Or maybe thrown from a vehicle."

"That could explain how the twin cab was damaged," Hine said.

Read moaned softly.

"Let's get moving," Taine said.

"Give me Read," said Eriksen.

Taine didn't want to let him go, but he wasn't Superman. He wasn't even Batman. They might have miles to cover before they found help. He wouldn't be able to do it on his own. Gingerly, he passed the private over, Hine helping to ease Read's passage from one set of shoulders to the next.

"Thanks."

"No problem."

They trudged on, eventually arriving at Rotoaira.

Peeling blue signage was their only welcome. The tiny town was deserted. In the tired campground, a dozen caravans with faded curtains waited for happier times.

Eriksen didn't stop. He strode straight past a jetty that had seen better days and straight into the lake until he was standing waist deep. Then, gently releasing Read from his shoulders, and still supporting his weight, Eriksen let him slide into the water.

Woken by the cold and a fresh onslaught of pain, Read's scream fractured the silence. The sound startled a lone falcon which burst from the trees and glided over the water.

"Hold still, mate. It'll take out the heat," Eriksen said. "Gotta do what we can to save those boyish good looks of yours."

Read gasped. "Bastard!"

Taine grinned. It was the first time he'd ever heard Read swear. A good sign. The private was not only alive, he was fighting back.

Hine waded into the water. "I'll stay with him," she said to Eriksen. "I don't feel the cold much."

It was an understatement. Adapted to living in an underground cave where the sole entrance was via a water tunnel, Hine and her tribespeople could not only withstand the cold, they could remain submerged without air for up to half an hour.

Taine chafed at the delay, but every minute cooling that burn could make the difference to Read right now. *Every minute could make a difference to Jules, too.* He shook off his impatience. "We should check out the village," he said. "See if there's anything we can use."

"I'll wait here," said Pringle, dropping to sit cross-legged on the rickety jetty.

Taine's skin prickled. Because Pringle wanted a break? Why should that bother him? Or was it because he wasn't convinced that Pringle wasn't involved in the prison break?

Taine glanced sidelong at Eriksen, who was standing waist-deep in the water.

"You know what? I'll wait here with Pringle," Eriksen said, picking up the vibe. He waded out of the lake onto the sand, water dripping from his smock, then lifted his helmet, running his fingers through his hair before replacing it. "Lefty, see if you can find me a towel, would you? Come to think of it, some talcum would be nice."

Taine and Lefty jogged through the village, checking the sheds for vehicles.

"This is a fat lot of use," Lefty said as they closed the doors on yet another metal dinghy.

The next shed, though – if you could even call it that, since only the lichen was holding it up – hid a rusting tractor, fifty years old if it was a day.

"Bazinga," said Lefty.

Taine turned the key in the ignition. The tractor didn't so much as sputter. "What do you reckon? Could Eriksen get it going?" he asked.

Lefty shrugged. "Maybe." He nodded at the tools scattered on the ground. "Looks like someone already tried."

Taine held up his hand. "Wait, you hear that?"

"Hear what?"

"Sounded like someone shouting."

"Probably Read again. That burn's gotta hurt like hell."

Taine brought his index finger to his lips. The sound came again.

Lefty's eyes widened. "I hear it."

They left the shed, Taine skirting the near side of a red weatherboard house, while Lefty circled the building. They came together on the front veranda.

"Hello!" Taine called.

"Help me!"

Whoever was shouting, was inside the house. Taine tried the door. It was unlocked. He slid it open and stepped inside. Dominated by a home bar from the seventies, the front room was littered with spirit bottles and chip bags.

"Someone left in a hurry," Taine said quietly.

"In the middle of a fucking party," Lefty muttered. He grabbed a fire poker from a metal bucket behind the fireplace and brandished it like a sword. "I'll take point."

Taine moved aside, and Lefty proceeded down the hall, ducking his head into each room as they passed. At the end of the hall, the last door was closed.

"Are you still there? Don't go. Help!" A man's voice, youngish, with a French accent.

Lefty signalled to Taine, then kicked it open with his boot.

Taine resisted the urge to roll his eyes. *Too much television.*

Taine took in the scene: there were no orange jumpsuits, just a man lying on the floor, his hands tied behind his back with a paisley necktie, a leather belt strapping his feet to a chair. Around his neck was a soggy woman's scarf, a gag that he'd somehow managed to wriggle over his chin.

The man babbled, "Please!"

While Lefty played detective, checking the wardrobe and swishing the curtains aside with the poker, Taine cut the man free with his penknife.

He stood up and rubbed his wrists. "No need to look. There's no one."

"What happened here?"

"Some men came. They say they are the authorities, only it is not true. They took my girlfriend and locked me in here." He plucked at the knot of the scarf with greasy blackened fingers.

Taine stepped forward intending to slit the scarf with his penknife. "Were they wearing orange? Is your girlfriend's name Brigitte?"

The man's eyes widened, and he shrank away, backing up against the wall. "Don't touch me."

"Hey, it's okay," Lefty said, laying the poker on the bed and putting his hands in the air. "We *are* the authorities. New Zealand Defence

Force. I'm Lefty and this here is Sergeant McKenna. We ran into your friends earlier. They took McKenna's girl, too."

Technically Jules wasn't his girl, but now wasn't the time to split hairs.

Still wary, the man hesitated, his eyes flicking from Lefty to Taine and back again. When they didn't move, he took the penknife from Taine, cutting away the scarf, before handing it back. "My name is Alain. Don't say those men are my friends. They are not my friends."

"Don't worry," Lefty said, extending his hand. "They're not our friends either. You come with us, Alain. We're going after them as soon as we can get the tractor going."

"I already try," Alain said, returning the handshake. "I think it is foutu."

"Let's see what Eriksen says," Taine said.

"Wait." Lefty ducked into the bathroom. "I promised I'd get him a towel."

When they got back, Pringle and Eriksen were sitting on the jetty, eating muesli bars and drinking Cokes. They leaped to their feet when they saw the stranger.

Read and Hine emerged from the water. Lefty threw them both a towel with an added t-shirt for Read. Read's face tensed with pain.

"This is Alain," Taine said, filling them in.

"I'd better take a look at this tractor, then," Eriksen said when Taine had finished. He stood up and handed the sugary bars to Hine. She pulled a face.

"Sorry. There wasn't much left," Pringle said, cocking his head towards a kiosk opposite the camping ground, "Mostly snacks. Still, it'll fill the gap."

"I got you something tasty," Lefty said to Read. He dug in his pocket, lobbing something over.

Read winced as he caught it. "What's this?"

"Ibuprofen. Eight hundred milligrams. Found it in a cupboard."

Read's smile was grim. "Thanks."

"Sure," Lefty said. "Just don't go operating any heavy machinery."

CHAPTER THIRTEEN

State Highway One, northbound

"Take the next left," Barnes barked.

Damn. Shane turned the wheel and forced himself not to react. Where had Barnes gotten his hands on that local map? Shane had been counting on him thinking the checkpoint was on the northern end of Turangi. Instead, Barnes had played it safe, turning off before the Tokaanu bypass onto an industrial slip road.

"Where are we going now?" Ants asked.

"We're cutting inside Mount Pīhanga, taking the backway in to Tokaanu," Barnes replied.

"We're not stopping in Turangi, then?"

"No."

"But you said—"

Barnes turned on him. "Didn't you hear those army guys? There's a road block at Turangi."

"And if we can't see them, how are we going to know when to leave?" Ant's whine was getting on Shane's nerves, let alone his idiotic questions.

"We'll hole up somewhere, look for a radio, and as soon as we hear that the army are pulling out, we'll do the same."

Ants giggled, and Shane didn't know what was worse: that or the whine.

"Like a cat slipping in when you're closing the door, you mean?" Ants said.

"Exactly." Barnes nudged Shane in the shoulder with his elbow. "Turn left at Tokaanu Road."

With a rifle jammed in his ribs, Shane didn't have much choice. He'd have to come up with some other way to bring Barnes in and rescue the women. The two of them must be sick with fear. If only he had an opportunity to let Jules know he was on her side. He glanced up. That opportunity might be coming: Jules Asher was marching down the aisle.

Shane slowed the truck as much as he dared and braced himself to act.

Jules stopped in front of Barnes. "I've come to ask you to pull over."

"Why? You don't like our hospitality?" Barnes said.

Careful, Jules.

"Because," she said, "unlike your men back there, we girls can't hang it out the window when we need to go."

Barnes' face. He looked like a fly had flown into his mouth. Shane's adrenalin spiked. Barnes was dangerous and unpredictable, and Jules had shown him up in front of his men. Let's hope she hadn't bitten off more than she could chew. His body coiled and ready, Shane held his breath.

Waited.

Finally, Barnes laughed, his guffaws reverberating around the truck. The other men joined in. "Fuck me, she's funny, this one." He chuckled again. "Harris, pull over. Seems the ladies need a comfort stop."

Shane exhaled silently. She'd gotten away with it. He drove across the Tokaanu tail race and pulled over opposite a knoll. Mount Pīhanga loomed behind them.

The women clambered off the back of the Unimog.

"Shouldn't we watch them?" one of the men said.

"Sure, you watch them, Pete. Tell them to keep talking so we know where they are." Barnes smiled. "Mind you, if they're stupid enough to run, they won't get far." He caressed the barrel of the rifle. "Could even be fun rounding them up."

Shane shuddered. Barnes wasn't the sort who needed an excuse to kill someone.

Shane opened the driver's door.

In the passenger seat, Pope raised his rifle, pointing it at Shane's head. "Where do you think you're going?" he demanded.

"For a slash," Shane said. "You got a problem with that?"

"Yeah, I might go too," said one of the men. Several others murmured in agreement.

"What? Are you all girls or something? Make it quick," Barnes snapped.

A bunch of the men leapt off the back of the truck and disappeared into the scrub on either side of the road. Keeping his eye on the spot where the women had entered the trees, Shane walked ten metres up the road, then slipped into the trees himself. If he could circle around quickly, he might be able to signal Jules and let her know that he was on her side.

He crept through the scrub, listening hard for the women.

There was nothing. Just the quiet rustle of insects. Had they made a run for it? No, if they'd already run, the man guarding them would have sounded the alert. Besides, Jules would know running was too risky. Barnes couldn't let them get away this close to Turangi. Not when there was a chance of the women reaching the checkpoint. Unless the mountains stopped threatening and decided to blow for real. If that happened, there'd be no winners.

So, where were they? Shane strained to hear. He was running out of time. If he didn't come back to the Unimog soon, Barnes would come looking; and when he did, he'd be armed.

At last, Shane picked up a sob. Brigitte. They couldn't be far away then. Crouching, Shane followed Jules' murmurs as she tried to comfort the girl.

He'd almost reached them when, through the brush, he spied a flash of orange. Pete. Why would he be on this side of the women? Ignoring the scratch of its branches, Shane ducked into a tea tree out of sight.

His back to Shane, Pete leaned his rifle up against a tree. There was the soft whish of a zipper. He was taking a leak.

But that wasn't it at all.

Shane's eyes widened, and rage exploded in his temples. What the hell? *Fuck* that. As if being held hostage wasn't indignity enough. He stepped out from behind the tree and marched straight for Pete.

The man must have heard him coming because he looked over his shoulder, at the same time scrabbling to rearrange his clothing. "Hey!" he said. "What—"

He couldn't say anything more because Shane had his head in a chokehold. Shane locked his fingers under his elbow and applied pressure to the carotid sinus in Pete's neck. Held his grip while Pete thrashed. There were plenty of ways to get out of a hold like this – a grab to your opponent's balls, a bend and twist to reverse the hold and wrench your attacker's arm up his back – it seemed Pete didn't know them.

Seconds passed.

Pete's knees went from under him. Shane lowered him to the ground. "Serves you right, you piece of filth," Shane murmured in his ear.

He'd worry about how to explain it to Barnes later; right now he had to hurry. The whole prison gang would descend on him any minute. He had to get to Jules and alert her while he had the chance.

Shane pushed aside the bushes and marched into the glade.

Startled, Brigitte screamed and bolted. Shane grabbed for the girl's arm.

Jules pushed him off. "Get the hell away from her!"

"No wait—" Shane said.

But Jules was off after Brigitte, the pair of them crashing through the bracken.

Don't run, don't run. Shane sprang after them.

And leapt…

Sailing through the brush…

…and brought them both down. All three of them landed in a heap: Brigitte, then Jules, then Shane, like a collapsed rugby scrum. Brigitte wailed.

Men's shouts rang through the bushes.

Shane whispered in Jules' ear, "Please, you can't run. You'll never make it. Barnes is a killer; he'll shoot you both."

"Get away from me!" Jules thrust her elbow in his solar plexus, knocking the wind out of him, and pushing him off.

Wheezing, Shane sucked in a breath. "I'm on your side," he croaked.

She turned, her eyes flaring. "Why should I trust you?"

Shane grunted. "Do I look like I've got a death wish? You think I'd hitch a ride with Barnes for the fun of it? I'm NZDF: it's my job to keep you safe, that's why," he said.

She stopped still at that and looked him in the eye, and, as Barnes and Pope crashed into the thicket, their faces red and their guns raised, Shane thought he saw her nod.

"What the fuck, Harris!"

"I knew we shouldn't have trusted him," said Knife, who'd only just arrived. Pope yanked Brigitte to her feet, his fingers wrapped around her forearm. More men in orange clustered about them, Ants wrestled with Jules while the big Samoan trained his gun on her.

Stifling his anger, Shane put on an air of innocence, standing up and brushing off his tunic. "I stopped them, didn't I?"

Barnes cocked his head. He leaned back against a tree. "Yes, you did. And why exactly did you do that, Harris?"

Shane pushed back his shoulders and met Barnes squarely in the eye. "You know why. I told you before: I want to get out of here before this whole place starts to look like the surface of Mars. If these two had done a runner, you'd have had us wasting time chasing through the bush looking for them. I didn't sign on for any fox hunt. Hell no, when that roadblock comes down, I want to be on the truck ready to move out like you promised."

"He's lying," said one of the men.

Shane rolled his eyes. "I'm not the one wearing orange."

The man roared. He lunged for Shane, making a grab for Shane's tunic, one arm drawn back, the fist closed tight.

Knife swung on the guy's arm, dragging the attacker back. "Leave it, Climo. He's not worth it."

"What about Pete, then?" Climo screamed. "He's fucking unconscious. You can't tell me it was the women who did that!"

Barnes sighed. "Climo does have a point." He raised an eyebrow. "Didn't have to happen. All he had to do was keep it in his pants."

"Bullshit," Climo shouted. "He was doing his business, is all."

Stepping forward, Shane jabbed a finger in Climo's chest. "Yeah, he was doing his business." Jab. "Too right, he was doing his business. Because he's a bloody pervert."

Climo looked at Barnes. "You believe this shit? Surely, you're not going to trust this guy. We don't even know who the fuck he is."

As Barnes looked from Climo to Shane and back again, Shane let his hand drop. He'd done all he could. Would it be enough to convince Barnes?

Jules twisted out of Ants' grasp, took two steps forward, and kicked Shane swift and hard in the shin.

His eyes watering, Shane doubled over with pain.

Yes, that ought to do it.

Backroad to Turangi

A bit of a whizz with engines, Eriksen pulled out the starter motor, cleaned the wires with some Brasso he found on a shelf, and put it back in. The engine turned first time.

Incredulous, Alain shook his head. "I can't believe it. So simple."

"Usually is," said Eriksen.

"There's a boat trailer in the shed one bach over," Taine said, desperate to get moving. "We'll hook it to the tractor. The rest of us can ride in the dinghy. It can't be any bumpier than the quakes."

Minutes later, the three of them pulled up beside the jetty, Eriksen driving the tractor and Taine and Alain in the dinghy.

"Need a ride?" Eriksen quipped.

Taine put out a hand to help Read up, while the rest of them clambered in. The tractor rumbled beneath them. Eriksen took them out of the hamlet, turning right at the peeling blue signs and putting his foot down. They weren't going to break any land speed records. Not on these slow climbs with the trailer laden with six passengers. And the road littered with rocks. Still, it beat walking. To make up for the slow climbs, Eriksen made the most of the downhill, using their momentum to pick up speed.

"No wait! Watch out!" Pringle shouted.

Taine had been watching the rear. He whipped his head round in time to see the lahar power across the road and down into the valley.

Yanking on the wheel, Eriksen slammed on the brakes. They were as rusty as the starter, the tractor turning sharply.

Alain gasped.

The trailer jack-knifed, jolting them sideways, so they were jerked about like marionettes.

At the wheel of the tractor, Eriksen battled to get the vehicle under control.

"Hang on!" Taine shouted.

Hine yelped, her gloved hands slipping on the shiny surface of the dinghy. Read grabbed her by the arm. His feet braced in the bottom of the boat, he pulled back hard. Hine's torso swung wide, momentum dragging her out of the boat. Read's weight wasn't going to be enough to hold her. "McKenna!" he groaned.

Reflexes kicked in. Taine, leaning over Read, stretched out an arm and snatched Hine back by her clothes. Between them, they dragged her into the dinghy.

The trailer jerked, Taine's head whipping from side to side. They came to a halt: the tractor and trailer so close, they were almost touching.

Taine jumped down to check out what they were dealing with. Maybe they could follow it down the valley, or possibly use the boat... He rounded the tractor and his heart sank. The lahar wasn't only swift, it was deep. They weren't going to get past it. They would have to go back. Except, the other way was blocked, too.

"Looks like we're in for some serious bushwhacking," Lefty said, jumping down to join Taine. He leaned closer and lowered his voice, "That's going to be a helluva hard work on Read."

Taine turned on his heel. "Back in the boat."

"Boss?"

His foot on the wheel arch, Taine swung his leg over the side of the dinghy. "Eriksen, let's get this tractor on the road again. Head for Lake Rotopounamu. Pull in to the parking bay."

Caught on the hop, Lefty was still climbing into the boat as Eriksen brought the tractor round, pulling them away from the wash of rock and mud.

"If you're thinking of using the boat, it won't work, boss. Even if we could get the dinghy to the shore, Lake Rotopounamu doesn't *go* anywhere," Eriksen called over his shoulder. "None of these little lakes do."

"But it does have a loop track," Taine replied. "I saw the DOC sign earlier. We'll use the track to skirt the lake, then cut north across the ridge and descend into Turangi. That way we'll avoid the lahar, and the going should be easier."

Behind Read, Lefty raised an eyebrow. "We're going to go *over* Mount Pīhanga?"

"Just the foothills."

"Fuck," Lefty replied.

"It's not like we have a lot of options," said Pringle.

Alain dropped his head into his hands.

"It's okay," Hine said, touching him gently on the forearm.

"No," he said, twisting away from her. "It's not okay."

Hine's face softened. "It's a good plan. I promise you, if anyone can get us out of this, it will be Sergeant McKenna."

In the cramped dinghy it was impossible not to hear. Lefty smirked. Taine looked away, embarrassed.

"It's not that!" Alain said. He exhaled slowly through pursed lips. After a moment, he went on, "Before, in the village, the men who brought me to the house were supposed to kill me. They had a gun. They tied me up and they were going to do it. Then one of them said that when the mountains erupted, I'd be buried anyway. 'Why waste a good bullet when the mountain will do the job for them,' he said. So instead, they put a scarf in my mouth, so no one can hear, and they left me there."

"You're with the NZDF now," Read said. "No one is going to abandon you."

Alain gazed out to the right, towards Tongariro buried under layers of ash and cloud. "No," he whispered. "It is not that, either. We are taking too long. I'm afraid of what they do to Brigitte."

Taine nodded. He was afraid, too.

Maungapōhatu, Te Urewera Forest

After Wayne had pulled away, Temera sat in his fold-out lawn chair on the back porch in the sun. He stared off into the distance where the blue-grey silhouette of the Huia-rau mountain range broke the skyline, Te Maunga, on the end, the proudest of them all. Blowing in on the breeze, the ash mingled with insects and grass clippings, filling the air with debris. Temera's brain was buzzing with stuff too, all of it unconnected and none of it making any sense. A smoke would be good, only he'd left his cigarettes inside and he was too lazy to get up.

The sun glinted through the trees. Once, when he still had his gift, he'd seen a taniwha standing over there at the edge of the yard. Bold as brass, the monster had come right up to the porch. Nearly made Temera wet himself, he was so scared.

The trees bent, murmuring, "That was before though, when your little spirit guide used to visit you..." The words were so distinct, Temera could have sworn he'd heard them.

"...when you still had your gift."

Temera sat upright. *He'd definitely heard that.*

"Who's speaking?"

"All these years, all the times you've sat on this porch, and yet you don't know me. I am Te Maunga."

Te Maunga. The mountain? Temera turned his hand over and rolled the wrinkled skin between his fingers. I'm not asleep, and I'm still old.

The mountain chuckled, its voice rumbling inside Temera's head. "Isn't it about time you grew up, Temera? How old are you now? Eighty-five? Surely, the time for childhood games is over. Or are you so attached to your blanket and your night-light that you can't let them go?"

I'm dreaming.

Te Maunga said nothing.

"It's the wind in the trees. It must be. I've lost my gift," Temera said out loud.

"Or maybe it's your fear talking."

Temera got up and walked to the edge of the porch. The mountain had spoken in his mind as clear as the six am wake-up call on Wayne's phone. Maybe he hadn't lost his gift at all. Temera's old mātua had always said seeing wasn't the same for all matakite. What if a matakite's way of seeing could change? Their *process*? Even the mountains changed over time. Temera shook his head. Would he ever understand his gift fully? Nearly a century on this earth and still it baffled him. He touched the scorched fingerprint where Te Pūpū had left her calling card. "The fire demons were really here?" he whispered.

The needle of the mountain cut through the mist and ash. "That scorch mark isn't enough to convince you? Look deeper, Temera. What does your heart tell you?"

Temera clutched at the pūrerehua hanging at his neck. He breathed in deeply, inhaling the woody resins of the forest and coughing when a flake of ash tickled his throat. "I think, yes. The demons came to give me a warning. I just have to figure out what it means, what I'm supposed to do."

Te Maunga rumbled, "Look around you. At the ash. At the ground. Isn't it obvious? My cousins, the mountains, are restless again."

Temera knew it. He'd said as much earlier when he'd been listening to that reporter on the radio.

"I'd thought we were done with this. It was bad enough when this nonsense all started," Te Maunga said.

"Nonsense?"

"The feuding between my cousins over Pīhanga."

Temera knew the story. New Zealanders would have to have been asleep their whole lives *not* to have heard it. The battle between the sacred peaks, Te Kāhui Tupua, was such an important part of New Zealand's whakapapa, so vital to The People's heritage and identity that

106

the tale had been told more often than there were rings on a kauri tree. Temera's mātua had told him the story, and he'd learned it back in the day from his own mātua. It had been taught in schools and recorded in journals and books. Temera held back a grunt. These days it was probably up on that cloud-thingy that Wayne was always going on about, too.

The way it was told might have changed, yet the story was the same: the battle raging for days, the mountains all fighting for the hand of the mountain-goddess Pīhanga. The air had burned with their fury. Rocks and fire had filled the sky. The ground had jolted and shaken. When, at last, Mount Tongariro emerged as the victor, he gave his brothers one night to leave the battlegrounds. Vanquished, the brothers had scattered. Ruapehu and Ngāuruhoe had bowed their heads and moved off to the south, while their brother Putauaki had escaped to the east to settle at Rotorua. Taranaki, overcome with grief, had forged his way westwards to the coast, gouging a river of tears in his wake. The last of the brothers, Mount Tauhara fled to the northeast, turning back as dawn broke to gaze across the lake at his lost love. He'd been frozen there ever since.

"Tongariro won," Temera said. "It was all over long ago. Why dredge up that old feud?"

The mountain chortled. "You think it's as simple as that? All this time, Tongariro has sat there in his throne-room in the middle of the country, his head in the clouds, lording it over everyone, while his brothers have had to bury their humiliation and their hurt."

"They're still angry."

"Exactly."

"You think one of them intends to challenge him?"

"Maybe."

"Which mountain?"

Again, Te Maunga said nothing.

"Why are you telling me all this? What am I supposed to do? Hold back a mountain? I'm an old man, not Arnold-bloody-Schwarzenegger!" Temera sat heavily on the step and leaned his head against the veranda post.

A veil of thick mist rolled into the valley, obscuring the mountain, who chose, once more, to say nothing.

CHAPTER FOURTEEN

Central Plateau, near Lake Rotopounamu

On the way back to Lake Rotopounamu, they came across a white rental van travelling in the opposite direction.

"Where the heck did they come from?" Lefty said as Eriksen stopped the tractor. Jumping down from the dinghy, Taine ran across to the van. The woman in the driver's seat rolled down the window.

"Taine McKenna, NZDF," Taine said, extending his hand through the gap.

"Keira Skelton. Otago University," the woman said, returning his handshake. In her mid-thirties, she was broad-shouldered with an equally wide smile. The type who plays the heroine's best friend in a movie. She glanced at the tractor and dinghy and raised an eyebrow. "Wow. And I thought university funding sucked. Looks like army funding is even worse."

Taine grinned. "Tell me about it." He stooped to check out the van's occupants. There were two passengers: an older man sporting a seventies moustache, riding shotgun, and a thin dark-haired man sitting in the back. No orange jumpsuits.

Seeing him looking, Keira said, "These are my colleagues." She tilted her head to the passenger seat. "This is Taika Thompson and in the back is Jawad Ahmad." Thompson raised his hand in greeting. Ahmad ignored him and stared out the window.

"You're heading for a dead end," Taine said. "The road's blocked in both directions."

"Shit," Keira said. "Could this day get any more fucked up?"

"I told you not to stop," Ahmad said.

"We're planning to take the track at Lake Rotopounamu," Taine said. "Thought we'd skirt the lake and then cross the foothills of Pīhanga and drop down through the farmland into Tokaanu. You're welcome to join us."

Keira glanced at Thompson.

"Do you have a better idea?" he said.

"Not really," she said. "Where's this track then?"

"I'll show you if you like," Taine said, and, turning, he called to let Eriksen know he was riding with the geologists and he'd meet up with the rest of them at the parking bay. Then he climbed into the back seat beside Ahmad. "I'm surprised to see anyone still in this area," he said as he pulled the door closed. "Civil Defence evacuated everyone a couple of days ago. NZDF has been doing the sweep for stragglers."

"We spoke to the Civil Defence. The poor bastards were run off their feet. Looked as if they hadn't slept in days. Clague told them not to worry about us; that we could look after ourselves," Keira replied.

Ahmad snorted, his breath fogging up the window.

"Clague?" Taine asked.

"Our supervisor. In the back."

Taine looked over his shoulder into the back of the van where a man-sized black polythene bag lay amongst a bunch of badly-packed camping equipment.

"A vent opened under his feet while he was taking some last-minute readings this morning," Thompson said.

"I'm sorry."

"There was nothing anyone could have done," Thompson said.

"We were studying the earthquake swarm," Keira explained. "Relaying information back to the authorities after the GNS Science people upped and left. Well, we were – until the university pulled us off the mountain."

"We should have left, too. Everyone said we should go," Ahmad whined.

Taika twisted in his seat. "Well, we didn't, so shut up about it, okay?"

"We didn't want to leave Clague on the mountain," Keira said.

"He was a friend," Thompson said. "I'd worked with Robert for over a decade. I couldn't just abandon him."

Although Thompson couldn't see him, Taine nodded. Leaving any soldier in the field, even a dead one, was agony. If there was a chance of recovering the body for the family, you took that chance.

Keira took one hand off the steering wheel and laid it on Thompson's shoulder. "It took us a while to bring Clague's body down. He was…" Her voice cracked and she trailed off. "It wasn't easy."

"Looks like we'll have to leave him now, anyway," Thompson replied.

Keira put her hand back on the steering wheel to take the corner. "We did our best, Taika," she said. "Robert will understand."

"I hope so. He remarried a couple of years ago, did you know that? Has a young family. A daughter." He shook his head. "God. I don't even want to think about what I'm going to say to them."

"Chances are you won't have to. Seeing as we'll all be dead," Ahmad broke in.

"No one is going to die," Taine said softly.

"Tell that to Clague," Ahmad murmured.

Thompson turned. Hanging his arm over the seat, he hissed, "I thought I told you to shut it." Spittle flew, spotting Ahmad's hands.

"I'll say whatever I like," Ahmad said, wiping his palms on his pants, but Thompson's glare must have affected his nerve because he turned away.

Up ahead, Eriksen pulled in to the layby.

"End of the line," Keira announced. She parked the rental van off the road behind the dinghy. "All out for Tokaanu."

They piled out of the van and Taine made the introductions. When he was done, Ahmad stood in the middle of the road, sulking, while Keira opened the back of the van.

"Excuse me, Robert." She reached past the black bin bag. Grabbing a backpack, she set about stuffing items into it: water bottles, a sweatshirt, a notebook, a torch...

Pringle leaned in to the back of the van, his cheek resting on the side of the door. "You wouldn't happen to have a First Aid kit by any chance? Read was burned earlier; it'd be good to get some clean gauze on the wound."

"Yeah. We...um...we were using it earlier. It's somewhere in here." She started to rifle through the camping gear.

"It's here," Thompson said, opening the passenger door and lifting a green canvas bag from a compartment in the side of the door. He threw the bag over the van to Pringle, who carried it across to Read and Hine.

"What about a satellite phone?" Taine asked. "Got one of those?"

"Geez, I thought you army guys were supposed to be rescuing *us*?" Keira said.

"You said it yourself: universities get all the funding," Taine joked.

"Yeah, right," she scoffed. She rummaged through the sacks and handed him a plastic sat phone. A cheap model, but it would do the trick. "Just don't use up all my minutes."

Taine carried the phone to the edge of the layby, and, facing the bush, he punched in the number for James Arnold.

"McKenna," the major said when he came on the line. "I hope you're phoning to tell me you're on your way out of that infernal hellhole."

"Privates Miller, Bahr, and Parata are on their way to you. They're in a conservation truck carrying one of the Rangipō boys who was injured in the bus crash. I thought they'd have reached you by now."

"No sign yet, although that'll be because there's no one left at Waiouru. We pulled back to Taihape an hour ago."

"Their vehicle was beaten up when they left."

"I'll keep a look out for your men. What's your situation?" Arnold asked.

"I'm on Te Ponanga Saddle Road near Lake Rotopounamu."

"How many with you?"

"Four NZDF and five civilians."

"Vehicles?"

"We're on foot."

There was a pause as Arnold cursed under his breath. "Well, that explains the Morse Code."

"I'm not sure I understand, Boss."

"A private came in fifteen minutes ago; reported one of our Unimogs was headed for Turangi. He said the Unimog driver tapped out Morse Code on the chassis, warned him off. He couldn't see anything, but our man was pretty sure the escaped convicts were on board."

"Not just the convicts; they have two hostages. Jules Asher is one of them."

"Son of a bitch," Arnold said. "What the hell is the doc doing in there? Don't tell me, rescuing ducklings, I imagine. Well, this changes things if the bastards have taken hostages. With everyone concentrating on the evacuation effort, searching for escapees hasn't been a priority. Hell, the police figured when conditions deteriorated, the prisoners would come through a check point with their tails between their legs."

"I think that's unlikely. Barnes is no lamb. He's already killed half a dozen men and he isn't counting on doing time for it. If he comes through a checkpoint, it'll be with a small army at his back."

"Damn. He hasn't passed through Turangi yet."

"Which means he's still in the red-zone…"

"He might have gone off-road," Arnold said.

"He's already lost two vehicles today. I doubt he'd risk a third."

"Okay, you sit tight. I'll get a section to you and a couple of vehicles."

"It won't help, boss. The road access here is cut off on both sides. The mountains are spewing boulders and there are lahars and lava all over. Chances are whoever you send won't make it."

On the other end, Arnold huffed into the phone. "That'll be why the powers-that-be are pulling everyone out, turning half the island into an exclusion zone. The checkpoints are being pulled back another fifty kilometres as we speak."

"Any chance you can keep that information off the airways? It could be what Barnes is waiting for. We're heading over to Pīhanga now. With a bit of luck, we'll have made it over the mountain in a little over an hour."

"You're going after the hostages," Arnold said, as if he had expected nothing less. "You realise you'll be on your own."

"We're resourceful. We'll work something out. If you could get eyes on that rogue Unimog, it would help. Maybe get a drone in there?"

"Leave it with me," Arnold said, and he hung up.

When Taine turned around, Keira was looking at him. Holding out one hand for the sat phone, she put the other on her hip. "What's all this about convicts and hostages, then?"

Tokaanu village, southern end of Lake Taupō

Barnes ordered Harris to pull off highway 41 and onto the slip road that was Tokaanu's main drag.

"Jesus H. Christ, it's a fucking ghost town," Knife said.

"Straight out of a western. Complete with dust," said Pope.

"Look out for tumbleweeds," Climo quipped. "Or Clint Eastwood."

"Or Natalie Portman," said Knife.

"Yeah, Natalie Portman," Climo replied. "I wouldn't say no to a bit of that."

"I reckon she'd say no, though, Climo. Since your bit is so tiny."

Climo turned red and the men laughed. "Shuddup."

Barnes tuned them out, scanning the weed-filled gaps between the buildings. It looked quiet enough, although there might still be soldiers hanging about. McKenna's lot had been charged with picking up stragglers, and where there was one platoon of jarheads, there could easily be another. "Drive to the end of the main road," he said to Harris. "Slowly."

"What are we looking for?" Ants asked.

Barnes glared at him. Had he always been like this? Questioning every single decision. Barnes was starting to get why people said it was lonely at the top. The cunt's whiny voice was getting on his nerves.

Thank fuck, Ants got the message and shut the hell up. Harris rolled them through the town. It was another shithole. A blink-or-you'll-miss-it one-street town of miserable houses painted try-too-hard white. There was the usual church and corner dairy and a few shops catering to the tourist industry – a kayak company, a fishing shop, and a motel. The only new building stood opposite the motel. Three storeys high and not quite complete, it looked like it was holding up the fucking crane.

"Lookee-here, no one's home," Pope said.

"Stop the truck," Barnes ordered.

Harris stopped the Unimog in the middle of the road.

"Now what?" Ants asked.

Barnes gritted his teeth. "You and Eaton go look for a radio. Make sure you get some batteries. The rest of you check the houses for clothes. We're like bloody traffic lights in these overalls."

"And passports, right?" Ants said. "They should look for passports. We're going to need those to get out of the country."

Barnes resisted the urge to roll his eyes. That idiot really thought they were all going to get on a fucking plane together. Like this was the Sound of Music or something. Well, let him think that if it made him happy. Barnes clapped him on the shoulder. "Sure. Good thinking. Look for passports, money. Anything we can use."

Grinning, Ants scampered down the aisle, jumping over Pete who was laying on the floor, still groggy from the choke hold Harris put on him earlier.

Speak of the devil. Harris was getting to his feet. Like he owned the place.

Barnes thumped him in the middle of his chest, pushing him back into the chair. "Not you, soldier-man. You stay here where we can keep an eye on you."

Harris put his hands in the air. "Hey, take it easy. No need to get all aggro. I was going to jump down and stretch my legs. No harm in that, is there?"

Barnes felt his eyes narrowing. He had to admit, Harris was a cool one. A bit of a hero when it came to the women but happy enough to switch his allegiance when it suited his own interests. That last part made him dangerous because if you could swing one way, you could just as easily swing the other. Still, they might need his skills, and it wasn't like there was anywhere to run to; he was unarmed and outnumbered by twenty to one. What the hell? Let him stretch his fucking legs.

Barnes grunted. "All right. Give me the keys first. And stay near the truck. Taliava, you watch him."

"Sure, Barnes." Taliava waved his gun, shoving Harris along the aisle.

The pair jumped off the end of the truck, their combined two-hundred plus kilos, making the flatbed bounce.

"Sure, Barnes, sure," the science chick muttered under her breath. "Evasion, kidnapping, firearms offences...why not go the whole nine yards and add identity theft, too?"

Mouthy little bitch, that one. The smart ones always were. Barnes preferred them cowered and pliant, like the Frenchie. Come to think of it, he'd missed a nice interlude with her earlier when Asher had turned up in her truck at Rotoaira. Another reason the Asher woman ticked him off. If they were going to be holed up here for a while, there was no reason why he should miss out. When the boys came back and he knew what was what, there'd be nothing to stop him taking the little Frenchie for some quality time at the motel. Console her for losing that woofter boyfriend of hers.

In the meantime... Barnes thrust his face into Asher's, mashed his nose into her cheek. "I said you were funny, but you really are funny, you know that? You think anyone cares about what we're up to? Take a look around. It's a fucking state of emergency. Everyone has cleared out, busy saving their own arses, which means I can do whatever I fucking want."

"There'll be a reckoning. There always is. The army—"

Barnes stepped back, then cracked her hard across the cheek with the rifle butt. She cried out, bringing her hand to the cut. The Frenchie squealed, and cringed away, making herself small. She had her eyes down, concentrating on her hands, trying to pretend she was anywhere else but here. She'd do the same later, in the motel. Gave him a hard on thinking about it. Asher was tougher to crack.

He pushed his face close to hers again. "I don't want to hear another word from you about the army, you hear me?"

She wiped the blood off her cheek with the back of her hand. And looked him in the eye. "Me not saying it doesn't mean they won't come."

Barnes raked his hand through his hair. He'd hit her hard and still she insisted on having the last word. It was a pity some of his lot didn't have her balls.

He licked her ear. Felt her shudder as he ran his tongue the length of it. "Maybe," he murmured. "If you can't control your lippy little mouth, I can't guarantee I'll be able to control my friend Pete."

Obligingly, Pete picked that moment to emerge from his stupor. He hauled himself up onto a seat, gave Asher a salacious smile, and ran his zipper up and down. Worked a bloody treat. The bitch went white as a sheet. Clammed right up.

Barnes stalked to the back of the truck and swung his leg over the back, sitting half in and half out while he waited for the others to return.

CHAPTER FIFTEEN

Lake Rotopounamu track

A favourite weekend bush trail, the track around the lake was easily wide enough for them to walk two abreast. Taine had Eriksen take point while Lefty covered their six. Not that there was any need, but old habits die hard and those two knew better than most that forests have a way of hiding their secrets.

Taine sucked in a breath. Beneath the canopy, where the undergrowth was thick with ferns, the air smelled fresh. If it weren't for Rūaumoko grumbling underfoot, you'd be hard pushed to believe they were smack in the middle of a disaster zone.

"What's his problem anyway?" Thompson complained up ahead. "He's sulking like a spoiled teenager."

He was moaning about Ahmad. The young man had snubbed his colleagues, preferring to walk ahead of them in Eriksen's shadow, his head down like a battering ram. If he didn't watch out, he'd bowl straight into Eriksen.

"Lay off him, Taika," Keira replied, her voice low. "The poor kid's frightened. He's had to deal with Robert's death – which you have to admit wasn't pretty. And getting him off the mountain. You had a time of it, not barfing yourself. Then, for our troubles, we get snookered between two lahars."

"You forgot to add being roped into chasing after a bunch of armed criminals."

"I know, right? It's like something out of a Joe Ledger novel. All that's missing are the zombies. Jawad doesn't know how to react, that's all."

"You and I aren't falling apart."

"I want to, though," Keira said quietly. "Only what would be the point? It won't help us get home any quicker."

"Yeah," said Thompson. "This trip has been rough on us all."

"Not exactly your average field trip."

"No."

"So you'll try to be a bit nicer to Jawad?"

There was a pause and Thompson tilted his head back to look at the sky, his shaggy hair falling to his shoulders.

"Taika." Keira drew out the word.

"Okay, okay, I'll try," Thompson was saying. "It's just—"

Taine didn't hear the rest, dropping back out of hearing. "How's our patient doing?" he asked Hine.

"Not patient at all," she said. Taine noted that, in just a year, not only had she mastered English, she'd developed a pretty effective eye-roll. "The burn is bad, and I think painful, but the cold water has drawn out a lot of the heat. I believe he will live."

"Although the same can't be said for Pringle," Read said, deliberately loud. "I plan to murder him in his sleep. He nearly killed me, patching me up."

"You can thank me later," Pringle called from the rear.

Despite everything, they were upbeat. It was a good sign.

Alain was the last in the line. Taine fell in beside him, matching him stride for stride. After a time, the Frenchman said, "Brigitte and I walked on this route before. She liked it a lot. The trees and the lake. It was peaceful." His voice was thick with tension. "But now, for me, it feels different." Flaring his nostrils, he sucked in a breath. "Lonely."

Taine nodded. For the moment, Alain was holding it together. Taine would need to keep an eye on him. "The army are convinced Barnes and his men are still in the area. If that's true, we'll find them." Taine meant every word.

"Boss," Eriksen called from up ahead.

Taine jogged through the group. Eriksen was standing next to the conservation marker that announced the site as Long Beach, although the stretch of sand extended barely thirty metres. They'd arrived at the far end of the track.

Checking his map, Eriksen pointed northwards over the western flank of Mount Pīhanga. "We're going to have to do some bushwhacking until we hit the ridge."

"There's a chance we'll find a hiking track," Taine said. Jules wouldn't like them trampling all over vital habitats, but what choice did they have?

"Give me a minute to cut some solid branches," Eriksen said. "We'll use them to push through the bracken."

Taine turned. The others had caught up.

Kneeling at the water's edge, Keira refilled her water bottles. "We should all have a drink while we can," she said. "Lake Rotopounamu is a category one lake. That's some of the highest water quality you can get. Although, it might have dropped a point with all this ash."

Taking her lead, Alain crouched to cup his hands in the water, then lifted them to his mouth for a drink. When he raised his head, he said, "That tree was not on the ground when I came with Brigitte." Taine followed his gaze. A giant matai straddled the far end of the beach, its canopy half submerged in the water, the exposed branches frosted lightly with ash.

"Yeah, that looks recent," Lefty said, digging the heel of his boot in the sand. "Judging by the dust."

"It'll be this earthquake swarm," Ahmad replied. "We've been monitoring the shakes for the past month. These last few days, the readings have been off the scale."

"Ahmad's right. It's as if the mountain's been trying to shake some sense into us," Thompson said.

Their words must have woken Pīhanga, who turned in her bed, the earth jolting underfoot and knocking everyone off their feet. They clutched at the beach while the shaking continued, rattling their bones. Alain gasped.

"Crikey," Thompson exclaimed. The shaggy scientist curled his fingers in the sand. "This is a big one."

When the quaking finally subsided, Taine stood up. He put out a hand to help Keira. "Let's go."

They left the beach and set out; Taine, Eriksen, Lefty and Hine taking turns to hack a path through the bush, while Read suffered at the back of the group, grumbling about there being nothing wrong with him and how he was quite capable of thrashing a stick about. Taine ignored him, and concentrated on clearing the way, his t-shirt pulled up over his nose and mouth to keep out ash and debris. It was hot work, made worse by drifting gases which made their eyes water. After half an hour of toil, the ridge loomed before them and the bush thinned. Taine called a brief halt.

Keira stopped to take a drink, handing around her water bottle to the others.

All at once, an explosion rocked the bush. Taine caught Keira's look of surprise as the ground opened, erupting in a fountain of molten lava beneath her. Rocks the size of cats ejected from the chasm and the sky filled with billowing ash.

Taine gaped. Keira was gone. Vaporised. One second she was there and then, nothing. Like she'd triggered an anti-tank mine. There was no time to mourn. More lava bombs were exploding from the fissure, the deadly missiles crashing around them. Red hot lava spurted and flowed down the face of the mountain. It scorched a trail, like blackened rope, that curled through the bush towards the lake. Trees as old as time burst into flames before being engulfed by the lava. Near the edge of the chasm, the ground was collapsing. Eriksen, almost carried away by the boiling torrent, was saved only by Lefty's quick reflexes and the strength of his army smock. In seconds, the heat was treacherous, the stench of gas overwhelming.

"Make for high ground," Taine shouted.

Lefty led the way, navigating a path up the rise, running through the falling boulders like a winger on offence, Eriksen hot on his heels.

Taine scanned the area. Off to his left, Hine was crouched beside a solid beech trunk. It provided some protection, just not enough. A stone the size of a walnut made it past the trunk to glance off her helmet. Hine hunched closer to the tree. The lava bombs were coming thick and fast now, the noise strangely familiar, like the time he and Trigger had been holed up in a school in central Kabul...

It had been during Taliban's spring onslaught. The insurgents were pummelling the school with everything they had: rocket propelled-launchers and machine gun fire, while NATO air support pummelled the insurgents back.

The ground yawned and a new crack opened, shaking Taine from his memories.

"Hine, get out of there, now! Three o'clock. Follow my voice."

She didn't hesitate, bounding away as a volley of stone and rock ricocheted off the tree trunk. She scrambled for the slope. Eriksen stuck out his hand to help her to scuttle up over the rise. Exhaling in relief, Taine turned back to the fray.

Where were the rest of them?

His heart pounding, he squinted through the clouds of ash and steam. "Read!" Dammit. The visibility was close to nil and with too much interference from the lava, his NVGs would be useless.

Read's croak filtered through the raining stone, "Over here, boss."

Through the murk of rock and hellfire, Taine caught sight of his private making for the slope, his body crouched over to protect Alain.

"See if you can find some cover," Taine ordered.

"Got it." The pair disappeared over the rise.

Three to go. His body low, Taine swivelled, searching for the others. Had they been vaporised too? They'd been standing near Keira.

A burning rock whistled past him, its heat searing the air. The thud of it landing echoed in his chest. Taine turned to look: the rock had landed a metre from his feet, the force so strong the steaming boulder was half-buried in the ground.

They were running out of time. He had to find the scientists. "Thompson! Speak up, man! Where are you?"

"We're coming!" Taine followed the sound of Thompson's voice. Seconds passed. Finally, he glimpsed Thompson and Pringle. They were dragging Ahmad away from the spurting wall of lava. Was the boy injured? Taine strained to see.

"Keira!" Ahmad twisted sharply, shoving Pringle off him. Pringle stumbled. His arms wind-milled and his feet scrabbled on the rock-strewn mountainside. Taine leaped forward and grabbed him by the arm, steadying him while he regained his balance. Then he pushed him towards the ridge. "Follow the others."

Above them, Eriksen's voice cut through the ash, "Over here!"

Taine turned on his heel.

Desperate, Ahmad was determined to look for his colleague. "We have to go back!"

Thompson held his arms wide, blocking his way. "There's no point. She's gone, son."

"No! She's here somewhere. I know it!" Ahmad charged, preparing to thump the older man's chest, but Thompson ducked, tackling him around the legs. Then he picked Ahmad up and slung him over his back. Fortunately, Ahmad's light frame was no match for Thompson. "Put me down," he roared.

"Can't. Keira told me to be nice to you, and that means making sure you don't die."

"This way." Taine readied himself to fall in behind them as they passed, when a figure appeared at the edge of his vision. He paused. Hine? No, he'd made that mistake before. She was shorter and sturdier than the Tūrehu woman and with a darker complexion, and where Hine's dark hair was cropped short, this woman's fell down her back in waves like blackened lava. Standing in the thick of the fiery crater, her patu-club quivering at her hip, she curled a talon in his direction. "McKenna," she called. "This way."

Dark eyes beckoned. The wind whispered in his ears. His heart urged him to follow; his brain screamed no.

"Come," she cooed through sharpened teeth.

She'd asked for him. It was important. Blinking against the sucking heat, he took a step forward, the blistered sole of his boot wobbling on the edge of an abyss.

"McKenna!" Eriksen shouted.

The woman vanished.

Startled, Taine turned and scrambled for the rise.

Slopes of Mount Pīhanga

Taine ducked under the rocky outcrop, joining the others just after Thompson and Ahmad. Given the way the ground was shaking, hunkering here was a risk. For the moment though, it offered them some protection from the hailstorm of rock still raging on the other side of the ridge. They wouldn't be sticking around long. "Eriksen, report."

"One MIA, presumed dead. Everyone else accounted for."

One casualty. Exposed and caught by surprise, it could have been much worse. Sure, they were battered, their tunics were scorched and torn and, no doubt they all had bruises that they'd pay for tomorrow, but it was an acceptable loss.

Taine's heart slowed. It was no consolation.

"La pauvre," Alain whispered.

Ahmad stopped his struggling. Thompson let him go.

"Why did you stop?" Ahmad asked Taine. "Did you see her? Keira?"

Taine wiped his face with the back of his hand. "No. It was nothing. A trick of the light," he said.

"Yes," Hine agreed. The front of her helmet was sporting a couple of decent dings. "My people say sometimes, in the mist, we see our sharpest hopes."

"That's lovely. I've not heard that one before. What iwi is that, then?" Thompson asked. Taine looked up and caught Read's worried glance.

Quickly, Pringle put an arm around Ahmad's shoulders. "The important thing is that Keira didn't suffer. Isn't that right, Thompson?" he said, distracting the pair's focus away from a discussion about Hine's origins.

"Yes, of course. It was nothing like Robert, Ahmad. She won't have felt a thing."

Lefty interrupted the condolences. "I'm really sorry about your friend, but we should go. Who knows when the mountain will hit us with another bomb?"

"He's right." Taine stood. "Getting over the ridge doesn't mean we're out of danger. Even without encountering any volcanic activity, it's going to take us a while to reach the road."

They prepared to leave the safety of the outcrop, pulling their t-shirts back up over their noses and mouths. Those who had them, tightened their helmets. Alain bent to re-tie his shoelaces.

Lefty was the first to step out...only to duck back under cover, when a wave of tiny projectiles filled the air. Stones clattered off his helmet and pelted his shoulders.

He grimaced. "Ow," he said, rubbing at his shoulder. "Maybe we should wait a sec. It's raining bowling balls out there."

Taine crouched, picking up some of the pebbles accumulating like hailstones at the edge of the shelter. He turned them over in his hand.

Some rounded and others with sharp facets, they were milky yellow-green, like tumbled glass, and the size of twenty-cent pieces.

"These look like pounamu," he said.

"Greenstone?" Pringle replied. "Well, the lake we walked around is called Rotopounamu, wasn't it? So I guess that makes sense."

Scooping up a handful, Thompson examined the pebbles. "Except it's not greenstone. Pounamu is only found in the South Island. These are olivine, silicate minerals called fayalite, or forsterite, depending on their relative magnesium or iron content. Common enough. It's rock from the mantle that gets spewed out in volcanic eruptions."

"No kidding," Eriksen muttered.

Thompson ignored him. "I've seen it before, just never had it rain on me. Dun Mountain near Nelson is composed entirely of this stuff. I saw great handfuls of it when I went to Hawaii, the grains thrown up in the Kilauea eruption. But these little gems don't just come out of *our* earth, they come out of the ground on other celestial bodies too, because they've been found in meteorites."

Taking one of the pebbles out of Thompson's hand, Alain lifted it up to the light. "This one looks like an emerald."

"That'll be the magnesium content," Ahmad said.

"Exactly, Jawad. Gem-quality olivines – peridots – are the magnesium-rich variety, although ironically, it's the *iron* that gives them that deeper green colour."

"My country, Pakistan, has some of the highest quality gems. They're often mistaken for emeralds. Have been for about the past four millennia."

Taine couldn't tell if Thompson's jump to lecture mode was deliberate; either way it was doing the trick, drawing Ahmad's interest and taking the young man's mind off Keira's death. The two scientists were huddled together, inspecting the collection in Thompson's hand. "Bizarre, because we usually see olivine where tectonic plates are pushed *together*," the older man said.

"But the volcanic plateau is sinking, being pulled apart, as the Australian Plate rides over the Pacific plate—" said Ahmad.

"And it's mostly ignimbrite…"

Near the wall, Hine gazed out at the sky, her gloved hand resting on rock. "It's like the mountain is crying and these are her tears," she said.

"It seems she's crying herself out," Lefty said. "The stones are easing off."

Leaning out, Taine checked the sky. A single pebble struck his helmet. There would be fewer as they moved away from the source, and the bush canopy should help. By the time they got to the pasture further down the slopes, the stones might not reach them at all. That is, providing they didn't step on another lava bomb. On that score, all bets were off.

"Let's move out." Opening his hand and dropping the cluster of yellow-green stones, Taine stepped out into the open.

"On the bright side, it's all downhill from here," quipped Eriksen.

CHAPTER SIXTEEN

Tokaanu village

Knife lifted the roller door of the garage.

A car!

"Holy shit," he muttered. His pulse shifted up a gear. Glancing back, he cast his eyes over the street. Climo and Pope had just gone into the house about a block away, and Eaton and Ants were at the fishing shop.

No one was looking his way.

He slipped under the roller door and dropped it back to the floor. Well, there was no need to let everyone know, was there? He'd check the car out first. See what was what. It might not even go. Even so, his pulse thrummed in his veins. Because if the car *did* go, he'd grab himself some clothes and make a run for it. Flip the bird to that Barnes on the way out of town. The guy was off his fucking head anyway; telling everyone to look for passports and money, like they were going to drive off into the sunset together. No way he was buying that.

First things first: check out the car. Whoever used it last had parked it so there was more room on the driver's side. Would have helped if they'd rolled it forward a metre, too. Knife squeezed around the back of the car. A sky-blue Mazda Familia, it looked tidy enough. A 2002 model, it had probably been around the clock a half dozen times, but as long as there was a hundred kilometres left under the bonnet, he'd be in business.

He leaned forward and looked at the windscreen. The warrant of fitness was current. Fucking awesome. Putting his hand to the driver's window, he peered through the glass, checking the ignition. Shit. No keys. Without them, he'd need a drill and screwdriver to start it – not to mention time he didn't have.

He breathed deep. It was fine. No need to panic. If the car was here, then the keys would be somewhere in the house. It shouldn't be too hard to whip inside without any of the others seeing. Once he'd found the keys, he'd be outta here.

"Anyone checked this one?" the voice outside was faint but recognisable.

Knife cringed. Ants. Damn. If he saw the car it'd fuck everything up. The twat would run straight to Barnes. Knife had hung out a bit with Ants while they'd been inside, and he'd seemed okay, but ever since the bus had done a backflip, he'd turned into an arse-wipe, sucking up to Barnes like a calf at the teat. Like he had Stockholm Syndrome, or something. Guess you never really know a person until the shit hits the fan. If Knife wanted the car, he'd have to head Ants off. Grabbing the gun, he lifted the roller door halfway and ducked out of the garage.

Ants and Eaton were coming up the driveway.

"Find anything?" Eaton asked.

"An old Mazda," Knife said, jabbing his thumb behind him at the garage.

"Sweeeet."

"No use to us, though. No engine block."

Ants grimaced. "Fuck it."

"You guys find a radio?"

"Nah, there was nothing at the fishing shop. Owner must've taken it with them." Ants put his hand in his pocket and pulled out a wad of notes. Grinning, he waved them in Knife's face. "We emptied the cash register, instead."

"Niiiice," Knife said mimicking Ant's drawl. "But wasn't Barnes counting on you two to bring back a radio? Otherwise, how are we going to find out when the army pulls back? Probably not good to piss him off with the mood he's in right now. Maybe poke your nose in a couple of doors up at the ski hire place?"

"Good idea," Eaton said, tapping Ants on the back as he turned to go.

"Yeah, I reckon that'll be your best bet," Knife said. "I'll have a quick rummage through here and catch up with you when I'm done."

Ants lingered on the driveway. Staring at Knife, he stuffed the money back in his pockets.

"Ants, hurry the fuck up," Eaton said.

Ants turned on his heel and sauntered back down the drive. At long last, he disappeared past the next building.

Knife blew out a breath he hadn't known he'd been holding. Then, taking the broken concrete path between the garage and the house, he skipped up the porch steps and let himself into the kitchen.

What was it with these little towns? Stepping into one was like stepping back in time. The kitchen cupboards were caked with layers of paint and the catches were those 1960s jobs with stainless steel hooks.

Where have you put the car keys, people? No key rack, but there was a line of coat pegs by the door, a couple of large coats and an umbrella hanging on them. Knife put the gun down while he checked the coat pockets. No luck there: only spare change and a packet of Kleenex. Maybe they were in the kitchen drawers? He pulled out the drawer closest to the back door. This was more like it. Lined with plastic Contact, the drawer was full of junk: pens, string, Sellotape, a stack of receipts... Bingo! A set of car keys.

"Put those keys down and get out of my house."

Knife spun about. A middle-aged woman wearing baggy jeans blocked the hallway. Shit! While his back had been turned, the bitch had snuck in and picked up the gun. She was pointing it right at him and it looked like she could tell one end from the other.

He took a step back. Which was the knife drawer?

She snarled, "You can move away from there, too."

"Honestly, I'm not—"

"Now!"

He did as he was told. *Gonna need a new tack.*

Straightening up, he did that thing with his hands, like he was praying – the way the counsellors at the prison did when they wanted you to think they were sincere. "Mrs, you've got it all wrong. I'm here with Civil Defence."

"Cut the crap. I know you're not Civil Defence. My ex volunteered for years and he never carried a gun. I heard on the radio that a bunch of prisoners escaped from Rangipō, so I knew who you were the minute you lot drove into town."

A young woman appeared behind her in the hall, one hand on the wall and the other resting under a belly that had to be close to bursting. "Oh my god, Mum! What are you doing? Put that gun down."

Knife's mind raced. A man going through a check point on his own would be suspicious, unlike a man with his heavily pregnant wife. No way the authorities would suspect a thing; he'd be through that checkpoint and on his way to freedom. All he had to do was deal with the mother. Put a gag in her mouth and stick her in the closet, or something. By the time anyone found her, they'd be long gone.

He splayed his hands in front of him. "Let's just calm down, shall we? Miss, please tell your mother that she's mistaken. It's true that Civil Defence don't usually carry weapons, but it's also true that there are some escaped prisoners in the area. *That's* the reason we're armed. Our Civil Defence team has joined forces with the army to do a last sweep of the town. Evacuate everyone. We have to be sure no one's left behind."

The daughter's lip quivered. She was gobbing it.

Knife played his trump card. "You said you saw the truck drive through, so you know we came in on an army Unimog. Do you really think the NZDF would let a bunch of prisoners get hold of one of their trucks?"

The girl took a step forward. "Mum, please. You're being paranoid. We should go with Civil Defence. I haven't heard back from Lefty and I can't get through to anyone on my cell. The towers must be overloaded."

The old lady pursed her lips. "Go back to the bedroom, Lisa. Lock the door."

"Mum—"

"You should listen to your daughter. I'm here to help."

The old lady's eyes narrowed. "I suppose you'd like to help yourself to my jewellery too? The way your friend outside helped himself to the cash register at the fishing shop."

"Ah, you heard that."

"I did."

"Well, the thing is—" Knife ran at her. Ducked under the barrel. Grappled with the gun, trying to wrest it from her fingers. Her body shook with effort and her face went red. For a woman, she put up a good fight. That was motherlove for you. Panting, Knife strained to twist the firearm from her grip. He grunted. "Let go, you bitch."

The rifle went off. The old lady's neck exploded out the back, spraying the daughter with blood and gunk. The daughter's mouth made an 'o' and her breath came in little gasps.

The mother slumped to the floor.

Her eyes wide, her hand still holding her stomach, the daughter stumbled backwards.

Oh, no, you don't... Knife jumped over the mother and lunged for the daughter. He trod on the woman's arm, slipped in the blood, and thumped into the wall. Before he could recover, the girl slammed the bathroom door in his face. Knife heard the bolt slide to.

Shit-shit-shit-shit-shit.

Ants and Eaton were next door. They had to have heard the rifle. The others, too. They'd be on their way. Looks like he wouldn't be travelling with a wife, after all. Grabbing the rifle, Knife ran down the hall, not giving two shits that he was tromping on the mother. In the kitchen, he grabbed a raincoat off the hook and dashed out the back door.

Great. The garage had a side door. He turned the knob. It gave a little. Not locked, but the wooden jam was swollen. Knife stepped back and threw his shoulder at the door, practically falling into the garage when it gave way. Fuck. He'd forgotten that the roller door at the front wasn't fully open. He ran around the hood of the Mazda, past the driver's side, and flung up the door.

A block north, Pope was running this way.

Shit.

Knife ran to the car. He dived into the driver's seat. Heart in his throat, he turned the key in the ignition, put the car in reverse and floored it. Nearly took out Eaton as he swung into the road. He gunned the accelerator.

By the time his former mates opened fire, he was more than a football field away, heading south towards Turangi. The shots went wide.

So long, suckers.

Central Plateau, State Highway 41

Taine swung his leg over the fence and jumped to the ground, ignoring a pebble in his boot. He looked out over the valley, some of the tension of the past hour draining away. Across this paddock and they'd be at the road. The detour had worked, getting them past the lahar. Now he could go after Barnes.

They tramped down the grassy slope, skittering a bunch of jumpy cows.

"Poor things," Pringle said. 'Imagine being abandoned like that. Do you think they know what's going on?"

As far as Taine was concerned there was no doubt the animals could sense the danger erupting all around them. Their ears were alert to every sound and their eyes were white with fear. It was clear this herd had been well cared for. Kiwi farmers tended to get pretty attached to their livestock. This one had taken the time to feed the stock out before departing. It must have near killed him to leave them in the field. There'd been no time to transport stock animals out of the region, and releasing them during the evacuation only to be bowled over by panicked motorists didn't make much sense either.

"We should let them go," Alain said abruptly. 'There's no one around. We could open the gate."

Everyone looked at Taine, as if he was Noah and they were loading the ark. "If we let them go and the mountains don't erupt, the farmer will lose his livelihood," he said.

Eriksen scoffed. "*If* the mountains don't erupt."

"Much as I hate to agree with Adrian," Lefty said, "I reckon that ship has already sailed, Boss."

"At least, if we let them go, they'll have had a chance," Ahmad said.

Taine looked at the desperation in their faces.

"I wonder what the doc would say?" Read said, smirking.

Taine grinned back. "Go on, then," he said. It was one paddock; a small price to boost the group's morale.

Alain and Ahmad raced each other down the slope, both wanting to open the gate. The rest of the group followed the pair down the grassy slope, Taine scanning the township in the distance. Only another two kilometres to Turangi. How would they find Barnes without getting themselves captured too? He had no way of contacting Arnold; the sat phone Taine had used to call him earlier had perished in Keira's pack. Their cell phones had been useless all day, and in anticipation of a major catastrophic event, electricity to the town would've been cut, so there was a chance the landlines would be out of action too. Which meant their best hope of locating Barnes and freeing the hostages would be spotting Arnold's drone while it hovered over the Unimog – the equivalent of finding a diamond in a box of cornflakes.

Circling the cattle, Ahmad and Alain were playing at being Huntaways, clapping their hands and barking at the cows to drive them out of the paddock. If he wasn't so worried, Taine might have been tempted to join in the fun.

All at once, the sound of cracking and popping filled the air. Taine froze. Beside him, Lefty's head shot up.

"Sounds like more trees have gone down somewhere," Thompson said.

"Nope. That was gunfire," said Eriksen.

"Definitely gunfire," said Read.

Taine didn't have to give the order: instinctively his soldiers ran towards the road, while Pringle and Thompson, caught flatfooted by their sudden acceleration, hurried to catch up.

"Did anyone catch which direction it came from?" Taine called.

"Hard to tell with the wind," Eriksen replied. "Maybe west?"

"Yes. It came from that way," Hine said, gesturing to their left.

So Barnes was holed up in Tokaanu.

They reached the gate, where Alain and Ahmad were chasing the last of the cattle out of the paddock onto the highway.

"I need a volunteer to escort the civilians to safety," Taine said, leaping over the ditch to the road.

"I won't go," Alain said. "I will come with you to find Brigitte."

"I'm not leaving either," said Pringle. "I know those men. I can help."

"Look out!" Ahmad shouted. He pointed down the road towards Tokaanu.

A blue Mazda was speeding towards them as if the hounds of hell were in pursuit. Everyone jumped back onto the verge, but there was no way to move the cattle.

The driver swerved hard to the left. Brakes shrieked, and the car slewed sideways, narrowly missing the animals. The Mazda veered off the road. It charged over the ditch, throwing up fenceposts and plunged into the scrub, then ploughed headlong into a tree.

Taine scrambled up the bank and crossed the paddock to the crash site. It was too late for the driver. A branch had cored through his eye socket and exited the rear of skull, skewering him to the seat.

"Knife," Pringle said.

No one commented on the irony.

CHAPTER SEVENTEEN

Tokaanu village

Lisa jumped away from the door. She clutched at her belly and fixed her eyes on the door handle. Omigod. What if the bolt didn't hold? What if he broke the door down? She'd seen his face. Seen him shoot her mother. She was a witness! He'd have to kill her and her baby, too. She sucked in a breath. Her body was trembling all over. She couldn't stop herself from shaking. Her heart was pounding. Racing.

Ohmigod! Mum!

Steadying herself on the edge of the bathtub, Lisa clamped her teeth together, pushing back her hysteria, and listened. Outside, car tyres screamed. There was a batter of gunfire.

Her stomach lurched. No, no, no. She'd forgotten about the others. Mum had told her, hadn't she? Said they were a bunch of escaped prisoners. A whole truckload. Lisa hadn't believed her. Now they'd be on their way here to find out what had happened. They'd come into the house and find her. If she wanted to live, she needed to get out now. There was only one way – through the bathroom window.

Lisa stood on the side of the bath, leaning over the sink so she could look out the window and check there was no one outside. Thankfully, the side of the house was clear. She pushed the window open as far as it would go. At thirty-three weeks, the gap would be tight. Her hand on the wall, she placed her foot in the sink.

Wait!

If they found the door locked, they'd know someone had been in here. Putting her foot down, she got out of the bath, and tiptoed across the bathroom. Laid her ear to the door. When she was sure no one was in the hall, she slipped the bolt open. Then, climbing on the edge of the bath, she used the sink as a step to help her clamber over the sill.

It took some wiggling, but eventually she dropped quietly onto the grass. Her arms out to balance the baby weight, she stood under the bathroom window in her nightie, cardigan, and bare feet. She held her breath.

On the street, men were shouting. She didn't have much time. Lisa reached up with both hands and pulled the window closed, pressing it until the latch clicked. Raising her arms above her head was dangerous for the baby; even with the cervical stitch, her doctor had advised her against any stretching or lifting.

What are you even thinking? Like getting shot isn't dangerous for the baby!

Lisa stifled a sob, hit again with the image of Mum splayed out on the floor in a pool of blood. She scrubbed at her face with the back of her arm, wishing she'd dreamed the whole ugly thing, that Mum wasn't dead. The spatter on her nightdress told another story.

Don't think about it. Don't think about Mum. Just get away. Save the baby. Her hand under her tummy, Lisa darted across the lawn to the garage. She paused for a moment, unsure what to do. What if she hid in one of the hotels? No, it was too risky. The prisoners were checking all the houses, so they were bound to look in the hotels too. Where then?

She peeked out towards the road. Gasped.

Men were coming! She needed to get away from the house. Anywhere out of sight. Lisa held her breath, listening for the men's voices, waiting until they were on the other side of the garage. Then she rushed away from the building and ran as hard as she could across the road. It had been ages since she'd run anywhere. She was as slow as a walrus, lumbering along on her fat swollen legs. They'd see her, of course. How could they not? She kept running, expecting someone to yell at her to stop right where she was and don't move or they'd blow her head off.

No one yelled. No one had seen her. Panting heavily, Lisa pushed her way into the brush. She was careful not to go too far: the back of the town near the Hot Springs was riddled with steaming mud pools.

A band tightened across her belly and she drew in a breath of the sulphury air.

Oh geez. That hurts.

One hand gripping a thin manuka trunk, she dropped to her knees, the pain in her belly so intense she barely noticed the twigs scratching her arms and legs. She put her hands on the ground. Bit the inside of her cheek. *Please, baby, don't come yet.* The band tightened. *Be Braxton Hicks. Be Braxton Hicks.* Her heart thumping in terror, Lisa concentrated on her breathing: in, in, in, and blowing out slow. After a while, the contractions eased. When she was sure they were over, she took off her cardigan and bundled it into a ball. Then she lay face up on the ground with the bundle tucked beneath her hips. Not exactly what the doctor had in mind, but it would have to do for now.

What was happening at the house? She poked a hole in the brush and peeked through the gap. Shadows at the windows showed the men inside. She'd rest here until they'd gone. At least near the Hot Springs, the ground was warm. She tried not to think of Mum.

*

Barnes pushed Pope aside and barged into the house. The place looked like a fucking abattoir: blood and shit everywhere. Ants and Eaton emerged from the bedrooms.

"What the hell happened?"

Ants shrugged. "Knife was checking out the house. The old lady must have surprised him."

"Ants and I heard the shot from up the road and came running," Eaton said. "By the time we got here, Knife was already pulling out of the driveway. He wasn't wasting any time. Almost mowed us down."

"Yeah, well. You'd expect him to be in a hurry. Murder's a step up from fencing stolen goods, isn't it?" said Pope, who'd followed Barnes inside. Barnes didn't like his tone.

"We tried to stop him," Eaton said. He looked at Pope. "You were there; you saw us shoot at the car."

Ants pursed his lips. "I reckon Knife was already planning on doing a runner. He told us before that the car in the garage was fucked. Said the engine block was missing."

"And neither of you fucks bothered to check?"

"How were we supposed to know he was talking shit?" Ants whined.

"The guy could lie for England," Eaton said.

"Load up the Unimog," Barnes ordered, turning to leave. "We're going after him."

"What the hell for?" Ants called. "He'll be long gone."

Leaning against the kitchen bench, Pope smirked. "Yeah, Barnes. Let him go. What does it even matter?" The bastard was enjoying himself.

Barnes glowered. "Because we're in this together, that's why. Either we all make it out, or *no one* does."

"Pope's right. What does it matter?" Ants said, picking his way through the puddles to step over the body. "Knife isn't going to say anything. Why would he? Not after this."

"Personally, I'd like to get out of here before the shit hits the fan and the mountains blow up," Eaton said.

"We need to forget about Knife and stick to the plan," Pope said.

Barnes hesitated. In Knife's place, Barnes would have run too, and if he got caught, it was easy enough to point the finger at someone else for the old lady's death. And since Barnes was the most likely scapegoat, it meant Knife was a loose end that needed snipping. Pope was becoming a problem, too. Always putting his two cents in, stirring things up.

Butting heads with him wasn't the answer. It would only rile him up more and Ants and Eaton had already proved they were easily won over. Barnes needed the men on his side, at least until he was ready to cut them loose. "Okay, okay," he said. "Forget about Knife. You two find a radio yet?"

"Not yet," Ants said. "We were interrupted, weren't we?"

"Hurry it up, then. Tell the others that no one goes anywhere without someone else with them." Barnes clocked the look Eaton gave Ants. "You got something you want to say about that?"

Eaton dropped his eyes to stare at the corpse. "No."

"Good." Barnes turned on his heel and stalked out of the house.

*

Taine would have preferred that the civilians wait behind in Turangi. Instead, they'd voted to come. It was probably just as well; he'd never known his soldiers to be keen on playing babysitter. Taine placed the civilians in the middle of the group where they'd be the safest, then they'd set off at a run.

Younger and leaner, Ahmad and Alain were having no trouble keeping up with the members of Taine's section, but for Thompson, who was the better part of twenty years older and more than twenty kilos heavier, covering the two kilometres was a challenge. He was wheezing as if he had a chest cold, his face was red and blotchy, and his straggly hair was plastered to his head. Pringle wasn't faring much better, although he'd already walked ten kilometres in close country this morning while propping up Brooker. Still, Taine had to hand it to them: neither man was complaining. Their faces fixed with determination, they followed doggedly in Read's footsteps. Their suffering was nearly over: they were approaching the slip road to Tokaanu.

Eriksen called a halt, gesturing for silence while he scanned the area. He was right to exercise caution; Barnes might have posted sentries. Thompson did his best to stay silent, but his wheezing was loud enough to raise the dead. They were lucky: there didn't seem to be anyone guarding the turn off. When he was certain the road was clear, Eriksen signalled for them to move out, waving the MARS-L that Taine had recovered from the Mazda. The rifle was useless: the barrel mangled in the crash, although seen from a distance, an enemy wouldn't know that, especially one not familiar with NZDF ordnance.

The group moved forward, keeping close to the shrubs at the side of the road, Taine regretting not taking the time to empty the pebble out of his boot.

"Boss," Lefty said, keeping his voice low. "My ex, Lisa, her mum's place is around the corner. It's a couple of houses in on the right. I never heard whether one of the other sections picked them up."

Taine nodded. "Let's give everyone a breather here, while you and I go and take a look. Tell Eriksen to keep them out of sight."

"Cool. Thanks, Boss."

Taine and Lefty ran from building to building, their eyes peeled. They climbed the fence and weaved their way round the back of what looked like a holiday rental bach. Lefty paused, his back against the wall, and nodded down the street. The Unimog was parked in the middle of the road at the far end of town. Some of Barnes' men were clustered about it. *Damn.* He wanted to storm down there and strangle every one of them. He clenched his fists. They had to secure Lisa and her mother first. When that was done, he'd go after Barnes. Narrowing his eyes, Taine strained for a glimpse of Jules. If she was there, he couldn't make her out. Lefty pointed to their right, and they carried on.

Lisa's mother's property was modest, a sixties build, tidy, with a single garage on the front. They circled the house.

Lefty's eyes widened. He pointed at the steps.

Boot marks. In blood.

Taine ducked his head inside, then darted back. No one in the kitchen. He gestured to Lefty who slipped inside, keeping low, so he couldn't be seen at the windows. Taine followed him in.

"Holy shit!" Lefty whispered. "It's Lisa's mum."

Taine took in the scene. The hall was awash with blood and bone. Taine had been with the NZDF for over a decade, and during that time he had witnessed some pretty gruesome things, yet something about this made his stomach roil. It wasn't just the violence of the attack, but the fact that this wasn't a combat zone; it was a violation of someone's *home*, a place where you expected to feel safe.

The dead woman lay on her back on the floor surrounded by a halo of blood. Taine didn't have to turn her over to know that her shoulders and head had been obliterated, blown off in an exit wound the size of a small crater. Lefty checked the remaining rooms, calling quietly for Lisa, and Taine crouched to examine the mother. Her skin was cool but without rigor. That fitted what they knew. The woman's death was probably the cause of the gunfire they'd heard earlier, and the reason for the man's – Knife's – deadly flight in the Mazda.

Lefty appeared at the other end of the hall. "Lisa's not here," he said. "I've checked everywhere. Barnes must have taken her." It was a fair assumption. The bloody footprints said as much. "We should go," Lefty said.

Something wasn't quite right.

"Hang on," Taine said. Staying low, he stepped over the dead woman and stuck his head around the bathroom door. Inside, the green and white checker linoleum was smeared red-brown, consistent with Barnes' men tromping all over the scene. Stepping back, Taine opened and closed the door. "Look at the wall here, and the door jam," he whispered.

Lefty frowned in concentration. "It's clean." His head snapped up. "When the shot went off, Lisa was standing here," he concluded.

The logical thing would have been for her to lock herself in the bathroom.

Taine pulled back the shower curtain and checked the bathtub. Inside the bath, near the plug outlet, was a toe print.

"Clever girl," Lefty said. "She went out the window."

*

Apart from the usual corner dairy, there were only a few businesses in Tokaanu, all of them geared to coaxing as much as possible from tourist wallets. Rutledge, Grant, and Stedman were in the kayak hire place, a blocky tan building about halfway down the main drag. A classic warehouse layout with the front area given over to retail and equipment hire, a mezzanine floor housing the office and staff facilities, and at the rear, a concrete service area.

"I'll check down the back." Rutledge loped past a wall covered with a large map and a stand of brochures. He looked in doors as he passed: a toilet block, change room, and some showers stalls. Nothing too helpful there. On the back wall of the building, a rear exit stood next to a garage tilt-a-door. His heart sped up. There might be a vehicle bay out the back. Glancing back over his shoulder, Rutledge pulled opened the exit and checked outside. His shoulders dropped. Damn. No vehicles. Just a crude concrete ramp leading down to a narrow stream. Slightly wider than a paddle-width and mostly overgrown with weeds, the water course was clearly the start point for the kayakers' tours of the lake.

Wedging a broom in the door, Rutledge stepped outside. He walked along the bank of the stream for a few metres, then turned back to the hire warehouse.

Inside, Grant was sitting on the counter, drumming his heels on the upright.

"Find anything?" Rutledge asked.

"Sure did," Grant replied. "Eight yellow sit-on kayaks, twelve orange ones, thirty life jackets in different sizes, and an odd number of paddles."

"Very funny. I meant anything useful."

"There are a couple of sturdy kayak trolleys if someone would like to rickshaw me out of town." Grant meant it as a joke, but Rutledge latched on to the words. It was an idea.

Taking a step back so he could see the mezzanine, Rutledge called up to Stedman, "What about you? Anything?"

"No radio, but there's food in the staffroom," Stedman said as he emerged triumphant from one of the upstairs rooms, a block of cheese in one hand and a butter knife in the other.

"Well, bring it down, then," Grant called.

"Give me a sec." The metal rungs of the yellow industrial stairs vibrated as Stedman descended. Joining them, he slid the cheese onto the counter, then pulled a box of crackers from his overalls and hiffed them to Grant. "Here, open that."

Stedman unwrapped the cheese and carved off a large chunk, stuffing it in his mouth while he cut another.

A stack of six crackers in his fist, Grant snatched up the second hunk of cheese. "I like my cheese better melted on toast," he mumbled.

Stedman grunted. He lifted the block and offered the cheese to Rutledge. "No problem. Another day in this hellhole and everything will be melted."

They said nothing, just sat there eating, Grant still drumming his heels on the counter. Rutledge used the moment to size up his companions. If he had a choice, he'd prefer to do this alone, but there were worse men than Grant and Stedman. He could have been paired up with Ants, for example. Even so, he would have to be careful how he played this. A wrong move could get him killed.

He took the cardboard box from Grant and helped himself to a cracker. "Look at us all running around like chooks with our heads chopped off, doing everything Barnes tells us," he said.

"Tell me about it," Stedman said, slicing himself more cheese.

"It's like we're his minions."

"You can talk, Rutledge," Grant said. "Weren't you the one who yanked out the starter cables on the Unimog?"

"And the way I heard it, you sold out the French guy," Rutledge replied quietly.

Grant rolled his eyes. "That's bullshit."

"Yeah?" Rutledge said. "Do you see him with us? Barnes left him stranded at the lake. For all we know, he might be dead."

"It wasn't just me. Stedman was there, too."

"Don't drag me into it."

"Don't you get it?" Rutledge said. "We're all involved one way or the other because Barnes *wants* it that way."

Grant stopped his drumming. "What are you saying, Rutledge?"

Rutledge held his index finger to his lips. Handing the crackers to Stedman, he crossed the shop and checked the door at the front of the building. When he joined them again, he kept his voice low, "The longer we stick with Barnes, the worse our chances."

Grant scoffed. "He's the one with the Unimog."

"He's also the one with four murders on his head, one of them a prison guard. Do you really think the police are going to let him walk out of here?"

"He's got hostages."

Rutledge shrugged. "They don't know that."

Grant got off the counter. He eyed the door nervously. "Fuck," he said, as if he was just realising the shit they were in.

Narrowing his eyes, Stedman's bushy eyebrows bunched even closer. He leaned over the counter. "What's your plan?"

Rutledge waved his hand at the kayaks on their trolleys.

Grant buried his face in his palms and shook his head. "I was joking when I said we should use the trolleys as rickshaws."

"Not the trolleys: the kayaks. We paddle across the lake."

"You're out of your mind," Stedman said. "Do you have any idea how far it is to Taupō?"

Rutledge crossed to the map and searched the fine-print until he found what he was looking for. "As the crow flies from Tokaanu village to Taupō..." He traced a line with his finger. "...forty-six kilometres," he said.

Shaking his head, Grant kicked at the counter with his toe. "Good one, Rutledge. Great plan. It'd take us all night, and that's providing we don't end up paddling around in circles in the dark."

"Who said anything about kayaking all the way across? All we have to do is get to one of the other towns around the lake. We could paddle east to Bulli or Hatepe." Rutledge picked them out on the map. "Or we go west to Omori—"

"I vote west," Stedman cut in. "We pull up at Omori. The settlement is bigger than Tokaanu, so we'll have a better chance of picking up a car, and we can take the road north from there into the Waikato-King Country district. No one will be looking for us there."

Rutledge checked the map. "Tokaanu to Omori direct...that's six kilometres. It'd take us maybe an hour."

"We'd be shot of Barnes," Stedman murmured.

"And further away from the mountains."

"Seeing as you've got it all thought out, tell me this: how are we going to get the kayaks to the edge of the lake? The Unimog is right in the middle of the road. Someone's bound to see us, and I don't plan on getting a bullet in my back," Grant said.

"Yeah, we don't want to end up like Perenia."

Rutledge smiled. They might still be arguing, but they'd both said 'we'. He was winning them over. Leaving the map, he returned to the counter. "There's a stream out back that runs down to the lake," he said. "I took a gawk earlier and it looks like it's well hidden behind trees and weeds, which means we can lock the front door and go out the back way without anyone seeing us. Paddle off into the sunset." He gestured with his arms, as if he was paddling a kayak. "It'll be as if we were never here. By the time Barnes realises we're missing, we could be pulling up on the beach at Omori."

"There's more food and canned drinks up in the staff room," Stedman said, starting for the stairs.

"Everything we need is here," Rutledge said, "wetsuits, lifejackets, torches..." he trailed off.

Stedman stopped. He turned slowly. Together, the pair of them looked at Grant and for a second the warehouse boomed with silence. If they couldn't persuade him, Stedman and Rutledge would have to prevent Grant from running back to Barnes and telling tales.

Grant's eyes flicked back to the door, a look of fear on his face. Rutledge almost felt sorry for him. The poor fuck was stuck between a rock and a hard place. The only question was: which way would he jump?

"Just as long as the bloody lake doesn't erupt while we're out there."

Rutledge exhaled. He gestured to the stack of kayaks. "You get your choice of yellow or orange..."

"Give me a yellow one," Grant said, peeling off his prison jumpsuit. "I'm fucking sick of orange."

*

Lisa scrubbed the snot off her face with the hem of her nightie. She had to move. She was getting cold and a twig was digging into her hip, giving her grief. Lifting the cardigan from under her hips, she shifted slowly onto her side. Her lower back ached, although it didn't feel like a contraction. Most likely, she'd strained it when she'd dropped down from the bathroom window. She let out a cackle, quickly covering her mouth with her hand.

It's okay, it's okay. Don't think about it.

She took a deep breath. She must have been here a while; she couldn't smell the sulphur any more. She couldn't lie here forever.

Mum had not only offered to look after Lisa when TJ had taken the job on the rig; she'd given up her life to save her and the baby, so it was Lisa's responsibility to make sure they survived. But the prisoners were armed, and they were prepared to kill anyone who got in their way – *no, she would not cry* – so getting out of Tokaanu would have to wait until after they'd gone. In the meantime, she needed somewhere safe to hide. Where? Back at the house? She couldn't go home. Mum was still there, and Lisa didn't think she could bear to look at her like that. Maybe the hot pools? It was only a few hundred metres away and they had a sick bay. Plus, there were toilets and showers there, and a kiosk with food. And the best part was, there was a bell on the door.

If anyone came, she'd nip behind the complex and hide on the thermal walk out the back. There: having a plan helped. She already felt better.

Peeping through the bracken, she checked across the road. Things had quieted down at the house. She was getting to her hands and knees when she caught a flash of movement.

Someone was coming.

Lisa held her breath.

Two soldiers. Her heart leapt. The army were here, and she recognised that gait. It was Lefty. He'd come for her. Tying her cardigan around her neck, Lisa gripped the scratchy manuka and hauled herself to her feet. She had to hurry, or he'd leave without her. Shoving away the branches that clung to her nightie, she pushed through the brush and ran into the open.

CHAPTER EIGHTEEN

Tokaanu village

In their hidey hole at the edge of the village, Thompson hunched with the others under the cover of the bush. Some time ago, McKenna and Lefty had skirted the corner of a house and disappeared. Now, they were waiting for the pair to come back with more information about where the hostages were being held before deciding how to proceed.

Suddenly, a pregnant woman burst from the trees, her nightdress snagging as she ran across the road towards the house.

"Shit," swore Eriksen. "That's Lefty's ex, Lisa."

'It's okay. Lefty will look out for her. She's making for the house," Ahmad said.

"Not okay," Read hissed. "Incoming at two o'clock."

No idea what he was talking about, Thompson followed the flick of the private's head. The sweat on his back froze. Two men in orange overalls were coming out of a nearby building. Both of them had rifles slung across their shoulders.

"That's Ants on the left and the other one is Eaton," Pringle whispered. "He's okay, but I wouldn't trust Ants as far as I could throw him. That man would sell his own mother if there was something in it for him."

"Maybe they don't see her," Alain whispered. "They are going the other way."

Thompson winced. Even from here, the flapping of the girl's nightdress was like a white flag of surrender.

Ants swivelled. "Hey!"

Lisa squealed. Panicked, she leapt forward, veering away from the prisoners.

"That's it. I'm going," Read said.

Eriksen thrust his rifle across Read's body, blocking his way. "Stand down, Read," he said. "Those guys are armed."

Read grasped the barrel of the rifle. "Give me the rifle, then."

"No can do, mate. McKenna said to stay out of sight until he'd conducted a recce."

Frustrated, Read shoved at the weapon, pushing it away from him. "McKenna hasn't seen her, has he? He didn't know this was going to happen. That woman's pregnant and she's out there *on her own*."

Lying beside Thompson, Pringle got to his hands and knees. "I'll go. This is all my fault anyway. I know those men. Maybe I can get them to listen to me."

This time it was Read who blocked the way, grabbing the prison officer by the jacket and pulling him back down. "Are you crazy, Karl? After what they did to your colleague? They'll shoot you on sight."

"None of us are doing anything," Eriksen said. "Any one of us shows ourselves, and they're likely to open fire. If not, they'll know we're on their case and we'll have lost the element of surprise. If we're going to save *anyone*, we're going to have to sit tight and see how this plays out. And Read, you fucking do so much as twitch and I'll knock you out myself."

Thompson swung his attention back to the street. Walking swiftly in their direction, the prisoners were coming after Lisa, Ants taking a second to glance over his shoulder at the far end of the settlement.

Lisa sobbed and ran on, her hand supporting her belly. It was obvious they would outrun her. There was nowhere for the poor kid to go.

Thompson didn't know why he did it, but the next thing he knew he'd slipped quietly away from the group, crouch-running behind the trees until he was standing with his back against the wall of a shed. He sneaked a peek around the corner of the structure. In the time it had taken Thompson to get here, Eaton had seized Lisa, his fingers tight around her upper arms. Lisa's face was stricken but not beaten.

"Who have we got here?" Ants asked.

Lisa glared at him. "None of your fucking business." She kicked out her foot, missing him, connecting only with air, but the gesture of defiance was enough to convince Thompson that he liked her already.

Ants lifted the hem of Lisa's nightdress with the barrel of the rifle. "Bit of blood on your PJs here, girl." His expression hardened. "You know what I think? I think you witnessed something in that house over there. I think maybe that old lady drowning in a pool of her own blood might be someone you know."

Lisa growled low in her throat.

"You know she didn't die straight away?" Ants went on, his words crueller than heartbreak. "Tragic really. When I got there, she was still breathing. Wheezy pitiful little breaths…"

Lisa bucked in Eaton's grip, digging in with her elbows, attempting to wrestle herself free.

"Keep still, will you?" Eaton snarled.

Thompson glanced back towards the copse where the others were hiding. Out of sight of the prisoners, Eriksen and Read were gesturing frantically for him to stay out of sight.

Thompson ignored them, peering around the corner in time to see Lisa bring her heel down on Eaton's shin.

Eaton swore between gritted teeth. Not letting go, he walloped her in the face, splitting her lip. Tears welled in Lisa's eyes.

"Well, he did ask you nicely."

"You pig," Lisa said through bloodied lips.

Ants took a step towards her, his posture full of menace. "*What* did you say?"

Enough of this. Thompson stepped out from behind the shed. "Stop," he said. "Let her go."

All three of them spun.

Ants' smile made Thompson's stomach shrink. He lifted the rifle to his shoulder, aiming it at Thompson. "And who the hell are you?"

Thompson nodded at Lisa. "I'm her father. The baby's grandfather." *Where had that come from?* Lisa's eyes fluttered, still she didn't let on.

"Aw, isn't that sweet? Daddy rides in on his white charger."

"Let her go. Please. I can pay you both, make it worth your while."

"Yeah, I don't think so," Ants said, his index finger hovering ominously on the trigger. "We haven't got time to pop down to the bank with you right now."

"I have it on me."

Ants laughed. "You expect me to believe you have a couple of hundred thou in your wallet? Because my colleague and I don't discuss terms for anything less."

Thompson squared his shoulders. "I have it."

Eaton grunted. "Yeah, right," he said.

"I swear."

Ants frowned. "Well, show us then."

Thompson slipped his hand into his pocket.

Ants adjusted the rifle. "And don't fuck with me."

His back damp with sweat, Thompson opened his palm. "They're emeralds," he said.

Despite the earth's shaking, it was as if everything had stilled: Thompson's breathing, his heart, even the ash stopped falling, as the men contemplated the gems in his palm.

Eaton licked his lips. "Ants," he said, "maybe we could consider his offer?"

"Hang on," Ants said. "How do we know they're real?

"Why else would I have a bunch of emeralds in my pocket? The government's evacuating everyone from the area – do you really think I'd leave something this valuable behind?"

"Where'd they come from?" Eaton asked.

"An emerald mine."

Ants swung the rifle at Lisa's belly, and she gasped. "I asked a civil question."

"Okay, sorry! Just don't shoot okay? I used to be a jeweller," Thompson lied through his teeth. "After my business failed I didn't trust banks very much."

"Yeah, that figures," said Eaton. "Fucking banks."

"You can have them all, but you have to let Lisa go."

Ants' nostrils flared, and he broke into a grin. "Sure. That sounds fair. We'll give her to you when you've handed over the emeralds." Thompson's spine tingled. Working with students for a couple of decades tended to sharpen your bullshit antenna. Right now, Thompson's was pinging like crazy. He'd blown it. Ants clearly had no intention of handing over the girl. Unless…

"Take them. They're all yours." Thompson threw the olivine on the ground, the gems scattering at Ants' feet.

"What the hell!" Ants dropped to one knee to scoop up the tiny stones.

"NZDF. Stay where you are!" Eriksen's voice was hard as flint.

Thompson glanced back. Protected by the shed where Thompson had sheltered earlier, the soldier had Knife's mangled gun trained on Ants. Talk about timing! Ants had lowered his rifle while stooping to grab the gems, and Eaton couldn't very well go for his while clutching Lisa like a human shield.

Already Eaton had cottoned on that Lisa was his ticket out of danger. Still gripping the girl, he backed away. When he reached the curve in the road, he flung her away and sprinted out of sight. Her nightdress billowing, Lisa ran for cover at a nearby house.

Ants watched Eaton go, then got to his feet.

"Stop right there," Eriksen said. "Throw the rifle down in front of you."

Instead, Ants turned and pointed the gun at Thompson. Thompson's blood froze in his veins. When he'd pointed the rifle at Thompson earlier, Ants had the upper hand. This was different. On the defensive, Ants would be dangerous. What if he panicked and squeezed the trigger? Thompson should have run when he'd had the chance.

"I said drop the rifle."

Ants didn't flinch. He took a step back. "I just worked something out. You're NZDF and I'm a New Zealand citizen, which means you can't shoot me." Bolder, he went on. "Now if you were to see me shoot Lisa's daddy here, you could return fire, but then he'd be dead, wouldn't he?"

Eriksen paused. "Looks like we have a stalemate," he said.

"Looks like we do." The gun still on Thompson, Ants shuffled backwards. "So I think I'll take my leave."

It was like a scene from a western, Thompson not breathing again until the outlaw disappeared.

Maungapōhatu, Te Urewera Forest

The sisters of darkness were back. In the lengthening shadows of the late afternoon, the sight of them hovering at the treeline made Temera's toes curl. As visitors go, even an election doorknocker would be more welcome.

May as well find out what they want.

Drying his hands on a tea towel, he stepped out onto the porch.

Always the shy one, Te Hoata melted further into the trees, even as Te Pūpū slipped out of the shade and into the light. Her bronze skin gleamed in the sunlight. Temera lifted his hand to shield his eyes.

"Time for you to make a journey, matakite," Te Pūpū said.

"To where? To what end?" Temera replied. "It would help if I knew what I was supposed to do."

For a moment, the demon didn't answer. Wielding her patu, she mimed slicing and hacking at an imaginary warrior.

Temera's blood chilled in his veins.

"Why does he ask what he already knows?" she said finally.

"He clings to the past. Misses his spirit guide," Te Hoata called from deep in the shadows.

Te Pūpū continued her hacking.

"They grieve so hard," said Te Hoata. "Remember the chief Ngātoro-i-rangi. How he grieved when Ngāuruhoe died."

"It's about the earthquakes," Temera blurted. "The volcanoes."

Both sisters cackled. Te Pūpū lunged and slashed, eviscerating her unseen enemy.

A kernel of anger hardened in Temera's chest. "I get that there's danger. I just don't understand what I'm supposed to do!"

Te Pūpū stood back from her broken foe. "Isn't it obvious? You must stop it, little seer. Speak to the mountains," she said and, stepping back, she withdrew into the trees.

Temera ran down the stairs after her. "Wait! What if they won't listen?"

Te Hoata's thready whisper curled through the misty undergrowth, "Then the People will suffer. Many will die."

Temera sank to his knees on the grass.

Tokaanu village

There was no one left in the bushes. Congregated behind the shed with Eriksen, the group stepped into the road the minute the convicts disappeared around the bend.

Eriksen rolled his eyes. "Good one, Read. I thought I told you to stay where you were."

Thompson didn't catch the soldier's response. Still trembling from the encounter with the convicts, he rested his hands on his knees and drew in a breath, nearly choking when Ahmad clapped him on the back. "Way to go, Thompson. That was awesome. From now on, I'm going to call you Indiana Jones."

Straightening, Thompson grinned. "It was all Lisa's doing. If she hadn't gone along with the ruse, things could have been different. She's a brave woman."

"I better go and find her," Eriksen said. "Poor thing has to be half out of her tree with fright."

"I'll come with you," Pringle said.

They started off down the road, Eriksen calling back over his shoulder to his comrades. "Read, Hine, you should get the civilians back under—"

The soldier's voice was drowned out by a roar, like water crashing at the bottom of a waterfall. Thompson recognised it immediately. Well, he *had* spent most of his adult life as a volcanologist. Although, being on the spot like this wasn't something he'd bargained on.

Ahmad had cottoned on too. His eyes grew round. "Oh no!"

"Get to high ground," Thompson screamed over the din. Seconds later the mud flow burst into town.

They scattered. Thompson ran too, although he couldn't help glancing back at the lahar. The wall of mud barrelled towards him. In truth, it was a small one, but still, it was incredible: the unmitigated power of raging mud as it plunged down the hill and across the road. Hyper-concentrated flow by the looks of it, since the slurry was thinner than concrete. Was it caused by a crater lake breaching high up in the mountains? Or a volcanic landslide mixing with the falling ash? Or had the recent volcanic activity provoked an ice melt... Whatever. The result was the same: a flotilla of deadly mud and rock, rollicking towards them faster than a ruddy bullet train.

Thompson blinked. Although, it was odd that should come this way. Lahars popped up every other day on the central plateau, but mostly over by Tangiwai. This definitely wasn't a typical route.

Then again, nothing about today had been typical.

"Thompson!" Ahmad shouted, dragging him from his stupor. The young man grabbed him by the elbow. "You want to get yourself killed? Come on!"

CHAPTER NINETEEN

Tokaanu village

From inside the Unimog, Jules watched Barnes flick the lighter on and off, on and off, on and off. He'd been pacing back and forth across the road, dicking around with that lighter for the past twenty minutes. Jules lifted her hand to her face, to where Barnes had struck her with the rifle, wincing as she wiped away the smear of blood. The man was rattled. Any pretence at civility had disintegrated.

Although no one had told them specifically what those gunshots had been about, Jules had picked up from their conversation that one of the convicts had done a runner. Now Barnes was paranoid about anyone heading off on their own in case they got the same idea. Everyone had been regrouped into twos or threes and sent off again in search of the precious radio, with only Pete, Taliava and Barnes waiting behind at the truck.

So even freedom had its shackles.

There was a shout from further along the road. Jules looked up. Barnes stopped his pacing to peer through the ash. "What's going on now?" he said.

Shifting towards the tailgate where she could see better, Jules caught a blur of movement at the far end of the township. With his rifle slung over his back, Eaton was running towards them at full burst.

"Taliava, go and find out what's going on," Barnes said.

The Samoan jogged forward, as someone else – Ants – came dashing around the bend.

"Maybe they found something," said Pete. He ambled forward to stand beside Barnes and Harris.

Barnes flicked the lighter. "Better be a bloody radio."

Taliava had reached Eaton, who was doubled over and breathing hard. Seconds later, Eaton stood up, gesturing and pointing back the way he'd come.

"What's up with Eaton?" Pete said. "Looks like he needs a fucking defibrillator."

Jules caught another movement: this time in the foreground. It was Shane, raising his hand to the back of his neck as if to scratch. No, not a scratch – *a signal*. What was he trying to tell her? That they should run? Had he noticed the change in mood, too?

The hair on Jules' neck stood on end. Barnes and his men had their backs turned. There was no one watching. Jules couldn't take the truck – Barnes had the keys – but she and Brigitte could climb over the seats, get out the driver's door, and slip away... Jules grasped Brigitte's hand. If Shane was signalling them, they should act now. Barnes was getting way too volatile and there was no telling what he'd do when he snapped. Best to be well out of reach. "Brigitte," she murmured. "No one's looking. We should go. Move slowly, though. We don't want to attract their attention."

Her eyes flashed white and Brigitte looked away, determined not to make eye contact.

"Brigitte—"

The girl shook her head. She wasn't going to budge. Jules pushed down her frustration. It wasn't Brigitte's fault. The poor thing was so stricken with fear. Jules glanced down the road. They were running out of time. Taliava and Eaton were running back to Barnes now, Ants a hundred metres behind them.

Getting to her feet, Jules tugged at Brigitte's hand. "Time to go, honey."

Still fifty metres away, Taliava hollered, "Eaton says the army have showed up. The group from the farmhouse. They're up that way." He pointed back towards the far end of town.

"Fuck," Barnes said and, turning, he fixed his eyes on Jules.

Shit. Jules froze. What would he do? Her blood hammered.

Barnes' stare hardened. It was clear he'd guessed what she'd been up to. He raised the rifle to his shoulder. "Sit down." His voice was cold.

Jules did as she was told, moving slowly, even while her pulse raced. They'd missed their chance to escape, but it didn't matter because the cavalry had arrived: Taine, Read, Lefty, Eriksen, and Hine. In her bones, she'd known they'd come. Her eyes on Barnes, she used her peripheral vision to scan the buildings and the scrub on either side of the road. If there were army personnel out there, she wouldn't see them unless they chose to reveal themselves. But it was a relief to know Taine would be moving heaven and earth to free them.

If Barnes doesn't kill us first.

The ground shook. Jules clutched at air. She fumbled for a handhold and found nothing. Outside, Barnes staggered sideways. Another jolt, and this time Jules managed to grab the side of the truck. She clung on, Brigitte's fingernails digging deep into her forearm.

The shaking went on and on. Not just another rumble but an all-out blast, as deafening as the roar of water shooting over Huka Falls. Wooden buildings swayed and groaned. Brigitte screamed. Through the rear of the truck, she saw the men being tossed off their feet. And again, as they tried to stand. The earth was bucking and kicking like a rodeo bull. Jules hung on.

Oh God. The road! It was splitting. They could all see it coming. Barnes, Taliava, Pete, Shane, Eaton: *all* of them were struggling to their feet, battling against the tremors, desperate to scramble clear of the chasm that was unzipping the street from neck to navel.

Flat-footed with shock, adrenalin finally kicked in and Jules went into overdrive. Stay here and they'd be engulfed by the pit. She and Brigitte had to get out of the truck. Now. She leapt up, dragging Brigitte towards the rear of the truck, tugging at her, pleading. They didn't get far. Violent spasms threw them sideways as more massive jolts ripped through the Unimog. Another chance missed. Brigitte whimpered, clinging to Jules, both of them staring in horror as the rift tore towards them, the road falling away like two halves of a melon.

The crack snaked beneath them and the truck wobbled...

...and tipped.

Brigitte shrieked.

Jules wrapped Brigitte in her arms and held on. She held her breath, time coming to a standstill, while all around them was a chaos of colour and noise and hurt. Somehow, through it all, Taine's voice reached her.

Jules.

Her heart broke with the pain of it. So, this was how it would end. The irony was too much. Wasn't this exactly why she'd broken up with him in the first place? To spare herself the hurt of losing him. How wrong she'd been. So much time wasted. She almost laughed. It's true what they say about your life flashing before your eyes in that moment before you die: all she could see was Taine.

With a sickening graunch of crushing metal, the truck crashed into the chasm.

*

Pringle stared. Some rescue. They'd only just got to Lisa after Eriksen had seen off Eaton and Ants and now this. A deluge of mud and water was coming at them from both sides, forking like a snake's tongue around the shed behind them. Thick and dark, it surged wide, taking the line of least resistance, rushing downwards towards the lake. Within seconds, they were cut off from the others, surrounded by the deadly flow of mud.

"Quickly, into the house," Eriksen yelled, pointing to the building Taine and Lefty had entered earlier. "Go straight through and out the back. We have to get ahead of it."

Pringle dashed for the house.

Suddenly, out of nowhere, Ants shoved him aside. He was looking for an escape, too. He leaped up the porch stairs and darted down the hall. Pringle caught the flash of light as he opened the far door. Eriksen's hunch had been a good one. These older houses typically had a hall that ran from front to back like an animal's gullet, the rooms branching from that central channel. Pringle ran into the kitchen and stopped dead. In front of him, the hall was a crime scene from a TV show. There was blood smeared across the wall, traipsed all over the floor, and in the middle of it all, a woman's body lay twisted in a puddle of rusted blood.

Lisa and then Eriksen appeared behind him.

Lisa moaned. "Mum!" she whispered. She thrust her hand against the wall, her knees collapsing beneath her. Eriksen grabbed her, easing her gently to the floor where she reached out, laying her hand on her mother's leg, her fingers caressing the fabric. "Oh God."

"Lisa. Listen to me. We can't help your mum now," Eriksen said. "We need to get you to safety."

Pringle hoped there was time. Stepping carefully over the body, he raced down the hall, while Eriksen was telling the girl, "It's what she would have wanted."

Reaching the open door, Pringle burst out the far side of the house. He stood on the steps, his chest heaving, and swallowed hard. Everything was happening too fast. Like a serpent, the water was wrapping its coils around the house, its deadly hiss making Pringle's hair stand on end. Already the two branches of the lahar were coming together, closing off their escape. The muddy torrent was rising, closing in.

Pringle scanned the area. No sign of Ants anywhere. Maybe the convict had been swallowed by the torrent, his skin flayed and his body consumed, as the river of mud thundered forward. Or maybe he'd got lucky and found a way through the gap in the split second before the two prongs had come together. One thing was certain: they weren't getting out this way.

Mud swirling around his ankles, he turned and raced inside, slamming the door closed against the mud.

Eriksen was picking his way down the narrow hall, Lisa in his arms. Rather than argue, the soldier had carried her over her mother's blood. "Pringle?"

"We're cut off."

"Shit."

Lisa's eyes widened in terror.

As one, they looked back at the front door where the mud was beating at the reinforced-glass inset, climbing upwards, looking for a way in.

Eriksen broke the spell. "Pringle, we need to get higher. Find a way to get up on the roof."

It was their only chance. Pringle rushed into the nearest bedroom, but one look at the windows and he knew getting out that way was out of the question. In seconds the deathly wash had risen by more than a metre. The brown tide was already sweeping past the window, branches and rocks roiling beneath the surface. On his own, Pringle might make it. He could slip out the top window onto the sill and use his upper body strength to lean out and haul himself onto the roof. While the water was halfway up the building, there was a chance. If he went now…

He dismissed the thought. He'd be leaving Eriksen with the girl. Lisa would never have the strength to fight the current and Eriksen was like McKenna, the sort to kill himself trying to save her. Suddenly, a branch smashed into the window. The pane buckled, imploding inwards, glass and debris surging into the room.

Pringle leaped back into the hall and yanked the door closed. "It's a no go this way."

"Try the other side."

Pringle ran the length of the hall, ignoring the dead woman on the floor, checking each of the rooms in turn. Everywhere, the windows were buckling and cracking under the strain, mud pushing against the glass, blocking out the light. Pringle shut each door against the inevitable deluge, although it wouldn't hold anything back for long.

With the doors closed, the hall was dark, as if they were already entombed.

Lisa sobbed.

"Any bright ideas?" Eriksen said. "Now would be a good time."

"Through the roof?" Pringle suggested.

"The attic!" Lisa cried. "Mum uses it for storage. There's a drop-down ladder."

"Where?" Eriksen said.

She pointed, Pringle catching the movement in the gloom. "That way, near the back door."

"I'm on it." His heart thudding, Pringle scanned the ceiling for the trapdoor. There! Set into the ceiling panels and painted the same dull cream, the trapdoor was almost invisible, its handle nothing more than a cup hook. Pringle jumped for it and missed.

"Oh God, the pole to pull it down is in the bedroom wardrobe," Lisa wailed.

"Here, you take Lisa," Eriksen said, impatient.

"No! I've got this," Pringle insisted, and ramming his back against one wall and his feet against the other, he shimmied up the gap until he was high enough to grab the hook. Not wanting to swing down in case he damaged the ladder with his weight, he slid down the wall, pulling the ladder down as he descended.

His feet had scarcely touched the floor when the glass in the back door gave way and the water rushed in. It swept into the hall like stampeding cattle, a thundering brown mass with a head of barbed horns.

"Go, go, go, man," Eriksen shouted. "I'll hand Lisa up to you."

Anticipating his command, Pringle was already scrambling up the flimsy rungs. At the top, he turned and grabbed Lisa under the armpits while Eriksen, now halfway up the ladder, shoved his shoulders under her hips. The two of them fell through the gap together, Eriksen swinging up into the attic as the ladder shuddered, taken out by the wave. Muted by the roar of the lahar, the ladder thumped the wall once before it disappeared out the door.

"Mum," Lisa said softly. Pringle's heart contracted at the anguish in her voice. They hadn't even seen her go.

Pringle stared through the gap where the wave surged unabated through the house. For a moment, he was mesmerised by the churn of the current, debris appearing and disappearing in the murky water: a branch, a piece of siding, a blue ice cream container. A wrong step up here, and they'd be dead.

"Careful," he warned. "The ceiling's only particle board. Try and keep to the joists."

Sometime in the house's past someone had stored a spare interior door in the crawl space. On his hands and knees, Pringle grabbed it and swung it across the gap. Even as he lay it flat over the attic entrance, it was clear the mud beneath them was still rising, but at least they'd won some time.

The gap plugged, Pringle turned. With no skylights or windows, he could barely see the others in the gloom. Eriksen was thumping and swearing not far away – plenty loud enough to be heard over the rush of the lahar. What was he doing? It didn't take long for his eyes to adjust. Eriksen was trying to prise the roofing off the joists using the barrel of the gun. His big body cramped in the tight space, the soldier struggled to gain leverage. Except leverage wasn't the issue. The rifle was too thick to fit in the gap. After several frustrated attempts, Eriksen turned the rifle around and smashed the stock at the roof, Pringle's teeth ringing with the vibrations. It was a waste of time. All that effort, and all he'd done was dent the metal.

Eventually, Eriksen slumped back on his haunches. He breathed deeply. "Well, that was a fat lot of use," he said. "Lisa, what's in the boxes?"

"Sentimental stuff. Memorabilia. Old photos—"

"Any old tools? Something thin, like a screwdriver?"

A screwdriver.

Pringle slipped his hand into his pocket and pulled out the screwdriver he'd taken from the shed with the smoker. "Will this do?"

Eriksen's teeth glowed white in the darkness. "You just happened to have a screwdriver in your pocket?"

"I was an excellent boy scout," Pringle quipped, passing it over to the soldier.

"You could have said something."

"Sorry, forgot I had it."

Eriksen jammed the blade underneath the roofing, pulling the metal away from the roof joists. All he'd needed was some grip. In minutes, he'd cleared a foot-long gap between parallel struts. Then he thrust the rifle into the gap, tearing through the building paper and peeling back the cladding like a banana skin. Eriksen hauled himself onto the roof before pulling Lisa through – Pringle kneeling so she could climb up his body, using his knee, and then his shoulder, as steps. When the girl was safely on the roof, Pringle clambered through the gap.

"Watch out. It's slippery," Eriksen said. The soldier's boots were covered in mud, his pants soaked to the thigh. They'd come so close to losing him: any longer downstairs and Eriksen would have been dragged away with the current.

One hand grasping the ridge, Pringle crouched on the roof and looked out at the tsunami of mud and rock surging on either side of them. His heart fell. That was it, then. The end of the road. They were stuck on a rooftop island. Unless the lahar receded, their chances of surviving were slim to nothing.

"Don't suppose you've got your Fairy Godmother in that pocket?" Eriksen said quietly.

CHAPTER TWENTY

Tokaanu village

Barnes stormed into the kayak hire at the centre of town, Taliava and Eaton on his heels. With the ground shaking up a storm outside, the solid cinder-brick building was a damn sight safer than being out in the open.

"Fuck, did you see that?" said Pete, who was last to arrive. "The truck fell down a hole with the women still in it. It fell down a sinkhole. The whole fucking caboodle. Good thing, too. It'll keep those army blokes busy. They can't be looking for us while they've got their hands full saving the world, can they?"

"Yeah, good thing they're not looking for us, seeing as *you just handed Harris your gun*," Eaton said.

"Well what did you want me to do?" Pete snapped. "Jump in after it? The ground opened up, didn't it? It was like a scene out of Jaws. I had to let it go or I would've ended up in there myself."

"Better you than the Unimog," Eaton said.

"The fuck, Eaton," Pete bleated.

Barnes tuned out their whining while he looked around. The usual set up: retail section was up front while the hire gear took up the bulk of the warehouse space. Like lots of these tin-pot places, this one sold a bit of everything: beach shoes, kids' rash shirts, magazines, sun hats, and, in one corner, some end-of-run camping gear…including some camp knives. Barnes helped himself to one. He peeled off the backing and slipped the knife into his belt before stepping across to check out the cash register. He yanked out the drawer. Empty. The business owners had left town in a hurry though, not even bothering to clear away a half-eaten box of crackers and some greasy plastic wrap. Barnes frowned. That wasn't usual. From what he'd seen, people tended to clean up before they left – it was creepy as fuck. Barnes didn't get it. Why waste time cleaning up a place if it was going to be blown to smithereens? But everywhere they'd been today had been the same. It was like people were offering up their homes as a sacrifice.

Except here, where the owners had left without even bothering to clear their lunch off the counter.

"Pete," Eaton was saying, his speech deliberately slow as if he were talking to a child. "In case you hadn't realised, that truck was our ticket to freedom, and the women were supposed to be leverage. They were the penny to pay the ferryman. Without them, we aren't going to be driving through any roadblocks."

Barnes whipped his head up. Was that a door creaking? "Shhhh," he said. Waving a hand at the others, he strained to hear over the rumble of the earthquakes. Was someone else in here with them?

Taliava joined him, his rifle at the ready. "Something up?"

"Who was supposed to be scouting this building?" Barnes whispered.

"Rutledge and Grant and I don't know…maybe Climo? Definitely Rutledge and Grant."

Barnes put a finger to his lips and pointed to the rear of the building. "Eaton, keep a look out," he said. He crept past a wall of maps, towards the rear of the building. Taliava followed him. The back door was ajar, a broom handle holding it open. Barnes burst outside, the door banging hard against the outside wall on his way through.

Through the scrub, the yellow of the lifejacket was like a beacon. Someone was using the creek to escape. Barnes fired. There was a shout. Damn. It wasn't a clean shot. There was too much scrub and crap in the way; Barnes had only winged him.

Barnes aimed again, waiting for an opening, when across the creek, someone else opened fire. Rifle fire.

"Shit." Barnes hustled backwards, shoving Taliava in the stomach with his elbow. "Inside! Hurry."

He slammed the door shut. "Watch this door," he said to Taliava, then he ran up the stairs to the mezzanine, the iron rungs clanging underfoot. Sprinting along the landing, he took the first door on the right. Checked the window. Not close enough. He ducked out, skipped the next office, and entered the third. His back against the wall, he peeked through the glass. His eyes narrowed.

The owners hadn't left their lunch out. Instead, one of his own had betrayed him. Barnes would make the bastard pay.

He pushed open the window. In the distance, the kayaker was making for the lake, his arm action determined. Barnes had been sure he'd winged him. No matter. He was a dead man. Barnes watched the ash for a moment, taking account of the wind, then he slowed his breathing, sighted the target, waiting until the splash of yellow emerged through the trees…

He squeezed the trigger. The shot exploded, the noise loud enough to wake the dead. The figure in the kayak jerked then slumped forward. The recoil, when it hit, was oddly satisfying. Barnes stepped back from the window and rolled his shoulder. Sniffing, he wiped his nose with the back of his hand. Job done. A clean death, which was more than the bastard deserved.

Someone was shouting downstairs. Barnes left the office and went to the end of the mezzanine. "What now?" he called down to the others.

"It's Grant. He came in the back way," Taliava replied.

Interesting.

Barnes went downstairs. Holding Grant by the back of his t-shirt, the Samoan had confiscated the gun, which lay on the floor several steps away.

"Well?" Barnes leaned back against the counter and took the lighter out of his pocket.

Hunched over, Grant peered out from under his brows. He had that look, like a cow at the freezing works. Barnes should know, since he'd worked there for the better part of a decade. The days he went. Mostly, the stupid cows were oblivious, serene right up to the moment they were slaughtered, but some of them, their eyes went white and they shifted their feet and you could tell they were antsy. Just like Grant right now.

"Lucky you came when you did, Barnesy," he blathered. "Rutledge and Stedman were doing a runner. Taking the creek out back. I tried to stop them. Well, you heard me shoot, right?"

Barnes cocked a brow. He flicked the lighter, igniting the flame.

"It was Rutledge's idea," Grant rabbited on. "He convinced Stedman we could paddle to Omori, get a car there."

Barnes flicked the lighter off.

"I just went along with it, you know. Wasn't my idea. When did I ever have an idea? But it was two against one, so I had to play along."

"You were just pretending?"

"Yes."

"And instead, you waited until their backs were turned. That was smart," Barnes said quietly.

Taliava stepped away from Grant.

Grant's eyes flashed with fear. "No, Barnes. Please. You gotta believe me. I'm with you, man. I'm loyal. I was just humouring them, you know? Rutledge and Stedman didn't give me any choice. They were going to kill me."

"Yeah, I can understand. You didn't have any choice."

"Exactly."

"Give him back his gun, Taliava."

"Barnes."

"No, no, Taliava. Grant did his best. I mean, it was a Catch 22, wasn't it? It's clear that Rutledge and Stedman were the ringleaders and

Grant was just going along with it. And obviously, he's sorry for the misunderstanding. I reckon he deserves a second chance."

The lighter safely back in his pocket, Barnes stepped forward and kicked the rifle towards Grant. Still wary, Grant's eyes stayed fixed on him as he bent to pick it up.

"We should probably make sure no one else has the same idea, though."

"'Course." Grant's voice trembled. "What did you have in mind?" He tried to look causal, but Barnes saw his finger hover over the trigger.

"Shoot the bottom out of the kayaks. Every one of them. That ought to send the message. What do you reckon? Can you do that?"

Grant smiled. "Yep, I can do that. Sure." He turned and opened fire on the kayaks.

The trolleys jumped in fright as Grant riddled the plastic carcasses with holes. He was getting right into it. Smoking up the place. Like his enthusiasm was proof he was innocent.

While he was occupied blasting them, Barnes stepped over to the camping section, grabbed a butane cannister, and angling it away from himself, stabbed it with the camp knife. Then he took out the lighter and ignited the gas, the camp cannister making a pretty decent flame thrower. Grant was facing the other way when Barnes torched him. Dripping flames, Grant staggered forward into a trolley, toppling the kayaks which tumbled off in a row like gaudy oversized dominoes.

Another earthquake rocked the building, the rumble drowning out the man's screams.

Near the door, Pete took a step back, a look of horror on his face.

"You got something you want to say?" Barnes said quietly.

Pete swallowed. He shook his head.

"You?"

Eaton shrugged.

"Let's get out of here, then," said Barnes.

They took the rear door, Barnes tossing the cannister back inside the warehouse before closing it behind him. He grinned. He was back in control.

*

Knocked off his feet, Taine could only stare helplessly as the Unimog toppled into the pit with Jules inside it. There was nothing he could do. The grind of metal and breaking glass made his chest ache.

"Jules!"

Taine got up. The earth protested. It kicked and heaved beneath his feet. His body low and his arms outstretched to keep his balance, he held firm and advanced three steps. He had to get to Jules. But he was slammed face-first onto the ground.

What? Lefty had leapt on him and was pinning him down.

"Let me go, Lefty!" Taine tried to throw the private off, but it was no use; they'd trained together and Lefty knew to cover the move. Taine swore under his breath.

"Not yet, Boss. We'll get the doc as soon as the shaking stops," Lefty said. "And we'll look for Lisa, too."

Taine gritted his teeth, but if a hothead like Lefty could hold his nerve, then Taine could do the same. Damn these earthquakes. Would the ground *ever* stop rolling? It was tossing them about like popcorn. Taine raised his eyes, unable to look away as the fissure ate up the road. Having devoured the vehicle, the tear in the earth plunged onwards, veering off the tar seal and running under the corner of the hotel. The front of the building slumped into the pit, the roof listing downwards and then, suddenly, like a zipper snagged on fabric, the rent in the earth stopped and the shaking slowed.

Thank the gods.

Taine threw Lefty off him and ran towards the chasm. If Barnes and his henchmen wanted to shoot him, let them have at it. He wasn't stopping for anyone.

Metres from the trench, he lay on his stomach and belly-crawled towards the edge on his elbows.

A voice called from behind him. "Can you see them?" It was Harris. Taine kept moving. "Not yet."

"Hey Hairy," Lefty exclaimed from the rear. "Welcome back. Where's your mate, Barnes?"

"Took off when he saw I had a gun."

"One gun. And they had how many?"

"Four."

"I guess that makes the odds about even."

Harris chuckled. "It was a gimme, too. Guy named Pete dropped his, trying to get away from the pit." His tone grew sombre. "They'll be back, though. Barnes will be looking for leverage to help him get out of town."

Taine tuned them out, concentrating on reaching the edge. He peered over the side. Below, in a mess of twisted metal, the Unimog lay on its side against a backdrop of black. "Jules!"

The only reply was the low rumbling of shifting ground.

"Jules!" he called again, irritated at the panic in his voice. "Come on! Talk to me. Are you okay?"

At last, a faint scuffling carried over the grumbling of the earth, and her face appeared from the driver's window. "Taine. I'm okay. We're both okay."

Taine swallowed, relief seeping into his limbs. Dishevelled and smeared with blood, she was stuck in a crumpled truck in the bottom of a trench, but she was alive. It was all that mattered. He could work with alive.

"How's it look, Boss?" Harris called.

Taine glanced over his shoulder. He grinned. "They're okay."

"Brilliant. Lefty's gone hunting for some rope."

Nodding, Taine turned back to Jules, careful not to knock any dirt into the pit. "Jules, what's the situation down there?"

Her dark eyes looked up at him. "Brigitte rolled under a bench seat in the crash. The metal's bent and now her hip is stuck. I'm going to need help getting her out."

Taine's mind raced. He couldn't afford to wait for Lefty. The earthquakes could start up again at any minute and cracks like this had been known to close. He sized up the trench. It wasn't that far: the Unimog was six, maybe seven metres down. Easy enough if you knew how to fall. "I'll jump down," he said.

"No! Don't do that," Jules said quickly, a tremor in her voice. "The Unimog is still sliding. I'm worried that it'll fall further."

Taine felt the blood drain from his face. That darkness surrounding the Unimog wasn't dirt. It was a hole who-knew-how-deep.

Jules smiled. "You know how I'm not a big fan of ledges." She nibbled her lip.

Taine's chest tightened. "Hold on, okay? We're coming to get you out."

She was still looking up at him from the wreckage when he shuffled back from the edge. He crawled clear of the loose earth and got to his feet, just as Lefty arrived back at a run, a couple of nylon ropes slung over his shoulder. "Found them in a fishing store," he said. "Let's do this." He cast about for somewhere to tie off the rope.

Taine took it from him. "We can't haul them out here. Even if we weren't being thrown around by the quakes, the ground near the edge is too soft. We'll risk burying them. And Jules says they're not on solid ground either, just wedged between the walls. If the truck gets jostled enough, it could fall even further."

Harris groaned. "Could this day get any worse?"

"What about the motel roof?" Lefty said pointing to the collapsed end of the building where buckled sheets of barnyard-red roofing metal slumped into the pit. "We could walk down the roof into the pit and find out what we're up against?"

"It's an idea," Taine said.

"Worth a go," Harris agreed.

Keeping away from the edge of the ravine, the three of them sprinted north to the end of the trench.

Taine had planned to descend himself, but Lefty had the shorter rope and was already threading it around his waist to create a Swiss seat. He carried both ends between his legs, Harris helping him to work them under the ropes at the back. Then, he squatted twice to tighten the rope seat. Meanwhile, Taine tied the longer rope to one of the motel veranda struts using a basic running bowline. He frowned. For safety's sake, he and Harris would need to use their body weights to anchor the line. That last quake had been powerful enough to collapse the corner of the building; who knew what it had done to the rest of this structure?

Lefty clipped his carabiner to the line, hooking it to his improvised harness. "Good to go then?"

"Wait!" Harris tied a stopper knot to the end of the main line, then clapped Lefty on the shoulder. "All good," he said, taking up the line.

"One on rappel," Lefty quipped, and he disappeared over the side.

The wait was interminable. Slower than treacle. What must it be like for Jules and Brigitte, dangling over the pit? His hands gripping the rope, Taine blinked ash out of his eyes. Finally, Lefty's voice carried over the shifting earth. "Coming up."

Taine and Harris dug their boots into the ground and hauled him in, Lefty beginning his report even before they'd dragged him over the lip. "The pit's shallower here – about four metres deep – then it slopes away heading south. We'd need a fireman's ladder to get to the Unimog and even then, it'd be touch and go – given that the whole thing could go down any minute." He unclipped his carabiner from the line.

"It's still the safest way," Taine said.

Harris' brow furrowed. "Not necessarily," he said, and he took off behind the mote, calling, "Come on!"

"What about the rope?" Lefty asked.

"Just leave it!" Taine dashed behind the motel after Harris, who was already emerging on the far side of the ravine. Not slowing, Taine peered through the ash to see his corporal climb into the cab of a small crane that was parked alongside a building under construction. Taine wanted to whoop with elation. Bloody hell, Hairy. A hydraulic crane. It was inspired. They could lift the women out without even touching the sides.

Taine and Lefty were still twenty metres away from the crane, when the vehicle roared to life. Of course, it did. Why bother to lock anything in a single-street town where the population was less than two hundred people? Towns like these, you couldn't even fart in your sleep without everyone knowing. Taine put on a spurt of speed, racing to catch up, while Hairy drove the vehicle towards the edge of the trench.

"Not too close," Taine called. Any further and the crane would follow the Unimog into the trench, crushing Jules and Brigitte.

Hairy stopped the crane.

Taine thrust his head into the cab. "Any idea how to operate one of these?"

"Can't be that hard, can it? Give me a second to complete the operator training." His face fixed in concertation as he fiddled with the controls, Taine and Lefty jumping out of the way while he practised swinging the boom through its angle of articulation, extending the lugs, and engaging the counterweights. The movements were as jerky as all hell, Hairy about as proficient as a teenager on his learner licence, but it would have to do. It was their best chance of getting Jules out of the hellhole.

"Okay. I reckon that's a pass," Hairy announced. "Let's do this." He raised the boom and lowered the hook block. Taine stepped onto the hook, hanging onto the cable with one hand and using the other to direct Hairy. The corporal swung the boom around, then he lowered the hook block into the trench, spooling it out with Taine on it, while Lefty crawled on his belly to the edge of the pit, ready to relay instructions as soon as Taine lost sight of Hairy at the controls.

Come on!

Taine dropped into the darkness, descending slowly like a performer in some bizarre circus act. Below him at the window of the Unimog, Jules watched the sky, her face pinched with tension.

He threw her a reassuring smile. *Not long now and we'll have you out of there.*

Suddenly, the air above them cracked with gunfire. The cable jerked to a stop.

Ash falling around him, Taine cranked his head back, straining to see. "Lefty? What's going on?"

"It's coming from somewhere up the road," Lefty called back. "Doesn't sound good. Want me to get Hairy to pull you up?"

"No. Jules and Brigitte first."

"Got it." Lifting his hand, Lefty signalled to Hairy to keep going. The cable re-started and Taine descended again. He was just past halfway when the cable lurched, jolting him hard from one side to the other like a pendulum bob. Eerie vibrations filled the trench and the low rumble began again in earnest.

CHAPTER TWENTY-ONE

Tokaanu village

Thompson gave it everything, his legs and lungs burning from the effort.

Up ahead, Read was urging everyone on. They'd already lost sight of Lisa and Eriksen and the prison guard. Thompson hoped they'd got clear.

"Hurry!" Ahmad shouted.

The ground thundered and bucked. Someone, somewhere, had it in for them. Thompson staggered, somehow managing to stay upright.

All at once, two men in orange jumpsuits burst from a building to his left.

More convicts! Thompson's heart jumped in fright, but the men in orange had no interest in him or anyone else. They were just trying to get clear of the wall of mud.

Read had seen them. "Go!" he screamed to Thompson, one eye on the men, "follow Hine." Thompson veered left, following the soldier-woman to higher ground. He'd almost made it when one of the convicts tripped. Still running, Thompson swivelled.

Panicked, the man scrabbled to get up. "Pope! Wait!" he shouted to his friend.

Hardly a friend: Pope wasn't stopping for anyone, running on without a glance. Instead, it was Read who dashed back towards the man and the lahar.

That boy had some sort of death wish.

Thompson's conscience pricked. He should go back and help. He turned to go, but Hine grabbed him by the shoulders.

"No," she said. "It's fine. Matt will bring him."

Thompson wished he had her confidence. The lahar was careering by now, like the proverbial runaway freight train. It was spreading too, consuming everything it touched. If they didn't hurry, the two men would get swept away.

Thompson watched, his heart in his throat as Read grabbed the man by the arm, pulling him upright. Still clutching his rifle, the convict was beyond panic now. He slipped a second time, stumbling like a hapless damsel on the cover of an old ghost story…

Thompson held his breath.

Read grabbed the barrel of the gun and used it to drag the convict along, pulling him clear of the mud flow. *That does it.* Thompson twisted out of Hine's grasp, and ran back to help, the two of them using a fireman's lift to carry him to safety.

"Thanks," the man said, when they set him down. He glanced down the road to where his friend had disappeared. "Name's Climo. You saved my hide back there."

"You're welcome," Read replied. "I'll be keeping the rifle, though."

Climo nodded. "Fair dues."

Ahmad reappeared. "Come quick. There's a man who needs our help over here." He scampered back behind a row of houses.

They followed him through the scrub to where a man in a life vest lay unconscious near a small stream. Read and Hine crouched beside him, assessing his injuries.

"Alain and I saved him," Ahmad said to Thompson. "We pulled him out of the water." It was only then that Thompson realised both men were soaked to the waist.

"Jeepers, that's a bullet hole. He's been shot in the back," Read said and he handed the confiscated gun to Thompson. "You know how to use one of these?"

Thompson nodded. "Did a bit of hunting with my brother in the day."

"Keep an eye out. Including on that one." He nodded towards Climo. Thompson wanted to say that shooting a few rabbits wasn't the same as shooting a human, but the soldier had already turned his attention back to the injured man.

"At first, we thought he might be dead, but he is still breathing," Alain explained. "He is not wearing orange, but he is one of the prisoners. I remember him from Rotoaira. He took me to repair the tractor."

Climo leaned in. "Yep, he's from Rangipō. That's Stedman," he said.

Giving the newcomer a sideways look, Alain grunted. "Then maybe it is better if we leave him in the river."

"Hey, he's a good guy."

Alain whirled. "Really?" He sidled up to Climo, his chin jutted forward. "So why was he in the prison then?"

Climo put his hands on his hips. "You don't know anything about anything. Half the prison are only in there because the other guy could afford a better lawyer."

"That is your answer?" Alain said. "That's it? They are in prison because they are poor? Excuse me if I don't believe it."

Climo shrugged and turned away. "Up to you."

Thompson had to agree with Climo that prisons everywhere were filled with people whose chief crime was their lack of privilege, but Climo's expression and that shrug enraged the Frenchman, who grabbed him by his overalls and yanked him backwards.

"You kidnapped my girlfriend then tied me up and left me for dead!"

"Guys..." Thompson said.

Climo ignored him. "That wasn't me," he said rounding on Alain, "and in case you didn't notice, they left me behind back there too, so don't go thinking you're anything special."

Thompson shivered. He swung the rifle to Alain, then Climo, and back again. What the hell! He couldn't just shoot one of them over an argument.

Read got to his feet. "That's enough!" He stepped between the two men. "Both of you."

"This is all because of the prisoners. Without them, we would all be out of here by now," Alain grumbled.

Read glared at him, and he shut up. Climo said nothing.

Ahmad and Hine had relieved Stedman of his gun and his life jacket. The man was coming to. He mewled in pain, his breaths coming in tight shallow gasps. Where was the blood? Thompson had expected a bloodbath, but his t-shirt was as clean as a whistle. Hine lifted the fabric and Thompson grimaced. One side of Stedman's body was purple with bruising. So he hadn't got away scot-free, but how the man had survived was nothing short of a miracle. Was it the distance between Stedman and the shooter that had saved him? Had there been obstacles – trees or maybe a fence – that had slowed the bullet, or was it something to do with the angle of the shot? Could it have been the polystyrene life jacket, or the fact that he'd tumbled into the cold water of the stream that helped to reduce the internal bleeding. Maybe it was a combination of things?

Or just pure luck?

"Merde," Alain said. "Qu'il a de la chance, celui-là."

"He's lucky, all right," Ahmad said.

"Yeah?" Climo said. "Well, he won't be so lucky if Barnes gets hold of him. Neither of us will."

Alain was opening his mouth to say something when the pop of gunfire erupted from somewhere further up the road.

Everyone ducked, Thompson laying on his stomach in the brush next to Ahmad, while Hine protected Stedman with her own body. The gunfire went on.

"Matt, we can't stay out here in the open," she said, her voice calm. "We need to find some decent cover."

The gunfire stopped abruptly and Read got to his feet. "We should find McKenna and Lefty first. That might have been them under fire. They're unarmed."

"We've got two guns now," Hine said.

"For all the good it'll do," Climo muttered under his breath. "Barnes isn't going to give up. The guy's a fucking psycho."

The Frenchman stood up. His lips thinned. He looked like he was about to explode.

"Alain, give me a hand with Stedman," Read said, closing down any further discussion.

*

Dammit. Another earthquake. "Jules, hang on!"

Taking his own advice, Taine gripped tight to the cable, ignoring the bite of metal in his palms. Rubble showered from above. The walls collapsing in? He whipped his head up...

Lefty's legs were dangling in the void. The edge of the trench was collapsing, falling away beneath him. Taine leaned out, hanging off the cable, stretching both arms wide as if to catch him. It was ridiculous. He'd have to be made of rubber to reach that far, but he stretched still further when Lefty slipped another metre – the private running in space, like that big-jowled dog in the old Warner cartoons.

Only, it wasn't funny.

Debris fell in a waterfall into the pit.

Then Hairy was there, pulling Lefty upwards through loose dirt. His feet were just disappearing when a boulder tumbled from the walls.

Fuck.

Holding on to the cable, Taine tucked his feet to his chest, then thrust them outwards, the momentum launching him sideways and away from the falling projectile. The rock grazed his back; so close, he heard the scrape of it against the fabric of his tunic. Then it struck the edge of the Unimog and glanced away, its clatter reverberating in the trench. Taine held his breath. *Please don't let it fall...*

More dirt bounced onto the vehicle, jumping once, then twice, like popcorn in a pan. The truck didn't move. Breathing out, Taine dropped his boot back onto the hook.

But the earth wasn't finished with them: the hook Taine was standing on swung hard into the side of the pit, hurling him into the bank.

Taine hit the wall. The air was knocked from his lungs. His helmet went flying. Wrenched free from his grip, the cable arced away. Taine slid, clutching at the earth, desperate to slow his fall. If he hit too hard, the whole house of cards could come down.

Still snatching at the wall, he landed on the Unimog as softly as he could, his shoulder taking the impact. It didn't help. His extra hundred-plus kilos was the straw that broke the camel's back – the vehicle tipped downwards. It slipped another metre. The grit and dirt he'd dislodged was making the surface slippery. Taine struggled for purchase.

Jules gasped. Her eyes widened. "Taine!" Leaning out the window, she threw out her hand. Taine clasped it, wrapped his hand around hers.

Her fingers were warm…

Jules heaved with all her might – all tiny fifty kilos of her – dragging him up the slope to her side of the vehicle. It was enough to get his feet under him. He scrambled to her side of the vehicle and crouched beside her.

"Hey," she said. She chewed the inside of her cheek.

"Hey."

"Thanks for coming."

"It's not going to hold."

The truck shifted beneath them, as if the gods were listening.

"Lefty! Dammit. We're going to need that rope," Taine roared. He looked up. Thank God, Lefty and Hairy had it covered: Hairy had pulled in the cable and Lefty was clambering across the boom, reaching for the hook. Still, it was going to be tight.

"Jules, when Hairy lets down the cable, I'm going to hand you up to Lefty."

"I can't leave Brigitte."

"I'll get her."

The hook stopped metres above the vehicle. Up in the cab and not able to see or hear them, it was Harris' best guess. It'd have to do.

Taine lifted Jules up to Lefty, the private's arm bulging as he strained under Jules' weight.

"Hey, doc."

"Hi, Lefty."

Harris' face appeared at the edge of the pit. "Go!" Taine yelled. Harris disappeared and seconds later the cable ascended, Lefty and Jules blotting the light, then growing smaller.

Maungapōhatu, Te Urewera Forest
Right then. Enough of this stuffing around.

Temera stalked into the middle of the lawn, the grassy clods sticking to his feet, and pulled the pūrerehua from inside his shirt. He smoothed the wooden blade under his fingertips, the action taking him back to his boyhood and the day he'd climbed the big hill up behind Lake Rotorua with his tutor. It was there that Mātua Rata had shown him the magic of the bullroarer for the first time...

Temera turned the object over in his hand. "So how's it supposed to work?"

"I believe it's in the particular music of the blade: a combination of the instrument's shape, its surface korero – the carvings – and the material itself. These days pūrerehua are made of different woods, but in the days of our ancestors, they were made of stone. Even the string attachment is significant. All these things influence the sound of the music when the musician swings and whirls the instrument."

"The magic is in the music itself then," Temera had concluded, pleased with himself. "The way it makes you feel." It wasn't so hard, now he'd figured it out.

Mātua smiled. "Ah, but Temera, you forget about the musician. If you give two guitarists the same guitar, do they make the same music?"

Well, that had started Temera guessing. Was it something to do with the musician's skill? Or the speed and size of the circles the little instrument traced as it was whirled through the air? The tune itself? One by one, Matua rejected all his suggestions.

"Well, am I even close?" Temera said crossly.

"You're close."

Temera huffed, impatient. He lay back on the ground and chewed on his lip. The clouds passed overhead. He was just about to drift off when the answer came to him. He sat up abruptly. "It's about the wairua, isn't it?"

"Uhuh."

"Is that why they call it soul music?"

"What do you think?"

"I think, yes. If you want a song to be meaningful, you have to put your heart into it. I think when you play a pūrerehua, especially one you've made yourself, then you put your whole soul, your wairua, into the performance. You play it so the voice of your spirit travels through the string, through the blade, and through the music. That way the song becomes like a prayer, or a chant. A song of the soul."

Mātua had cuffed Temera's hair affectionately with the flat of his hand. "You know what? I reckon you're not as dumb as you look."

Excited, Temera faced his tutor. "Holy shit!"

The old man grinned.

It was too cool for words. The pūrerehua was like a telephone, linking the living and the dead, a connection between the spirit world and the earthly realm.

"This...this...it's amazing."

"You think?"

After that, Temera had lain on the ground, his hands cradling his head, once again watching the drift of the clouds.

In his ear, Mātua continued the lesson, his old voice mellow. "As well as being a beautiful object, the pūrerehua's uses are many. The right man can use it to call forth a soul-mate, farewell a loved one, even summon the rain..."

Temera planted his feet, his weight balanced. He could do this. He'd done it before, hadn't he? His childhood spirit guide had left him, but Temera could still *see*; the demons had proved that. All he had to do was channel his wairua into the blade.

He lifted the bullroarer and swung it, twirling it above his head, slowly at first, then gaining speed. He let out the flaxen string to extend the instrument's reach. The string snapped taut, its hum deepening as the blade sliced through the air. Temera focussed his mind, concentrating on Taine McKenna, who wore a pūrerehua which was the twin of his own, carved at the same time by a man who would become such an important part of Temera's life. He imagined the soldier on the central plateau helping with the evacuation. He didn't know for sure, but knowing McKenna, he had to be there. Where else would he be?

Temera's arm burned. Inside his shirt, sweat trickled down his back.

Come on, work!

He scrunched his eyes tight and threw his hips into the action.

The pūrerehua buzzed over his head. Nothing happened.

Who did he think he was, anyway? Tom bloody Jones?

All this was doing was giving him a sore arm.

Blowing out hard, he let the string drop, the blade circling aimlessly for a turn before it too fell to the ground.

This was useless. A waste of time. He'd tried so many times already, why should it suddenly work now? If the pūrerehua was like a telephone, then McKenna had missed a helluva lot of calls. Winding up the instrument, Temera stuffed it into his pants. Well, that was that, wasn't it? He'd done everything he could.

Mātua's chuckle sounded in his head.

Temera bristled. He had. He'd tried everything. He'd come home to Maungapōhatu, hadn't he? Given up the creature comforts of living with his whānau. If he concentrated any harder, steam would start pouring from his ears.

At the treeline, Temera picked at the bark of a beech with his fingernail.

Maybe there *was* something he hadn't tried.

Turning on his heel, he stalked back to his spot in the middle of the lawn, pulled out the bullroarer, and unravelled the string. Kicking a clump of grass from his insole, he re-set his feet, and twirled the string. The bullroarer lifted into the air, soaring upwards on the breeze.

Temera turned too, the string humming in his hand.

He faced the mountain. "Te Maunga!" he called.

"What is it? What do you want?" Te Maunga's voice seemed to travel through the string, the vibrations rumbling in Temera's chest.

"I need your help."

"I already helped you."

"Look, I get it. I took the morepork for granted. Content to let her guide me, I got lazy, didn't I? I never bothered to learn the route to the spirit realm. But you know the way: You're Te Maunga, sacred mountain of the Tūhoe. You could show me; be my spirit guide."

"Gah! You ask too much. I'm too old to leave my mountain-bed."

"I'm not asking you to go anywhere. Just show me the way. If I'm going to stop your cousins from laying waste to the land and destroying our People, then I'm going to need help."

The mountain ducked its head and refused to reply. A brace of clouds scudded by, obscuring the craggy face of Te Maunga.

"You asked me before if my fear was holding me back!" Temera shouted. "I'm not afraid. I just need help."

The earth shook, the grass rolling beneath his feet. Even the ash floating on the air seemed to hover in fright. Temera dug his toes into the earth and held his stance, the bullroarer in his hands.

The mists parted and Te Maunga spoke. "Take care to remember the route, because from here on, you'll have to find the way for yourself."

"Thank you," Temera breathed. "Thank you." Then he straightened his arm, rotated his wrist, and let the pūrerehua fly.

*

At point, Hine stopped the group, signalling for them to wait, then she peered around the side of the building.

The muddy deluge poured across the road. Full of sticks and branches, it had surrounded a house, and was hurtling onwards towards the highway. For a moment, she watched, mesmerised by its force. The waves of mud danced and bubbled, like a child running away from its mother and delighting in the freedom.

Then Hine saw another movement, a flash of orange in the distance. Barnes' men were disappearing behind a small shed. Hine counted four. Was Barnes with them? A dozen prisoners had left the farmhouse in the Unimog. Where were the others? And where were Eriksen, Lisa and Pringle?

Hine pressed her back to the wall while she weighed her options. With five civilians in her charge, including one who might betray them, she wouldn't risk a confrontation with Barnes. They should find somewhere safe to hide the civilians, and then she or Matt would go looking for McKenna.

Her decision made, Hine checked the street again.

Still, the lahar thundered by, confident and unyielding. But this time, she saw something else. Eriksen had appeared on the roof of the house. Seconds later, Pringle appeared beside him. With the house surrounded by the lahar, they'd broken through the roof! They were safe enough for now, but the mud was a bloodthirsty enemy. They didn't have much time.

Hine pulled away from the wall and signalled to the party to follow her.

*

Taine ducked through the driver's door into the Unimog, moving gingerly in case his weight caused the vehicle to shift. Inside, it was dark. Dirt and stones rattled through the truck, trickling downwards into the pit.

Allowing his eyes a moment to adjust, Taine scanned the interior. The girl was trapped under the bench seat that ran the length of the vehicle. Taine could see the problem: the seat base had bent in the crash, wedging her in, although it'd probably saved her from being flung from the truck when it fell.

Keeping his steps slow and measured, Taine inched his way across to her.

"Brigitte? I'm Taine McKenna," he said, barely daring to fill his lungs in case the extra weight tipped them into the abyss.

The vehicle groaned.

He took another step. "Do you remember me? I was at the farmhouse." On the plus side, talking drowned out the Unimog's whine.

The girl sniffed. "You're Jules' friend. She said you would come for us."

"I'll let you in on a secret. Alain came for you, too."

171

She gasped. "Alain is alive? They didn't shoot him? Where is he?" Her eyes filled with tears and she twisted in a futile attempt to see to the top of the trench.

"Let's get you out, so you can see him." Taine slipped his fingertips under the bench seat on either side of the girl's hip. The space was awkward, but it was the best he could manage. "I'm going to try and lift it. Roll away if you can, okay?"

The girl nodded.

Taine took a deep breath and counted, "On three...one...two...three." His back flat, he bunched his leg muscles and deadlifted the seat. The bench gave a little, but not enough to allow her to escape. He set it back. Some of the screws attaching the bench to the floor were loose, though. Another heave might do it...

"Let's try that again—"

The truck squealed – one of those discordant backboard-scraping notes that a band plays in warm up. The cab nosedived. The entire Unimog, Taine and Brigitte still inside it, slid...and slid...finally jamming against the walls.

Taine clung to the bench, his feet dangling towards the windscreen.

They were no longer moving, but still Brigitte wailed, "Stop! Please! We're going to fall."

She needn't have worried. There would be no second attempt to move the seat now. The slope was too steep, and the truck could plummet any second.

Taine looked back through the truck to the top of the pit. Lefty was at the edge again, directing, as Hairy lowered the hook a third time. Taine waited for it to arrive, then snapped the hook through bars of the bench. He signalled to Lefty before hooking his elbow through the bench and the other arm around Brigitte. Up top, he heard Lefty's shout. The cable went taut. The metal bench screeched. The cable tightened... tighter...

This had better work.

At last, the loose rivets popped, and the bench flew out of the truck with Taine and Brigitte still holding it.

Seconds later, the Unimog crashed to the bottom of the pit.

*

Taine and Brigitte were dangling in the chasm, still clinging to the bench seat, when a drone flitted by.

So Arnold had come through. Good. With the drone's camera footage, there'd be no need for paperwork explaining how Taine had lost a Unimog.

CHAPTER TWENTY-TWO

Tokaanu village

Barnes flung Pope hard against the wall of the shed. In a split-second, he had the knife to his neck. "Where've you been?"

Pope put his hands in the air. "Dodging rivers of mud. In case you hadn't noticed, the whole place is going to shit."

"Where are the others? Climo? Smithy?"

"Smithy's dead. He copped it back near the farmhouse. His head hit the road when he fell off the twin cab, remember? Climo, I don't know. Dead probably. Around the bend behind us, there's a lahar barrelling across the road. The mud was coming for us, and I saw him go down. Didn't see what happened after that."

"What about Ants?" Taliava asked.

"Haven't seen him."

"He sold us out," Eaton murmured.

Releasing Pope, Barnes turned and jabbed the tip of the blade in Eaton's direction. "What are you on about?"

"We had a hostage, a girl, only Ants traded her for some emeralds her father had. Just one of those stones could buy off a busload of people, so I reckon he's taken the gems and done a bunk. If he isn't dead in the trench."

"Why didn't you tell us this before?" Pete said.

"Yes, why didn't you tell us this before?" Barnes parroted. He slapped the flat of the blade against his palm.

"No time, was there?" Eaton said, shifting nervously, his eyes darting to the knife. "Like Pope said, the whole place has been going to shit."

"So that's it: we're all that's left then," Taliava said, obviously accepting Eaton's story about the emeralds. "Six of us."

"We should leave," Pope announced, like he was the one in charge. "Forget the radio. If the roadblocks are still there, I say we run right through them."

"Yeah, except the Unimog's gone," Pete said. "So that's not happening."

Pope thumped the wall of the shed with his fist. "Damn. Someone took the Unimog? I suppose it was Harris. Shouldn't have trusted him. Bloody turncoat."

"Nah, it wasn't Harris." Pete giggled. "Wasn't any of his army mates either. The truck fell in a bloody trench. One minute it was right next to us, and next thing you know it was in the ditch—"

Pope's head shot up. He turned on his heel. "What's this about the army?"

"You heard right. They're here," Eaton said. "McKenna and his choir boys."

"Well, that's just great, isn't it? What are we supposed to do now?" Pope asked.

They all looked at Barnes.

Christ, it was like herding a bunch of toddlers. Any minute now they'd be asking him to wipe their bums, too. What was that saying about great power and great responsibility? Great pain in the arse, more like. They were doing his head in. He couldn't wait to cut them loose. All of them. Even Taliava. He just needed to pick his moment. Until then, he needed to keep them sweet because while they were loyal, they were useful. Especially if things came to a head with McKenna.

"We keep looking, don't we?" he said at last. "We need to find a car or a boat, anything to get us out of here."

He stifled his annoyance as Eaton and Taliava exchanged glances.

Pope adjusted the MARS-L. "And McKenna?"

Barnes rubbed his chin and pushed away from the wall. "Give him a wide berth."

"So, are we still looking for a radio?" Pete asked, hurrying to catch up. "Barnes?"

Pope gave Pete a shove. "Forget about the blasted radio."

*

Taine stepped off the hook and into Jules' hug.

She mumbled into his chest. "You did it. You're safe. Oh my god, Taine, I was so scared."

Taine rested his cheek on the top of her head – a gesture so familiar it was painful. The moment didn't last though, because Brigitte needed Jules, too. "Jules!"

Jules pulled away from Taine to wrap the girl in her arms. "I told you my friends would come, didn't I?"

Taine frowned. They weren't out of danger yet. They weren't exactly standing on solid ground and there was still a bunch of armed convicts running amuck.

"Nice work, Boss."

Taine dragged his eyes back as Lefty offered him his hand.

"Not so bad yourself, private," Taine said, retuning the handshake. Across the road, Hairy was climbing out of the cab.

"Hairy," Taine said, stepping over to shake his hand in turn. "Thank you." He clapped a hand on Hairy's shoulder, while Lefty retrieved the rifle from the crane cab.

"Any time, Boss," Hairy said.

"I'll see what I can do about reversing that court martial."

Hairy broke into a grin. "Appreciate that."

"And maybe getting you some crane training—"

"McKenna," Lefty warned, and he raised the gun. "Incoming."

Taine spun.

It was Hine, Read, and the others, but there was an addition – a man in an orange jumpsuit – and Read and Alain were supporting a second newcomer.

Taine tensed. Had Barnes' man taken control of the group?

No, Hine was at point and Thompson was armed, too. At the rear of the group, the academic looked like a cat who'd just realised the neighbour's dog was out of the yard.

"Alain!" Brigitte was squealing with excitement. She abandoned Jules and ran to meet him, showering him with kisses, which he was powerless to stop since he had his hands full.

"This is Stedman," Read said as they approached. "Luckiest man alive. Like Superman this one: bullets bounce right off him. And this is Climo. We picked him up trying to surf a lahar."

Hairy stepped forward. "Those are Barnes' Rangipō boys."

"And neither of them will be giving us any trouble," Read replied. "On their mothers' lives. They just want to get out of here alive."

"On that point, we need to get moving," Lefty said. "We still need to find Lisa. She's somewhere in town—"

"We know where she is. She's with Eriksen and Pringle," Hine said, her eyes wide. "We saw them on our way here."

"Fantastic," Lefty said.

"Yeah, about that." Thompson grimaced.

*

Pringle stood on the rooftop, surveying the devastation. Any hopes he'd had of the lahar abating were fading. Crossing the street at right angles, the mud wall surged around the house and plunged onwards. Pringle couldn't see beyond the highway, but he'd lay bets the wave veered at the canal, taking the easiest course down to the lake.

All around them, the mud battered the house's brick cladding with the treasures it'd collected on its voyage from somewhere up in the mountains. Tyres, trees branches, even a child's trike had rushed past them on the wave. Minutes ago, a letterbox had smacked into the side of the house, the impact causing it to flip over the roof, just missing Lisa.

Between Eriksen and Pringle, with one hand gripping the roof and the other cradling her belly, Lisa sobbed. Pringle would have liked to comfort her, but what could he say that would make a difference? All of them were up shit creek, but she was expecting a baby. An innocent soul about to be wiped out before it ever saw the sunlight – although perhaps that was kinder.

The monster wave kept coming. Its girth had spread, the lahar now as wide as a school gymnasium, bulging even wider in places where it had been forced to skirt the buildings blocking its path. For how long, though? How long would they have before the sheer strength of the wave ripped the house off its foundations and them with it? Minutes? An hour?

Pringle felt Eriksen's hand on his shoulder and he shuddered, acknowledging a farewell salute between two unlikely comrades who'd joined forces against a greater foe.

"Hold tight, everyone," Eriksen said. "Looks like the cavalry are coming!"

What? Pringle glanced at Eriksen. The man was *grinning*. Following Eriksen's gaze, Pringle squinted through the ash. He was right. The cavalry *was* on the way. Like Batman emerging from the mist, McKenna had rounded the bend and was racing towards them, Lefty hot on his heels. And behind them, with Corporal Harris in the cab, was an articulated crane.

Pringle's breath hitched. It wasn't over yet. There was still a chance they could get out of this. He crouched, patting Lisa's hand, hearing her gasp as he pointed to the convoy.

"Oh my god. That's Eddie!" she cried when she saw Lefty.

The rescuers were slowing, taking in the situation as they approached the lahar. They were wise to keep their distance. More people were coming: Hine and Read, Jules! McKenna had the hostages back.

From their rooftop vantage, Eriksen signalled to McKenna, pointing out the best location for the crane, out of the grasp of the swirling mud. Taking his cue, Harris positioned the crane at the edge of the mud. Pringle prayed it would be close enough to reach them. He held his breath, his heartbeat counting down the seconds while Harris rotated the boom, extending it to its full length before lowering the load hook.

Eriksen leaned out to grasp the hook.

Lisa squealed. She grabbed at Pringle's trousers.

Pringle turned. It was Ants. No wonder Pringle hadn't seen him earlier – he must've been climbing the leeward side of the building, clinging to a windowsill, or sitting on the lower side of the roof. Now, spying an opportunity to escape, the convict was climbing over the ridge of the roof, his rifle trained on them.

"I've got this." Eriksen let the hook swing idly by. He lifted Knife's rifle to his shoulder. "Stay where you are, man."

Ants stopped in his tracks. Only this time, there was no hiding the deformed barrel damaged by Knife's crash in the paddock.

One foot on either side of the ridge, Ants smirked. "Yeah, that mangled rifle isn't scaring me."

"Not doing it for you, huh?" Eriksen replied. "Well, how about the M4 my friend on the ground has trained at your head? That one scary enough for you?"

Ants hesitated. Pringle could almost see the cogs turning as he weighed the odds.

"Ants," Pringle warned, his hand outstretched. "Come on. You don't want to do this. It's not worth it. Squeeze that trigger and you'll never get off this roof alive."

"And don't go thinking this ash will throw off my friend's aim either," Eriksen added. "Lefty's a superb marksman. One of the best."

Lowering the rifle so it hung from its sling, Ants raised his hands. "Okay, okay. I don't want any trouble. All I want is off this roof, same as everyone else."

"And you will, but we're going to use our manners, aren't we?" Eriksen said. "Which means women and children go first." He signalled to Harris in the crane cab to bring the hook back, then he held out a hand to Lisa to help her up. When the load block was hovering within reach, Eriksen leaned forward to grab it.

All at once, Ants leapt across him, sailing through the air towards the hook.

Lisa screamed.

No shot came. They were too close. Lefty couldn't risk it.

Airborne, Ants' fingers touched the hook...

...and fell short.

The hook swung away, and Ants soared down the roof like a child on a water slide. He twisted, his fingers pawing the slippery roofing. He snatched at the plastic guttering.

Pringle jumped after him, sliding down the roofing on his rump, the nails tearing at his pants.

Ants yelped.

"Pringle, what the hell?" Eriksen shouted.

Ants had done some dumb things today, but Pringle couldn't just let him die.

Dangling over the edge of the roof, Ants clung to the gutter.

Pringle was nearing the edge. Still sliding, he flexed his foot and wedged his heel hard against the guttering to stop his momentum. He clenched his core and prayed the guttering wouldn't give way.

He hit the guttering and stopped.

Waited.

Nothing happened. It was holding.

Eyes frantic, Ants pawed at Pringle's foot. "Help me!"

With no time to celebrate, Pringle leaned over and grabbed the rifle sling stretched across Ants' back. Then, his feet braced against the guttering and body flat against the roof, he yanked upwards on the sling. His arms burned and the cords in his neck went taut. The gun tightened around Ants' shoulders. Little by little, Pringle hauled him over the edge, Ants heaving his leg over the rim just as the guttering snapped off. While they lay there panting, the white plastic was swallowed by the mud.

*

The arsewipes took Ants' gun. Made him wait on the far end of the roof.

"Any more funny business and we'll leave you to take your chances with the lahar," Eriksen said. "You got that?"

Ants said nothing. Instead, he glanced across the mud slick to check on the marksman. Bugger. Lefty's gun was still trained on him.

"Ants?" Pringle warned.

"Yeah, yeah, I heard the first time."

They left him there.

"Okay, Lisa, let's go," Eriksen said.

"Adrian, I don't think I can do this," she said.

"Yes, you can. Come on. Just don't look down."

Shaking her head, the woman tucked her hands under her armpits.

"Please. All you have to do is stand on the hook and Hairy will lower you to the ground."

"I can't hold my own weight any more, Adrian. As soon as the cable swings, I'll fall." She smiled weakly. "I might've gained a couple of kilos since I was dating Eddie."

"Hey, if the lady's not keen, I'm happy to go first," Ants called.

Eriksen shot him a glare.

"I'll go with you. Like a tandem parachute jump," Pringle said.

"Good idea, Pringle," Eriksen said. "Here you get on and I'll help Lisa up to you. Hurry."

One hand on the steel cable, Pringle jammed his foot into the hook. It swung wildly under his weight. Pringle waited for the movements to slow. Ants had to hand it to him; the man had nerves. "Pass her up," Pringle said.

The crane rocked.

"Shit, come on, Hairy. Hold it still," Eriksen said, as if the driver could hear him over the bellowing of the lahar.

Hairy. Eriksen had used the nickname, but he meant Harris. Ants smirked. Barnes should have known the soldier would jump ship the minute he got the chance. It was fine with Ants; Harris could jump like a jackrabbit for all he cared; just as long as he was prepared to get him off the roof.

The ground was breakdancing all over the place.

Fuck!

Ants clung to the ridgeline as the ground shook again, harder this time. The crane boom jerked to one side. Pringle's feet slipped from the hook and dangled in the air. Pringle was hanging out over the lahar, while down in the cab, Hairy struggled to keep the crane steady. The prison officer's face creased with concentration. He was slipping, losing his grip on the cable. Any second, he'd fall; Ants could feel it in his bones. And it was as if the lahar knew it too, because arms of mud reached up to grab him.

"Hairy, reel him in!" Eriksen screamed. Hairy couldn't hear, so Eriksen made a reeling motion, like a grinder on a yacht. It was the only answer – to reel Pringle in like a prize fish, find a new spot on the bank, and cast the line again.

Ants tingled with frustration. It was all very well saving Pringle, but he was *waiting* over here. He sucked the air in over his teeth. It was the same every time: a crisis came along, everyone else got sorted and, meanwhile, he was left waiting, wasn't he? All those re-starts back in foster care, Jimmy Brice getting spooked and fucking off when they knocked over the car dealership, and then, when the earthquakes started, the government bugging out and leaving them to rot at Rangipō. It was the story of his bloody life.

A thought crossed his mind: Hairy had better not lose the crane in the mud, or Ants would still be waiting on this roof when the house washed away.

Ants peered over the edge. *Thank god.* Hairy was doing it: he'd found some solid ground and was hauling Pringle in. Just a few more metres. Nearly...

Pringle saw his chance and jumped off the hook, tumbling to clear the lahar. Two men ran in to help drag him away from the wash. Ants recognised the sergeant, McKenna, and...

Well, would you look at that? The Frenchman made it out of Rotoaira.

*

Taine helped Pringle to his feet.

"Karl, are you okay?"

"Yeah, yeah, I'm fine." Pringle flicked a twig off his boot. "But we've got to get that hook back up on the roof to Lisa and Eriksen. I don't know how long the house will hold. Up there, it felt like it was made of straw." He turned to Lefty. "Lefty, can you keep that gun on Ants? Don't shoot him or anything, but maybe make some noise over his head if he moves. Eriksen will have his hands full helping Lisa." Pringle started towards the cab. "I better tell your corporal to keep the cable as short as he can..."

Already, Hairy was bringing the crane around, looking for a better position to re-launch the rescue – somewhere far enough from the lahar to be solid, yet close enough that the boom would still reach.

On the roof, Eriksen caught Taine's eye.

Taine gave him the thumbs up. He clutched his pūrerehua, feeling the carved kōrero beneath his fingers. The three on the roof seemed so far away...

"Taine!" From the heart of the Ureweras, Temera's voice, and the whirr of his pūrerehua, sounded in Taine's head. "Thank goodness, Te Maunga, we did it. We found a way through! Look, Taine, I need your help. I've had another vision."

"Temera, I'm pretty busy right now. A bunch of escaped prisoners are wreaking havoc—"

"Forget about them. It's the mountains we need to worry about. They're the real danger. They're going to blow up – explode – and when they do, bits of New Zealand are going to be scattered all over the Pacific."

Turning the crane parallel to the lahar, Hairy was engaging the counterweights.

"Yeah. It looks that way," Taine told Temera. "We're in Tokaanu, right under the Kāhui Tupua mountain range, and we're up to our armpits in lava bombs and lahars—"

An explosion sounded nearby. Taine's head snapped up. The lahar had taken another tack and engulfed a shed, the timbers cracking. "When we've shaken off some...obstacles...here, I intend to get my people out of out the area. Just as soon as I work out how."

"You don't understand," Temera said. "I need you to help stop the eruption."

Taine shook his head. His old friend had finally lost it. It was true they'd achieved some incredible things together but stopping an eruption? What did Temera think they were? A couple of demi-gods? Even Maui wouldn't be arrogant enough to take on the might of the god of earthquakes. If he was listening, Rūaumoko had to be laughing out loud in his underground lair.

"You don't believe me," Temera said, flatly.

"It's not that I don't believe—"

"It's okay. I get it. I know I sound crazy, like an old man who's gone ga-ga, but I know what I saw: the fire demons visited me and then the mountain, Te Maunga, spoke to me and..."

"Back up a bit. What's this about fire demons?"

"Te Pūpū and Te Hoata. They were the ones who warned me about the threat to Wayne when he was a toddler. If it weren't for them, he might have died."

"They actually visited you, though? You didn't just hear them in your head?"

"No." Temera laughed. "They came to the house. Twice. The first time, one of them left a scorch mark on the porch. They were as real as you or me."

They left a scorch mark? Taine thought of the warrior woman he'd seen dancing over the lava at the farmhouse, and then again when the lava bomb had killed poor Keira Skelton.

"What do they look like, these fire demons?"

"Like Wonder Woman in a piu piu. They've got dark skin and long hair and they're muscly. I reckon they'd give those guys on the World Wrestling Federation a run for their money."

"Then I've seen them. One of them, at least."

Temera paused. "Ah, they came to you, too? Then there *is* something to what they're saying."

Hairy had the boom out over the roof. Eriksen leaned out to grab for the hook.

"I don't know. Do you trust them?" Taine said.

"They saved Wayne."

"Then why exactly are they called demons? They didn't seem too friendly."

Temera sighed. In his mind, Taine heard the blade of his friend's pūrerehua, the twin of his own, whirr through the air. "I once sat at the knee of a great kaumatua who told me that the People are connected to the land. '*We are of the landscape,*' he said."

"My mother's people say the same thing," Taine replied.

"Then you'll know that the Tangata whenua, the People, won't survive if the mountains fall. Our mountain ancestors – Tongariro, Ngāuruhoe, Taranaki, Ruapehu, Tauhara, Pūtauaki – they're fighting over the mountain-maiden Pīhanga again. I reckon that trickster Rūaumoko, is revelling in it, whipping up their fury and making matters worse. He's always liked to make mischief."

Taine looked at the roiling power of the lahar. "What are we supposed to do against mountains?"

"Te Pūpū insists the eruption can be stopped if I talk to them, convince them to stop their arguing. I can't do that on my own. I need you to go to the mountains in my stead."

The timbers of the shed cracked again. If it went, it could take out the crane. "Temera, sorry, I have to go."

CHAPTER TWENTY-THREE

Tokaanu village

They'd just broken into a garage, when Eaton turned. "You hear shouting?" he asked.

Casting his eyes over the shelves of empty paint tins and stacks of old magazines, Barnes pricked up his ears. In the distance, shouts carried over the thrum of the lahar.

"Could be the army blokes," Pete said.

"Could be the others, too. Ants and Stedman. We should go look," Pope said.

"Barnesy?" Pete prompted.

Pope wasn't waiting for an answer. "I'm going," he said, and, turning on his heel, he strode out of the garage.

Barnes stared after him. He thought about putting a bullet in his back. Thought hard. Let's face it: the guy had been pushing his luck all day. Except shooting Pope would have consequences: Eaton would flip sides – already he was itching to go after Pope – and Pete might go too if he sensed the tide turning.

"Barnes?" Pete said again.

What did it hurt to have a look? Go with the flow. There was nothing useful in here. It was just junk: old reno projects and rusting garden tools.

"Yeah, good call," he said, keeping his voice upbeat. "It could be the others."

With Pope in the lead, the five of them ran from one building to another, keeping low as they crept closer to the lahar and whoever was doing the shouting. When they reached the bend in the road, they ducked behind a wooden fence – so old that the timbers curled up at the bottom. Barnes put his hands on the roughened top post and peeped over.

Christ!

The town looked like a scene from a disaster movie. An avalanche of mud and branches was surging across the road. The mud had surrounded a house, trapping people on the roof. Someone – no, not someone, fucking Harris – was trying to rescue them with a crane. Meanwhile, McKenna and his men were lined up like ducks at a shooting range, watching.

Barnes swore under his breath. He already knew McKenna was in town; still, it hurt to see it. The soldier was like a phoenix, always rising from the fucking ashes. And Barnes had completely forgotten about the crane. That had been a mistake…

"Fuck, is that Ants up on the roof?" Pete blurted. "How the hell did he get up there?"

"He's with that soldier I told you about," Eaton said. "And the girl, the one Ants gave up in return for the emeralds."

Barnes squinted. "What's he doing sitting over there by himself? Why doesn't he go for the hook?"

"One of the soldiers has his gun on him," Pete said, pointing. "Over there. See?"

"Hang on. We took their guns," Pope said. "How'd they get guns?"

Eaton snorted. "Pete here handed his over. Just gave it to Harris. 'Here you go Harris, help yourself.' May as well have tied a ribbon on it."

"Fucking leave it out, Eaton. I did not give it to him. He nabbed it while I was trying to stop myself from falling in the trench. Anyway, it was only one gun."

"Three," Taliava said. "I count three guns. Climo and Stedman are with them, so they must have taken theirs."

"We should do something," Pope interrupted. "Distract the soldiers, so Ants can get off the roof. We've still got the upper hand."

"You're just feeling bad for dumping Climo. Why should the rest of us risk our necks for him?" Eaton asked.

Barnes was thinking the same thing.

"Be a shame if those emeralds got washed away, though," said Pete.

*

On the roof, Ants sniffed. All of their grandiose plans for skipping the country had gone to hell. Down by the crane, McKenna had his whole gang in tow: the Frenchies were with him, Lisa's old man, even the Conservation chick. Seemed he'd got Climo and Stedman to switch camps, too.

That wasn't the worst of it: a shed to their left was cracking and creaking. Ants could hear it over the sound of the lahar. Any second now, it would break off its foundations. When it did, no doubt it would wipe out the house – and his chances of making it out alive.

The cracking sounded again. Ants' heart jumped, and he whirled, fixing his eyes on the shed. It was still standing. Further along the street though, near the bend, Pope and Eaton appeared from behind a fence. Flashes of white pierced the swirling ash. There was more cracking – *and it wasn't the shed.*

Ants got to his feet. It was gunfire! Pope and Eaton were firing on the soldiers as Barnes and Taliava surged from behind the fence. A diversion? Was that for him? Ants couldn't be sure. Everything was happening at once.

Cut off on one side by the lahar, McKenna's group had scattered, everyone running for cover between the houses. All except Lefty, who dropped to the ground and returned fire.

Climo got shot, struck in the crossfire. Dropped like a hat toppled in the wind, he lay flat out on the road, like he was sunbathing.

Ants sucked in a breath. Lefty had taken his eyes off Ants to protect the crane. Four against one, the soldier was holding them off too – forcing the Rangipō boys to take cover behind some buildings. Still, Lefty kept up the barrage.

Time for Ants to go, while Lefty was occupied.

Ants turned. *What on earth?* McKenna was climbing the crane, walking hand over hand up the boom, oblivious to the mud surging below. And Ants could see why: Eriksen couldn't hold the hook and lift Lisa at the same time. McKenna was coming to do the job that Pringle had failed to complete.

Really? They couldn't just ask me nicely?

A bullet pinged nearby. Too close. Ants ducked. His heart raced. Was that shot meant for him? Maybe this gunfight wasn't a distraction to get Ants off the roof. Maybe Barnes wanted to take him out to keep him from talking. Was that what had happened to Climo? Ants scanned the street trying to identify the shooter, but the place was lit up like the Las Vegas strip. McKenna's soldiers had joined the gunfight, firing back to cover their sergeant.

Through the racket, Ants heard the shed groan. Shit, it was going to go. He'd worry about Barnes later. Right now, he had to get to that hook.

Keeping low, Ants started across the roof.

McKenna had already reached the top of the boom. The sergeant didn't bother shimmying down the cable. Lying on his stomach on the boom, one arm wrapped around it and his lower leg hooked under it, he reached for Lisa. Eriksen lifted the girl, passing her up to McKenna. Their hands touched. The crane bucked.

Lisa screamed.

Quick as a cat, McKenna leaned forward and grabbed her, gripping her hand in his. The night dress billowed out, the girl swaying over the bubbling cauldron of mud. Too terrified to scream, she clamped her mouth shut. Even the gunfire seemed to stop as everyone waited to see if she would fall.

McKenna inched her upwards. The tendons in his neck tensed. He grimaced.

Lisa gasped.

"Come on, Boss," Eriksen urged, hovering beneath them on the roof. "You've got this."

Dragging the girl upwards, McKenna grunted with effort. Lisa managed to throw her leg over the boom.

In that moment, Ants realised McKenna wasn't going to risk climbing down the boom with the girl. Instead, he'd twisted his torso, signalling to Hairy to swing the boom around and lower them to the ground. Ants frowned. Reaching out to grasp the hook, Eriksen was planning on going, too. *The bastards never had any intention of getting me off this roof. They're leaving me behind.*

Ants lunged for Eriksen, tackling him by the legs and lifting him off his feet. Then he turned and tossed him sideways. Intent on catching the hook, Eriksen wasn't expecting the attack. Before he knew what had hit him, he fell into the hole in the roof.

Good riddance, too. With a bit of luck, he'll have gone through the ceiling.

"Oh my God! Adrian!" On the boom, the girl's screams could wake the dead.

The hook was still hovering in mid-air. Snatching it up, Ants thrust his boot into the gap. He glanced up. Saw McKenna's expression harden. Ants chuckled. What was the sergeant going to do? He couldn't save them both: it was either the girl or the soldier.

It was a no brainer – since McKenna had the bird in hand. Ants giggled at his own joke.

Eriksen's head appeared at the hole.

So, he wasn't dead. As good as, though.

Clambering through the ragged metal, he got to his feet. His army tunic was torn and, underneath it, his shoulder was bleeding. The look on his face was priceless.

"Not so great when the shoe's on the other foot, is it?" Ants taunted. Already, the cable was drifting away from the roof.

"Ants. Come on," Eriksen said.

Ants grinned. "You were happy enough to leave me."

"Eriksen, the shed's going to go," McKenna yelled.

"Ants. Quit mucking around."

"I'm sure Harris won't mind sending the cable back."

The shed smashed off its foundations.

"Eriksen!" McKenna roared.

Eriksen leaped.

*

Leaving the others to the gunfight, Barnes slipped behind the buildings and made his way towards the lahar. Bloody Harris, farting about trying to play the hero. He was going to put that crane in the mud, and then what? It would be all over. Barnes wanted that crane. It was his ride out of here. And while Eaton and Pope and Taliava were fucking around fending off McKenna's soldiers, Barnes intended to get it. Hell, he could ditch them all and drive away. Take the road to the west of the lake. Run the roadblocks. Go for broke.

He ducked around a carport and his sleeve caught on something. He turned to see what he'd snagged it on.

Taliava's big fist was clenched in the sleeve of his overalls. "Where are you going?" Taliava demanded.

"I want that fucking crane." Barnes tried to shake him off.

Taliava only tightened his grip. "Don't do it. Ants is up there, and that woman is *pregnant!*"

Barnes stopped struggling and put all the menace he could muster into his stare, reminding Taliava exactly what was at stake if Barnes didn't get what he wanted.

Taliava's face crumpled and he backed away.

*

Diving headlong through the air, Eriksen didn't look down. He streamlined his body, tensed his core, and fixed his eyes on the cable. Then he prayed.

Time dragged.

When he was certain he'd fall short, positive he would plunge into the mud, his fingers found the cable. He clenched his fists around it, savouring the burn of the metal on his palms. But carried by the momentum, his body didn't stop. Eriksen clung on.

He swung out, then back.

Above him on the cable, Ants swore.

The swinging slowed and Eriksen flexed his arms, engaging his bones to carry the weight. He was facing Ants' chest. There was no place on the hook to anchor his foot – Ants had claimed that spot – but at least he'd made it off the roof, and in the nick of time too. Below him, a chunk of concrete the size of a concrete mixer had washed down the lahar and smashed into the house, ripping away the corner, wounding the building. Mud gushed into the gap, dragging away bricks and drywall. The mud swept into the house, scouring out everything. Dangling like a plumb-bob on a line, Eriksen couldn't help but stare. The devastation was hypnotic. A lethal surge of mud...

Eriksen's arms burned. His shoulders ached. He breathed deep. All he had to do was hang on. McKenna would get him out of this. When had the sergeant ever let them down? Any minute, he'd have Hairy bring the boom around.

The cable rattled and jerked.

There, the crane was moving. Not long now: maybe the time it took to pump out four sets of bench presses.

Up on the boom, McKenna's shout carried on the air, his voice calm in the chaos.

Ants kicked him in the thigh. It would've been one doozy of a Charley Horse if Eriksen hadn't been dangling in the air. As it was, his legs swung out like a piñata. He clung to the cable, his chest aching with the strain.

Ants lined up his boot to kick again.

Lisa screamed.

He wasn't imagining it, then. Ants was trying to kill him.

Come on, Hairy. A little help here.

The kick landed and Eriksen oscillated like a pendulum.

Shit. If he kept this up, he'd lose his grip. Maybe he could climb over Ants, get himself up on the boom beside McKenna and Lisa. He glanced up and caught Ants' smile. Eriksen shivered. There would be no getting past him.

When the third kick came, Eriksen lost his grip, slipping down the cable. He snatched at the lifeline, finally clamping his sweaty fingers around the cable at the level of Ants' knees. The next blow would be to his face. But no kick came. Instead, Ants leaned down to fumble with the rifles slung over Eriksen's shoulders.

Eriksen froze. Ants wouldn't be able to lift them off, but that didn't mean he couldn't fire one. Eriksen was powerless to stop him. The safety clicked.

"You squeeze that trigger and you'll be sorry," Eriksen whispered.

"You shouldn't have left me," Ants said.

Eriksen's leg exploded in fire. He roared. White heat flooded his body and his hand slipped, the remaining arm nearly yanked from its socket. Curled around the cable, his fingers were slick. One kick from Ants and he'd be gone. It didn't matter. He was gone, anyway, his lifeblood pumping into the lahar. He glanced up at McKenna.

One last thing maybe.

Grappling with his free hand, he reached around to the rifles on his back. He put his finger in the housing – which one, he didn't know – and flicked his thumb. Then he dragged the rifle round, thrust it in Ants' belly. His shoulder screamed when he leaned back.

"No!" Ants yelled.

In his mind's eye, he pictured Little Ed. He squeezed the trigger. *The mangled gun, then.*

*

Thompson huddled behind the deck of someone's house, his knees shaking with fear and rage. As if they didn't have enough trouble, the prisoners had decided to pick a fight, turning the town into a war zone. It was infernal, Thompson's bones rattling with the blasts. He could only imagine what it must be like for Lefty. Lying on the road, the soldier was firing up the street at the prisoners, drawing their attention away from McKenna, who was up on the boom trying to rescue the group on the roof. Meanwhile, Read had grabbed the rifle from Thompson, shouting something about doubling back, then he and Hine had disappeared,

Thompson glanced around. He hadn't seen what had happened to Pringle, although Alain and Brigitte were hunkered a few metres away, their backs against the wall. Dammit, where was Ahmad? He'd made a promise to Keira to look out for him.

"Either of you seen Ahmad?" he called.

"Last time I saw him, he was helping Jules carry Stedman over there," Alain said. He pointed to a rusted-out shipping container covered in graffiti. The side door was ajar. Not exactly the Bank of England, but if that's where they were, they should be safe enough.

Brigitte drew in a breath. "Attention!" she hissed. "Look!"

Thompson spun. He looked over the deck. An armed man in orange overalls was running parallel to the lahar.

"That's Barnes," Alain said, his voice dripping with disdain.

"Salopard," Brigitte muttered.

Thompson frowned. The hair on his neck bristled. Barnes was deliberately staying out of Lefty's line of sight. He was heading for the crane! Through the ash, Thompson saw him raise the gun and point it at Hairy. The soldier took his hands from the controls.

No! He can't have the crane. There are people up there.

Thompson turned to Alain. "You two, get in the house," he said.

"What—"

Thompson didn't wait to hear the rest. He burst from behind the deck, running alongside the lahar. This close to the rush of mud, the noise was crippling. Thompson sprinted, his legs protesting.

Please don't shoot me.

There was a shot, but it wasn't for him. It'd come from up on the crane. Distracted, Barnes and Harris looked up.

Thompson saw his chance. Barnes hadn't seen him coming, the bulk of the crane hiding his approach. Putting his head down, he charged full tit at Barnes, hitting him in the guts and sending him flying. While he was rolling on the ground, straining to suck in a breath, Thompson snatched up the rifle.

"Hairy, come on!" McKenna yelled from up high.

Something was happening. Harris fumbled for the controls, desperate to move the boom. An explosion rocked the air.

Thompson jumped in fright, turning as Eriksen and Ants plunged into the lahar. Thompson spied a boot and then they were gone, both men swallowed by the mud.

"Don't move."

Shit, he'd looked away from Barnes.

But it was Pringle who'd spoken, because when Thompson looked back, Barnes was still on the ground, a garden fork aimed at his head.

CHAPTER TWENTY-FOUR

Tokaanu, Waihi Bay

Thompson sat on a log, the rifle across his knee and his boots in the pumice. He was helping Pringle keep an eye on the prisoners, while the soldiers came up with a plan to get them out of here. It wasn't a big group. Of the thirty men who'd left Rangipō, only six were left. Pringle had found the last one hiding in an outside laundry. Pringle had locked him in, then gone back to retrieve him when the gunfight was over.

Breaking away from Brigitte and Alain, Lisa came and sat beside him. She was still in her nightie, but someone had found her a Chiefs rugby sweatshirt to wear over the top.

"Hi, Dad," she said, and she lay her head on his shoulder.

He patted her gently on her head. "Good to see you're safe, honey."

They smiled. For a while, they said nothing, content to sit there as if they really were father and daughter, the pair of them watching while Hairy wrote a message in the sand for the army drone that had been hovering about.

"All the tech these days and we're still writing messages in the sand," Thompson quipped.

"Yeah. It's crazy."

He flicked his head towards the soldiers. "How's Lefty doing?"

Lisa smoothed the nightdress over her knees. "Not so great. They used to fight like a couple of alley cats, but Adrian was his best friend."

Thompson nodded. He'd only known the two men for an afternoon and he'd got the same impression. "I'm sorry about your mum," he said. "She was so brave. I hear she saved your life."

Lisa nodded, her lips tight. She sat up and scrubbed the tears out of her eyes. "Look, I don't know what's going to happen now. Maybe we'll get out, maybe we won't… Anyway, I wanted to thank you for what you did."

Thompson patted her knee. "Nothing to thank me for, love. Your mother and I are really proud of you."

Tears welled again, and she leaned over and kissed him on the cheek. "I'd better go and thank Pringle and McKenna." She stood up, shaking out her nightdress.

They glanced along the beach at the sergeant. McKenna was pacing in circles, clutching that bullroarer around his neck and talking to himself. Mourning his friend.

"Maybe leave him a bit," Thompson suggested. "Speak to Pringle first."

When she'd left, Barnes jeered at Thompson from the huddle of prisoners on the beach. "Boohoo. Everyone's so sad." He dropped his lower lip.

"Shut up, Barnes. People are grieving. Everyone's lost someone today."

"Your daughter's safe."

Thompson looked across to Lisa, chatting with Pringle. "Yes, she is."

"Cost you your emeralds, though, didn't it? That's got to hurt. They're still in Ants' pocket by the way – probably somewhere at the bottom of the lake by now. Your life savings, down the gurgler."

Thompson's anger flared. He got to his feet. "There are plenty more where those came from. I found those emeralds up on the mountain." He nodded towards Pīhanga. "We were on the western ridge when a lava bomb exploded, ejecting them into the air. Great handfuls of them, falling from the sky."

Barnes smirked. "In case you hadn't noticed, the supervolcano's about to explode. Even if you survive, Mount Pīhanga could be gone."

"Yes, but if we survive, I'll be free to come and look, won't I?" Thompson retorted. "Unlike some others I can think of."

"Don't listen to him," Eaton said, nudging Barnes with his shoulder. "He's just trying to get in your head."

Thompson turned away. It was petty of him to take it out on Barnes. The man might have contributed to Eriksen's death and he'd obviously intended for Alain to die, but he'd had nothing to do with Clague or Keira's deaths. Barnes was a nobody. A nothing. It had been the *mountains* that had killed Thompson's friends, and the mountains were capable of so much more. You didn't need to be a seismologist to figure that out. In the end, there wasn't much chance of any of them making it out of here, let alone coming back.

*

Looking out over the lake, Jules didn't turn when Taine approached. "I guess there are worse places to spend your last hours," she said. Her hair was sprinkled with bits of ash.

"Temera thinks we can stop it," he said.

She turned. "Stop what?"

"The earthquakes. The eruption. Everything."

"Taine…"

"I know it sounds crazy, but I've been talking to him and some of it makes sense."

Her brow furrowed in tiny creases. "What makes sense?"

This was always the hard part: Jules' scientific mind needing to make sense of his spiritual connection to Temera. It was an enigma even to Taine, the way their respective wairua intersected, each influencing the other. It wasn't that Jules didn't believe it – she'd seen too much not to believe – she just didn't understand it.

"You know, the way history repeats. Temera says the Kāhui Tupua mountains are fighting over Pīhanga again."

"Like the legend?"

"Exactly. He thinks that's why there's been so much volcanic activity. Initially, it was just a theory – you know how Temera loves his stories – but then the fire demons Te Pūpū and Te Hoata visited him and told him he should do something about it. Those two really put the wind up him." He smiled. "He described them as Wonder Women in piu piu."

Jules' head snapped up. Her eyes widened.

"He's not just some old man, Jules. He's been right before."

"I know. What are the chances he's wrong this time?"

They were quiet. A slab of timber floated by.

"What do you have to do?"

"We have to talk to the mountains, get them to stop."

"All of them?"

"It'll be Taranaki or Tauhara, since those mountains fought the hardest for her. Before Tongariro banished them."

"Well, that's that then. You can't get to either one of them. Taranaki is two hundred kilometres away and—"

"I don't think it's Taranaki. Temera's been listening on the radio and there's been no reports of earthquakes there. I think it'll be Tauhara."

She shook her head. "Still too far."

Taine didn't reply.

"You're kidding, right?" She flung out her arm towards Taupō. "How are you going to get there? If we had boats, we'd be using them to get out of here."

"Hine. She's going to swim me across the lake."

The look on Jules' face said it all: as if he was running away to join the circus.

"Taine, no. Hine can't possibly haul you that far. It's got to be forty kilometres, at least."

Taine shrugged. "She says she can do it."

"Taine." Her voice barely a whisper. "Please, don't. You can't tolerate the cold the way Hine can. Being submerged for that long could kill you. The water temperature is less than twelve degrees."

"I can't ask Hine to go on her own. What's she going to do when she gets there? Temera needs my help, Jules. I have to go."

Jules hugged her arms about her body and rocked herself gently. Taine had seen the gesture before. She did it to protect herself from hurt. Because he was doing it again, wasn't he? Leaving her behind while he rushed off to save the world. Exactly what she'd accused him of when they'd parted. The thing is, he wished he could stay. More than anything, he wished he could sit on the wharf with her, the two of them dangling their feet in the lake while the world around them burned.

He wished he could, but he couldn't.

Leaving Hine with Lefty, Read came over to join them.

Taine tensed: Jules wasn't his only problem. How was he going to straighten this with his friend? Read hadn't wanted Hine to come in the first place. They'd almost lost her at the farmhouse, and then again when the lava bomb had taken Keira. No doubt he was worked up, stomping over here to demand Taine drop the idea. Hadn't he figured out yet that the Tūrehu woman was her own person, that Hine could make her own decisions, without anyone's permission.

"Hine's just told me," he announced.

"Good," Jules said. "You talk some sense into him, Matt, because he won't listen to me."

"We have to let them go, doc," Read said.

Taine gaped. If anything, he'd expected Read to put up the most resistance. Jules obviously thought so too, because her forehead crinkled.

"I don't understand. I thought you loved Hine," she said.

"I do love her."

"I suppose now you're going to tell me that she's a soldier first," Jules said.

Read exhaled, letting out his breath in a slow stream. Finally, he said, "Tell me this doc: how is it exactly that we found you here, in your conservation truck in the middle of a national emergency?"

"I came to look for the Chesterfield skink."

Read raised an eyebrow.

"No, you don't understand. I had permission from the minister to come. The skink isn't just endangered, it's on the brink of extinction and there was a sighting in the area last week, so I had to come. If there was an outside chance we could find a second population before..." Jules trailed off. She nibbled her lip.

Taking Jules' hand, Read gave it a pat. "You see, doc? You're not so different from the rest of us. Our Defence Force mission is to protect New Zealand lives, and yours is to save all its little beasties." Read chuckled. "Especially the reptiles: big ugly ones, little skinky ones…you kinda have a thing for reptiles." He bent to pick up a piece of pumice, flicking it into the lake where it bobbed on the surface. "Of course, I'd prefer that my friends didn't go. I'd rather go myself than risk the people I care about. If I had their skills, I'd already be gone."

Taine snorted.

Leaning closer to Jules, Read spoke from behind his hand. "You might find this hard to believe, doc, but some people say I'm impulsive."

Jules smiled at that. "Really?"

"We have to let them go," Read said. "It's only fair."

Jules' shoulders slumped, and she nodded.

*

Taine and Hine ran along the wharf, their boots thumping on the boards. One of the oldest structures in the country, and possibly the most photographed, it'd been built when the township had been a thriving trading and tourism outpost in the 1870s. When the council had renovated it, they'd retained some of the original timbers and all of its original length, all two hundred and fifty metres of it stretching into the lake. That meant they could avoid swimming through the muck and debris that had washed down the canal.

Taine wondered if Eriksen's body was here, submerged beneath the murky water…

Reaching the end of the wharf first, Hine took off her gloves, revealing the webbed syndactyly of her hands. She spread her fingers and rolled her shoulders. Then she took off her tunic, bunching it up, and dropping it on the wharf.

"Ready?" she asked.

Shucking his tunic, he added it to the pile. He would have liked to keep an outer layer, but the fabric's bulk would add drag. As it was, he was keeping his boots; he didn't want to make Hine's task even harder.

Taine tucked his pūrerehua into his t-shirt. "Ready," he replied. Together, they slipped into the chilly water of the crater lake.

"Hold tight to my belt," she instructed.

He might be the sergeant, but water was Hine's domain. Taine closed his fingers around the leather and gripped it tightly. Then Hine took a breath and dived, her paddle-hands cutting the surface and pulling them through the water, propelling them past the splinters and the silt into the middle of the lake. Economising her energy, Hine allowed them to glide the full length of the stroke, before repeating the motion of dragging her hands through the black liquid. Taine tried to help, kicking out with his legs and pulling his free arm through the water, but it was clear he was throwing off her rhythm so he stopped, contenting himself with breathing deep whenever his face broke the water and tapping her on the back when she forgot that, unlike her, he couldn't survive for longer than a couple of minutes without air. Each time he came up, Taine checked the wharf, watching it grow smaller in the distance.

Nearing Motutaiko Island, the sacred resting place of the famous chieftain Ngātoro-i-rangi, Hine pulled up. Taine let go of her and treaded water. He flexed his fingers to shake off the cold. All around them particles of ash fell from the sky, dissolving like candy floss where it hit the water. "Everything okay?"

Her eyes wide, Hine inclined her head to their left. Taine lifted his chin above the choppy water. A sit-on kayak was bobbing nearby, a man slumped forward over the paddles. Dark brown stains spattered the yellow plastic. He'd been shot in the back of the head. Although half his face and shoulder were little more than a pulpy mush, Taine recognised him from the farmhouse: it was the man who'd pulled the cables from the Unimog, leaving them stranded. Someone hadn't liked the idea of him leaving, either. Well, there was nothing they could do for him now.

"Let's go," Taine said, but Hine lifted her hand, showing him the short rope attached to the front of the kayak.

"We should take the little boat," she said. "Your lips are already blue."

"Good call." Taine pushed the convict into the water, though he hated to pollute the lake. As the man sank beneath the surface, Taine clambered into the kayak, while Hine tied the rope to her belt and pulled it tight.

Taine pushed his knees into the moulded plastic and took up the paddles. "All good," he said.

Turning, Hine plunged, striking out for Taupō. The kayak had less drag, and Taine was paddling, so they zipped across the lake, Hine surfacing every fifteen minutes.

Taine spared a moment to look back over his shoulder. Above the mountains, the late afternoon sun hovered in a cloud of pink-white ash, the scene reminding him of one of those old paintings of the Pink and White Terraces before they'd been buried under the Tarawera eruption. As vistas went, it was beautiful and peaceful. A cruel lie.

Taine faced forward again, towards Taupō and beyond that, Mount Tauhara.

Hine was tiring now, coming up for air more often, and Taine's own shoulders were burning from the effort of paddling. It was hard to imagine he'd ever been cold. Worse, the earthquakes were causing waves in the lake, the swell slowing their progress.

There was nothing else but to carry on. He dipped his paddle and dragged it through the waves.

When they neared Taupō, Taine hardly recognised the waterfront. On the main esplanade, the beach below the cliffs was gone, submerged by the tsunami effect of the waves. Instead, Taine and Hine were approaching the clifftop near the famous golf tee into the lake. If the raft with the golf hole was still anchored somewhere out in the lake, it was submerged too, because Taine hadn't seen it.

At the new shoreline, Taine jumped out of the kayak and helped Hine to higher ground, setting her down on the grass. Still tethered to the kayak, she rested on her hands and knees, breathing hard. Taine untied the rope at her waist and she rolled over, her arm covering her eyes. She was exhausted, and no wonder: apart from her Tūrehu kinsmen, Taine doubted anyone had witnessed what he'd just seen. It had been an epic swim. World beating. A swim that would take an ultra-swimming athlete two days, the warrior woman had achieved in a little over two hours.

It reminded Taine of a story his mother had told him about Hine Poupou. Abandoned on an island by her husband, Hine Poupou had swum eighty kilometres to freedom, helped by a kindly dolphin. Where was the dolphin to help this Hine? There was none; she'd done it on her own.

When she sat up, Taine patted her shoulder. She held his hand there a moment. "When I've recovered, I'm going straight back," she said.

He pointed down the slope to their right, where the Waikato River drained from the lake. "There'll be boats at the mouth of the river. Look for a tourist charter boat. A boat like that will carry a big group and should have fuel and first aid supplies on board. By the time you've retrieved everyone and brought them to this side of the lake, Major Arnold will have organised some transport. That is, if his boys aren't here already."

Hine nodded. "Go beat the mountain," she said. She didn't question the how, but then, the Tūrehu had their own secrets.

"Don't wait for me." Taine turned, searching for some way to get to the mountain. It wasn't far, only five kilometres from town, and another two to the summit, but who knew when the supervolcano would go up? He needed a vehicle. Even a bike would do. His eyes fell on the fire station with its clear-fronted garage doors. He gave an internal cheer –

there was still a truck inside. Running across the road, he lifted the garage doors.

Beside the truck, boots and jackets were lined up ready to go, like a set of Russian dolls laid side by side. Still in his t-shirt, Taine grabbed a fireman's jacket and put it on, then he swung into the truck. When he drove out, Hine lifted her hand. Returning her wave, he drove inland, touching the pūrerehua at his neck, to summon his friend.

"You took a fire engine," the old man chuckled in his head.

"We might die," he said. "And it's been on my bucket list."

"'Course it has."

When they reached the start of the Tauhara summit track, Taine parked the engine.

CHAPTER TWENTY-FIVE

Taupō-nui-a-tia, Tauhara

The first part of the track crossed some of the local farmland. Taine dashed through the paddocks, climbing fences and scattering the sheep. Dammit, he'd forgotten to take that pebble out of his boot. He passed through the two concrete water tanks that marked the start of the scrub. "Temera," he called.

"I'm here."

"I don't see the boy anywhere."

"He's gone. Grown up. With the morepork gone, my mountain ancestor, Te Maunga, guided me between the realms. Now I see everything as if I'm beside you and also above you."

The track cut steeply through the ferns, a small creek running alongside. It was late in the afternoon and vibrant greens were fading to grey. Taine sprang from rock to rock, bounding up the slope. He paused at the stream, cupping his hands for a drink. Tree trunks squeaked in the wind.

"Reminds me of home," Temera said.

Taine gazed at the canopy. "It doesn't feel right," he said.

"What do you mean?"

Taine wiped his mouth with the back of his hand. "Well, for a start, where are the lahars, the lava bombs, the cracking earth? All day I've been pitched and tossed as if I were on the deck of a ship, and the minute we get here, there's nothing. Just a bit of ash."

"I can't believe you're complaining."

Taine hauled them up the slope between two trees. "See any demons up there?"

"Good point," Temera said.

The ground was flattening out. He was nearing the summit, the breeze picking up as they left the shelter of the scrub. Even with the ash, the view was magnificent, with the lake in the forefront and, in the distance, the great peaks of Te Kāhui Tupua.

"Stop here," Temera whispered and he cited the old proverb, "Mehemea ka tuohu ahau me maunga teitei." *If I should bow my head let it be to a great mountain.* He was right. It didn't do to stand on the head of an ancestor.

Taine slowed, taking a moment to catch his breath. "Pūrerehua?" he asked.

"I think so."

Taine took out his bullroarer, and choosing a clearing, he began to play.

The string hummed, singing a trail to the spirit world.

Taine closed his eyes and saw the warrior step out of the ash. Broad and muscled, with tattoos to match his status, he was twice Taine's height with legs like puriri trunks and his back the width of a great canoe. The wairua-spirit of Tauhara. His voice rumbled like shifting rocks as he recited his pepeha, speaking the names and the deeds of his ancestors since the dawn of time.

When he had introduced himself, he flicked the tip of his taiaha-spear in Taine's direction. "Why are you here?" he demanded.

"Uncle,' Temera said respectfully, "we've come to beg you to cease your quarrel with your brother Tongariro. Your bickering has disturbed Rūaumoko and—"

Tauhara grunted. "Why are you bothering me with this? That argument was settled long ago."

"Settled? But what about the earthquakes and the ash?" Taine said.

"That has nothing to do with me." He turned to step back into the brume.

Dropping the bullroarer, Taine leaped forward to block his path. "No, you don't. You don't get to walk away. We need your help. If the earthquakes continue and the lake erupts, the People will die."

Tauhara swatted at Taine as if he was brushing away an insect. "Like I said, it has nothing to do with me."

Thrown to the ground, Taine turned his shoulder inwards, tumbling to regain his feet. "How can you say that?" he shouted. "*We are of the landscape*. The People are your children. Ignore us, and you turn your back on everything!"

Tauhara lunged, his spear at Taine's neck. "I turn my back on nothing! I have stood here at the end of the lake and watched while my life was taken from me. Not once have I looked away!"

"You need to look again." Taine pointed across the lake.

Tauhara turned his eyes to the horizon. In the dimming light, lava bombs flashed red in the distance, trails of red spilling down the mountain.

"Pīhanga," he whispered.

"She's tearing up the land," Temera said. "The People have fled."

Tauhara took a step closer to the edge of the cliff. "I don't understand," he rumbled. "I respected her wishes. All these years, we've never spoken. How could I have known she was unhappy?"

Tauhara might not have seen it, but Taine had. Heartbroken, Pīhanga was hurling stones into the sky. What had Hine said? *It's like the mountain is crying and these are her tears.* Maybe...

Taine took off his boot and shook out a tiny olivine pebble.

He smiled. "Let me show you," he said.

Taupō

Taine ran down the mountain, stumbling on rocks and crashing through branches in the gloom.

"Hurry," Tauhara called to them.

"What are we supposed to do when we get there?" Temera replied.

"Speak for me," Tauhara rumbled. "Tell her, tell Pīhanga..." His voice faded.

*

Back at the paddocks, Taine stretched out his stride, letting the slope of the mountain carry him downwards. At the track entrance, he slid into the fire engine, putting it into gear even before he'd closed the door. Then, skidding sideways, he burned out of the parking lot.

Temera clucked. "Wheelie in a fire engine."

"Bucket list," Taine reminded him.

They took the highway, accelerating towards the lake. Taine's mind raced. They'd go to the harbour, like he'd told Hine, and search for a boat. It was the fastest way. Who knows how much time they had?

They reached the lakefront. "Look!" Temera said, from over Taine's shoulder.

Out on the lake, a single craft – a charter boat – was heading south towards Tokaanu.

"She's leaving," Temera said. "We'll never catch her."

Taine put his foot on the accelerator, nearly tipping the engine as he screamed around the corner. He hoofed along the esplanade, driving parallel to the charter.

"She can't see you," Temera said.

Taine searched the dash for the right icons. He flicked the switches, turning on the sirens and the lights. The horn bellowed across the water.

The charter slowed, turning in towards the beach.

Temera laughed. "You and your bucket list," he shouted.

Minutes later, Taine had boarded the charter.

"We thought you'd be gone," Taine said, laying the axe on a seat.

He'd used 'we', but Hine didn't bat an eyelid. "The earthquakes caused a tide," she replied, "and washed all boats into a corner. I had to move a few to get to this one. It was the biggest. And it has a satellite phone."

"Did you get hold of Major Arnold?"

"I spoke to Private Dawson. She said to say thank you: the major had received Hairy's text and he's doing what he can to convince the brass. She didn't sound hopeful."

"That's okay. I left a spare fire engine parked back on the beach."

She grinned. "There's food behind me if you want it."

Lifting the lid of the chilly-bin, Taine grabbed the first thing he found – a bread roll – and crammed it in his mouth.

"So, what did your mountain say?" Hine asked.

"We made a mistake," Taine mumbled through the sandwich. "It isn't Tauhara causing the earthquakes. It's Pīhanga. That's why we have to go back."

"Taine," Temera's voice boomed in his head. "I hate to interrupt your afternoon tea, but things are getting worse."

Taine swallowed, the bread thick in his throat. Across the lake, a lava bomb was exploding on Pīhanga, rock and ash choking the sky.

"We'll have to turn around," Temera insisted.

"The boat's too slow," Taine agreed. "We'll never make it in time."

"Maybe the little rescue boat will be faster," Hine said, pointing to the rear. 'It's under the seats."

Taine figured she was talking about a life raft, but he ran down the centre of the craft anyway, checking under the seats until he found what she was talking about.

He almost went back and kissed her. A PVC self-inflatable Zodiac. It wasn't huge, but then Temera didn't take up much room. Was there an outboard? Taine opened every locker, eventually finding one, along with the boat's aluminium floor. It took less than ten minutes to assemble and launch, Taine standing in the boat while Hine handed him the outboard, which he mounted to the transom.

Passing him his axe and a torch, she unhitched the painter line.

"See you on the other side," he called.

Tokaanu village

At Tokaanu, the group were waiting, drawn by the sound of the motor. Taking care to avoid the floating timber, Taine manoeuvred the craft towards the beach. He cut the outboard and leaped out of the boat, splashing the last few metres to help Hairy drag it out of the water. Then he pulled off to one side to talk to Jules and Read.

"Hine's fine," he said, answering Read's unspoken question. "She's following in a charter boat. When she gets here, I'll need you to load everyone on and get them back to Taupō as quickly as you can. There's transport on the beach."

"Wait. You're not coming with us?" Read asked.

"What happened?" Jules said. "I thought you said—"

"We got the wrong mountain. The problem isn't Tauhara, it's Pīhanga."

Lifting his helmet, Read ran a hand through his hair "You're going back to Pīhanga? You can't be serious. McKenna, you saw what it was like, saw what happened to Keira Skelton, and that was hours ago..." Read must have seen the look on Jules' face because he clamped his mouth shut and pursed his lips. Eventually, he said, "In that case, I'm going with you."

"Not this time, Read."

"McKenna, you can't—"

Taine held up his hand. "Matt, I'd give anything to have you with me, but we have six prisoners and six civilians in our charge. Hine has swum the length of the lake, and Lefty just lost his best friend. I'm going to need you to help Hairy."

"You're going to face the mountain on your own?" Jules' eyes clouded.

Taine gave her arm a squeeze. "Not alone. I'll have Temera with me." He turned to go.

"Taine."

His heart lurched. If only he had time...

He turned back.

Jules paused, like she was wrestling with something. "Before, you said there were six prisoners," she said finally. "Now there are four: Barnes and Taliava skipped out an hour ago. Hairy made the call not to go after them. He said enough lives had been lost."

"They have any weapons?" he asked, tightening his grip on the axe.

She shook her head. "It was just the two of them, and they're unarmed. One of the prisoners thought they were making a run for Omori. Hairy said that was their decision; everyone's been cleared out of there, anyway." She nibbled her cheek.

Taine nodded slowly.

"Thanks for the heads-up." Then he ran.

Rotorua township

By the time Wayne pulled into the house, it was late. Pania was waiting for him on the back porch. Leaning against the doorframe, she was wearing her dressing gown, her hands wrapped around a mug of tea.

She was going to kill him.

Wayne locked the car, listening for the clunk before crossing the lawn to the porch.

"Wayne?" Her face was pinched with worry.

Here it comes...

"Where's your uncle?"

Wayne brushed past her, stepping into the laundry to shuck off his trainers. "I couldn't get him to come home." He closed the door on her for a moment, hanging his jacket on the hook on the back.

When he opened it, she was still there, hovering in the kitchen.

"Why not?"

"I couldn't convince him to come, that's all. I tried all afternoon." Puffing his cheeks, he stepped past her into the lounge. "You know what he's like."

"Wayne—" Pania trailed after him.

Wayne sat heavily on the sofa, picked up the remote, and started surfing through the channels, the TV on mute. "Look, please don't start, babe. I'm tired, okay? It took me twice as long as usual to get back. The roads are chocka-block with everyone leaving Taupō, trying to put some distance between them and the mountains."

Pania put her mug on the coffee table, that silent gesture speaking volumes. Parking her bottom on the sofa's arm rest, she cocked her head in the direction of the TV. "The news is bad. They say it's getting worse."

Wayne nodded. "The earthquake swarms are making it hard to get around, even this far away from the epicentre. There are cracks in the road, trees down in places. I had to drive up on the shoulder to get around a fallen puriri tree out near Titiotonga."

"Sweetie, you have to go back."

Wayne sighed. "I wish he'd come back with me too, but he refused to come. What was I supposed to do? I couldn't exactly hogtie him. Maungapōhatu isn't in the official evacuation zone. We have to respect his wishes."

Pania slipped off the armrest onto the sofa beside him. Wayne put his arm around her and she snuggled into his chest like she usually did.

"I don't like it," she whispered.

"I don't like it either."

"It's just so isolated out there, and we can't even call him to make sure he's okay."

"Shit," Wayne said, putting her away from him and sitting up. "I promised Uncle Rawiri I'd call Taine McKenna."

He got up and went to the laundry, Pania calling from the lounge. "The soldier? Why? Has Uncle Rawiri had another premonition?"

Wayne rummaged in his jacket pocket for his phone. "Yeah, he had another vision: the fire demons who warned him about the geyser," he said through the door.

"Does he know what it means?"

"No, it's the same as always," Wayne said, joining her in the kitchen. He scrolled through his contacts list. "Danger. Foreboding. He doesn't know the details."

Wayne punched in the number for McKenna and put the phone to his ear, while Pania placed her cup in the dishwasher. The phone rang a few times, then went to voicemail, so Wayne hung up and sent a text instead.

"Wayne," Pania said softly.

"Yeah?" Still texting, Wayne didn't look up.

"I've been thinking about your uncle's gift. The other times – when he foresaw the geyser and saved your life, or that time he had the nightmare about McKenna and his friends when they were lost in the forest and needing help – it was always about saving other people. So, I was thinking; what if the danger was about him? Would he be able to see it?"

Wayne almost staggered as her words hit him head on and hard. Like the ABs entire front row. The thought had never occurred to him.

He nodded. "We'll drive back first thing in the morning."

CHAPTER TWENTY-SIX

Mount Pīhanga

To get to Pīhanga, Taine had to cut west around the lahar. The fireman's coat whistled as he ran. There was no need for a torch: streams of lava criss-crossed the slopes, illuminating the path like runway lighting. It was just as well: fissures were appearing everywhere, perfect for breaking an ankle, or a leg, or even swallowing him whole.

"Things are worse," he told Temera.

"Not entirely," Temera said. "At least there's no stone in your shoe."

Taine kept climbing.

He was nearing the western ridge when the top of the mountain exploded outwards, boulders tumbling down the ridges.

Taine dived for cover, dust and ash burning his lungs.

When he looked up, a crater had formed just beneath the summit, rivulets of lava spilling from the rim. Skipping across the rivers of red, the fire demons were heading up the mountain, their piu piu swishing around their legs. They were making for the crater.

"Taine, are you okay?" Taine heard the thrum of Temera's pūrerehua. Sitting up, he spat the ash from his lungs.

"Taine, come on, we have to hurry."

"The twisted sisters, did you see them?"

"Yeah, I saw them."

One of the demons turned. She flicked a blackened talon, and a plume of lava spurted from the ground, plunging down the hill towards him. Taine rolled away, grateful for the fireman's jacket.

"Te Pūpū," Temera said as Taine got up.

He hadn't fully regained his feet when a boulder hit him in the chest, throwing him down again, and knocking the axe right out of his hands.

The breath squeezed from his lungs, Taine tried to push the weight off his chest. Not a boulder: it was Barnes. Now Taine was the prisoner: Barnes' knee in his chest and a camping blade stuck to his throat.

"You are going to show me where the emeralds are," Barnes snarled, his knuckles in Taine's gorge.

The demon sisters vanished through the gaps in the flames.

"There are no emeralds," Taine said, keeping his voice even. He felt around for the axe. "They were olivine. They only look like emeralds. Like Fools' Gold."

Barnes pushed his face closer, the lava's glow shining on his cheeks. "You're lying."

"I'm telling you the truth. You're wasting your time, Barnes. Risking your life for nothing." Taine threw up a leg, trying to twist away. He didn't have time for this.

Barnes pressed the knife deeper. "Why are you here then, if it isn't to grab a handful for yourself?"

Taine had no answer. None that would satisfy Barnes.

"I thought so. Now, either you show me where the emeralds are, or I'll slit your throat."

The skin broke.

Suddenly, a big fist grabbed Barnes' hand, holding it. "Barnes. Leave him. Let's just go," Taliava said. "We don't need him to find the emeralds. That guy said they were everywhere. 'Handfuls of them,' he said. We just have to find them."

Barnes' eyes narrowed. Lifting the blade, he released the pressure on Taine's neck and sat back on his haunches. "Yeah, you're right. Let's just go." He got to his feet, then he swept Taliava's out from under him. The big Samoan went down heavily. Barnes stamped hard on his arm, before running up the mountain.

The crack of bone was tiny, scarcely perceptible over the mountain's tantrum, yet Taine had heard it. The arm hung at an angle. The big Samoan hadn't made a sound.

Eyes round, Taliava scrabbled backwards, his good hand fumbling behind him and finding a branch. He used it first to stand, then plunged it into a well of lava, so when he lifted it, the tip glowed red.

Taine stood. He found the axe and bent to pick it up. Maybe without Barnes, Taliava could turn himself around. Have a decent life. Pringle said that for most prisoners, all they needed was a second chance.

"Taliava, put the stick down. I'm not going to hurt you. Go back to town. There are boats at the lake. If you go now, you might make it."

Dropping the staff, Taliava hugged his arm against his chest, orange flames reflected in his eyes. "I can't leave," he rasped. "Barnes will kill my family. My daughter."

"Look at this place! He has to survive first." A rocket of lava whizzed, missing them both, but even after it had passed, Taine still felt its heat. "Go man. Hurry."

Taliava stared at him a second, then he ran. Taine wiped the blood from his throat and wished he could follow. Instead, he continued up the mountain, ducking through a clump of trees. He ploughed straight into Barnes.

Kneeling, the man was stuffing stones into his pockets.

Barnes looked up, his lip curling. "Back off, McKenna." He couldn't see Te Pūpū, behind him, raising her deadly talon.

"Barnes!" Taine warned.

Barnes leaped up, his eyes blazing. "I said back the fuck off." He pulled out the knife. "These are mine. You want some, you can go and find your own."

Baring pointed teeth, Te Pūpū drew a line in the air, searing a fissure on the ground. Barnes was oblivious to the danger.

Taine took a step forward. "Barnes!" he yelled.

It was a mistake.

Barnes backed away, dropping chest-deep into the crevasse. The blade went flying, and the demon cackled. Black smoke curled from the edges of the pit with a smell that made Taine want to hurl. Barnes whimpered through cracked lips.

"Help me," he rasped.

Taine ran to him, grabbing him by the arm, hauling on him. But the slit was closing, squeezing him in. Te Pūpū disappeared into the ashes, her screeches becoming distant.

"There's no time," Temera's voice sounded in his head.

Ignoring him, Taine tried again. Blackened and blistered, the skin of Barnes' arms came off in his hands. Barnes slipped further into the gap. Maybe if Taliava had been here, they might have been able to pull him free. On his own, Taine could do nothing.

Barnes mewled, his mouth bubbling.

Taine lifted the axe and finished it, several small stones tumbling from Barnes' hand.

"Taine! The mountain," Temera urged.

Taine ran up the rise to the crater. Whatever was about to happen, it would be there.

Now Te Pūpū blocked his way. Crouching, she thrust out her tongue and waved her patu-club, making the blade tremble.

Taine twirled the axe. "Let us through."

She thrust the club, slicing close to Taine's torso, shredding his coat.

"Why are you doing this?" Taine yelled.

She lunged again. "The matakite already knows."

Taine jumped away, his breath coming hard. He swung the axe, but already she'd stepped aside, his blade cutting only air. The demon was toying with him.

"Tell me, then," he said.

"Pīhanga summoned us," she said. "We came through secret tunnels under the earth, carrying the sacred embers as we did for Ngātoro-i-rangi." She pointed a talon at the earth and a stream of lava erupted near his feet.

"Why?" Taine asked, as he leapt away.

"Why what?"

"Why bring the fire?"

"Because he left," Te Pūpū said. "Went away and never spoke to her again. Anyone would be angry. She wanted Tauhara to know how angry she was."

"Not angry, heartbroken," Te Hoata called from the shadows.

"Yes, angry," barked Te Pūpū, hacking wildly with her patu. "She's angry now."

Taine parried with the axe. "But it was Pīhanga's idea. The battle, the terms. She agreed," Taine said.

"She made a mistake." Te Pūpū threw the blade to the ground, slicing a fissure in the rock. Taine had just seen what those fissures could do.

"She made a mistake and she's angry at him? Why didn't she say?"

"Look around," Te Pūpū said. "She's telling him now."

The ground rocked. A massive quake. Taine staggered, nearly stepping in the crack.

"It's done," Te Pūpū said, gleefully. "Rūaumoko's coming. She's woken him!"

"Quickly," Te Hoata urged, stepping out of the ashes. "You have to do it now."

"Do what? What are we supposed to do?" Temera demanded.

Cackling, Te Pūpū slipped sideways into the darkness between the flames. "Always they ask what they already know."

"Just tell us!" Temera shouted.

"You must give Pīhanga Tauhara's message," Te Hoata said. "Hurry! She's waited so long. Centuries..."

Taine shivered. Tauhara hadn't sent a message. There was no message.

"He sent us," Temera said. "We're his gift to her."

The ground shuddered, flames licking upwards all around them. Below them, the crater was dark and empty. Fathomless. At last, too late, Taine understood. "We're supposed to jump in there and die?"

"I can't see any other way."

"Well, that's easy for you to say. You're not really here."

Temera snorted. "My wairua is here. What's a body without a spirit?"

Taine dropped the axe. "If we do this, will it placate her?" he said. "We do this, and everyone else lives, right?"

"I think so," Temera replied.

"I would have preferred a taniwha or a kraken," Taine said.

"Too easy," Temera said. "Anything left on your bucket list?"

"Just one. I wish I'd sorted things with Jules."

"I'm sorry."

"It's okay."

"Maybe our wairua will walk together to Rēinga, to the jumping off place."

"I'd like that."

"Rūaumoko, Rūaumoko! He's coming!" Te Pūpū shrieked.

Taine stared into the mouth of the crater.

He stepped off the rim.

*

Inside the crater, the darkness was absolute. Wind whistled around him, like the whirr of his pūrerehua, and he was aware of Temera falling beside him in the darkness.

Taine would hit the bottom. His body would be smashed against the rock and earth. He would lie forever, the shifting earth grinding his bones to dust until eventually he became one with the mountain.

Was he afraid? Of the pain, perhaps. He prayed for an easy death, for a single fatal instant when his neck or spine would snap, and he would feel nothing more. Afterwards, his wairua would abandon the husk of tendon and sinew and walk north to where the two seas meet at the tip of the land, to Rēinga and Te Rerenga Wairua, the stepping off place of his mother's people. There his spirit-self would slip into the ocean, duck its head beneath the froth and spume, and begin the long journey to Hawaiki where his ancestors, and perhaps some friends, waited to welcome him to the underworld.

In the darkness, regret wrapped around him like fog. But why? Death was the way of all things. What was so bad about spending eternity with his friends and family?

As a soldier, death had always been a possibility, part of the job description. When he'd taken the vow to protect and serve, he'd known it could come to this. He'd been prepared to put his life on the line in the interests of his People. Why would he question that now, in the last seconds of his life? Because it was actually happening? Or because his death might hurt someone else more than it hurt him?

Yeah right; because he was *that* altruistic. The truth was, he was feeling sorry for himself because he'd never see Jules again. Never hold her again.

He laughed aloud. Jules had been right all along. He really did think of himself as some kind of comic book hero. Look how he'd jumped into a volcano, believing he could stop it from erupting and somehow save the entire bloody universe.

And yet Temera had believed it.

Then Temera was a bigger idiot than you.

Still, while there was a chance – even the smallest chance – that Jules and his friends might live, Taine would take it. He *had* taken it.

His shoulder brushed the wall. The air hummed. Death was coming, rushing up fast to greet him. Clutching his pūrerehua in his hand, Taine reached out to farewell his friend, but there was only emptiness. Taine held his breath and waited...

*

Temera was falling, spiralling downwards into Papatūānuku's earthy embrace. At first, he could sense Taine falling with him, but soon the rush of air and earth and ash overwhelmed him, and Temera lost him in the darkness.

Te Pūpū arrived to dance around him, her piu piu rustling in the wind.

"Have you come to gloat?"

Te Pūpū grinned through pointed teeth. "I've come to carry Tauhara's gift to Pīhanga."

"Will it be enough to stop her anger?" Temera asked. "Will she spare our People?"

Te Pūpū slapped the flattened blade of the patu against her thigh. "Always you ask. *What does this mean? What should I do?* You're a matakite, are you not?"

And always you answer with riddles. She wasn't going to tell him. Temera closed his eyes, held his pūrerehua to his heart, and sought the answer. Shrouded in mist, Temera's mountain ancestor, Te Maunga, reached into the ashes, his arms outstretched, and Temera saw what he had always known.

"Just do it," he whispered, his voice trembling.

"Are you afraid, little seer?" Te Pūpū cocked her head to one side. "I could come with you, if you like."

Temera's throat tightened. "No. I know the way."

Raising her blackened talon, the demon drew a line down his chest, searing a fissure through his ribcage. Temera's heart exploded in pain.

Far off in the darkness, a little morepork called.

*

Muscled arms wrapped around Taine and squeezed the breath from his lungs. Ah, the walls were closing in. Soon, he would suffocate. He closed his eyes.

There was a dull thud and the smell of fire and earth filled his nostrils.

"Your ancestors will just have to wait, seer," Te Hoata whispered in his ear. She set him on his feet and melted into the darkness.

Taine blinked. The black enveloped him, so dense it seemed to suck all the oxygen from the air.

He wasn't dead.

Not dead! She'd saved him.

Blind, he patted the walls. The ground grumbled beneath his fingers. *Wait. Come back!*

The demon was gone.

Taine grabbed his bullroarer. "Temera!" he shouted. "Temera."

He called until his throat was raw. Temera didn't answer.

He was alone. Why would Te Hoata save him just to let him die all over again? There was something he was missing.

Taine slid his hands along the wall and over a curve, tracing earth and rock and...an opening. There was a tunnel leading out of the pit. Taine's chest pounded. A route to the surface? It was a thin hope, but, given that seconds ago he'd expected to die, he wasn't about to look a gift horse in the mouth.

Pulling his t-shirt up over his face, and sliding his pūrerehua to the back, he dropped to his knees and crawled forward. It was slow going, with one hand on the wall, half crawling across the broken ground. By the time he found his way out – if he ever found his way out – the second Ice Age might have come and gone.

He kept on.

Every so often he would discover another passage leading away from the main tributary. There was a veritable labyrinth tucked away down here beneath the earth. Lava tubes probably: hundreds, possibly thousands, of underground trails stretching who-knew-how far. Most of them were too small for a man to crawl through, but the scratching noises said other creatures made use of them, either to hide from whatever was raging overhead or just to get from here to there, like a critter super-subterranean highway.

After a while, the main tunnel forked, both passages roughly the same size. Disoriented in the dark, Taine couldn't have said whether they sloped up or down. "Which way then?" he asked, his voice startling in the emptiness.

Something small skittered in front of him, barely moving the air. Taine reached out, his fingertips grazing a tiny scaled body. A wisp of a tail, thinner and smoother than a pencil, slipped through his grasp and the creature shied away. A gecko perhaps? Taine listened for its movements, strained so hard that his breathing was a sub-woofer in his ears. His pulse hammered at his temples. At last, a rustling reached him from off to his left.

"That way, you reckon?" Taine spoke into the gloom. He was asking a gecko for directions. Still, what did he have to lose? "Okay, this way it is, then." He plunged onwards, following the creature's scratching.

It was weird how, underground, you lost all sense of time. Taine didn't know how long he'd crawled. Fifteen minutes? An hour? Eventually, the tunnel narrowed to nothing. Taine reached out, his palms meeting rock. The lousy gecko had led him up the garden path to a dead end. He'd have to go back. Only, the gecko didn't seem interested in turning around. Taine could hear it darting over the rocks and dirt.

"Give it up, man. It's blocked," Taine said.

The gecko was determined to climb through. His persistence made Taine think: what if dirt had fallen in the recent earthquakes, and before that, this had been the way out? If there had been room for his shoulders to move, Taine might have shrugged. Instead, he scratched at the earth, pulling away the rocks. His fist punched through, his fingers grabbing at air. On the other side, the tunnel continued. The space was limited, but Taine kept digging, pushing the dirt behind him until he'd created a gap at the top. The gecko didn't wait, scurrying over the pile and into the tunnel on the other side. Taine pushed through the barrier. He blinked the dust out of his eyes. The tunnel here was narrower, forcing him to worm forward on his elbows. He spied a flash of movement up ahead.

Except to see movement, you need light!

Was that really a glow or a figment of his imagination? On his belly, he ramped forward, his eyes fixed on the tiny dot of light which grew and grew. Taine's hopes grew with it. It was a way out. Pīhanga had chosen to spare him. Or maybe it had been Temera's doing. In any case, it seemed there was such a thing as second chances.

Relief thundering through his veins, Taine reached the opening and looked out. His eyes watered at the sudden brightness. Opposite him across a chasm was another wall, but below him to the right was the mangled carcass of...*an army Unimog!* He was in the trench. He'd emerged at the northern end, higher up the slope. He'd have to pick his way carefully – there might be sinkholes, and nails or iron that could shred flesh – but if he followed the slope upwards, he might find the rope still tied to the veranda of the motel.

Taine shook his head with disbelief. A tiny gecko – no, not a gecko, a speckled skink – had shown him the way out. Taine gave the little creature a salute as it darted up the wall to the surface. Then, sucking in the night air, Taine pulled himself out of the tunnel and set his feet on the floor of the trench.

Tokaanu, Waihi Bay

Jules waited with Matt and Hine in the zodiac.

In the front of the boat, Taliava nursed his broken arm. He'd arrived back on the beach twenty minutes ago, his presence filling Jules with hope, but that had faded as the night had closed in.

Read patted Jules' arm. "Doc, we should go," he said quietly.

"Just a few more minutes," Jules said.

He was right. They should leave. Yet Jules didn't move. For a moment, the swell lifted the zodiac, then settled them back on the beach.

"What if the others have had to leave Taupō?" Hine asked.

"They'll leave a vehicle for us," Read reassured her. "Hairy and Lefty will make sure."

Jules stepped out of the boat. Freezing water splashed her legs. "You go," she said, giving the Zodiac a push to send it on its way.

"Jules—"

"Matt, please. I have to stay." She backed away. "I can't leave him."

"No, that's not what I mean. The shaking's stopped. It's stopped. Listen!"

Jules turned. On the skyline, tinged with pink, the lava bombs were no longer exploding. The ground was calm. Even the lahar seemed quiet.

She looked up.

Taine was walking down the street.

CHAPTER TWENTY-SEVEN

Maungapōhatu, Te Urewera Forest

For the second time in as many days, Wayne's tyres crunched on the gravel road leading to the Temera family homestead. In the passenger seat, wrapped in a fleece blanket, Pania gazed out the front window. Dark smudges weighed under her eyes. Neither of them had slept much, Pania even less than Wayne, waking before five and bringing him a cup of coffee so they could get on the road. Even leaving at a sparrow's fart, it had taken them over three hours to get to Maungapōhatu. After hearing the emergency had been lifted, every man and his dog had taken to the road. Most likely people who'd evacuated before the disaster were trying to get a jump on the traffic and get home. Which was all very well, only the authorities – those who hadn't been evacuated themselves – hadn't had five minutes to remove the debris yet. The downed puriri tree at Titiotonga had been hastily pushed to the side of the road and a banged-up orange cone left to mark the hazard. Meanwhile the traffic was backed up while the rubberneckers had a good gawk. It had been a slow trip.

Her elbow on the door, Pania tapped her fingernails on the window ledge. She sighed.

"Nearly there," he said to fill the silence.

Outside, the air was full of ash. It fluttered like snow, drifting down from the trees and hovering in the famous Te Urewera mist.

Where he'd stalled the truck, Wayne nudged the accelerator. There'd been no time to check the battery and he didn't want a repeat of yesterday. At last, the house appeared through the trees.

"You know he's probably asleep," Wayne said, but Pania was already unclicking her seat belt. She kicked the fleece into the footwell and opened the door before Wayne had had time to put the truck into park. Now she was running across the dewy grass to the house.

At the corner of the building, she stopped dead, her gasp telling him everything. "Wayne!" She put her hands to her mouth.

He ran.

In the end, though, there was nothing they could do. Uncle Rawiri was sitting on the porch. Wearing the same clothes he'd had on when Wayne had visited yesterday, his back was propped against the veranda post. In one hand, he was clutching the pūrerehua he'd carved in his potting shed back in Rotorua. His gaze, though, was on the mountain.

Her eyes wet with tears, Pania stepped into Wayne's arms. She wrapped her arms around his waist. "Wayne. I'm so sorry."

Wayne buried his face in her hair. "It's my fault. I should have listened to you and come back last night."

She raised her head to look at him. "No. You were right to leave him. He needed to be here. His heart, his soul, was here. I wish he hadn't been all alone, that's all."

The three of them sat on the porch together one last time, Uncle sleeping peacefully, and Wayne in the beach chair with Pania curled in his lap. Ash drifted and swirled on the breeze as the sun climbed over Te Maunga.

Much later, when Pania went to the bathroom to wash her face, Wayne slipped the pūrerehua out of his uncle's fingers and lifted it from around his neck. He turned it over in his hand and admired its workmanship. The flattened oblong blade had been cut from a piece of golden matai, the swooping whorls and dog-tooth notches carved with Uncle Rawiri's own hand. Wayne felt a sudden urge to play it. Just once.

A song for his uncle's wairua.

Stepping off the porch, he unravelled the string and let out the slack. He shucked off his jandals, kicking them into the grass. Then, his feet wide, and his toes curled in the earth, he lifted his arm and swung the pūrerehua. The string tightened and the blade hummed, the little instrument tracing a wide arc in the air. It sliced through the flakes of ash. Wayne twirled it faster...

...and faster...

...and faster.

Then he closed his eyes and listened to its music. It was soft and insistent, like the beat of a dragonfly's wings.

A voice murmured in his head.

Wayne's heart did a flip. His eyes flew open. Someone was speaking to him. But Wayne wasn't a matakite. Hardly. Uncle Rawiri used to joke that Wayne wouldn't see an elephant if it was standing on his foot.

On the porch, his great-uncle seemed to smile.

Wayne closed his eyes again and, in his mind, *two* blades whirred and whistled in unison.

"Temera?" the soldier's voice sounded in his head.

"McKenna. It's Wayne."

"Ah. He's really gone, then?"

Wayne didn't question how McKenna knew. He swallowed. "Yes."

"You're playing his pūrerehua. You know, he saved my life with it more than once."

Wayne nodded, tears pricking at the corners of his eyes. "I guess we're both going to miss him."

McKenna chuckled. "He could be bloody stubborn when he wanted to be."

"No arguments there."

"One of a kind."

"Yeah."

They were silent for a time, lulled by the blades as they flew on the breeze.

Eventually, McKenna said, "Will you join me in wishing him farewell on his journey to the spirit world?"

Warming to the rhythm of the blade, Wayne lifted his eyes to the grey-green peak of Te Maunga. "Of course."

THE END

GLOSSARY:

Aotearoa	land of the long white cloud, Māori name for New Zealand
bach (es)	(colloq.) beach house, typically modest with few amenities
charley horse	muscle spasm caused when thigh muscle is crushed to underlying bone
dunny / ies	(colloq.) crude outside toilet
full tit	(colloq.) Kiwi version of 'full tilt'
Hawaiki	mythological homeland of Polynesian peoples, Māori underworld
to hiff (something)	to throw, heave (typically Australian / New Zealand usage)
hongi	Māori salutation where noses are pressed together in greeting, a sharing of breath and souls
iwi	tribe
jandals	(collq.) from 'Japanese sandals', this is the Kiwi term for flip flops
karakia	prayer, chant, song
kaumātua	elder
matakite	seer, soothsayer
mātua	teacher, mentor
munted	(colloq.) Kiwi slang for damaged, wrecked, gone to shit
patu	flattened club made of wood or stone
pepeha	introduction which includes identity and heritage
piu piu	traditional skirt, apron
pounamu	greenstone, New Zealand jade
pūrerehua	bullroarer, musical instrument
taonga	treasure
tāne	husband, male, man
taiaha	long-handled spear
taniwha	monster, often a lizard or sea creature
Te Hoata	(and Te Pūpū) fire demon sisters
Te Maunga	sacred mountain of the Tūhoe people, part of the Te Urewera ranges
Te Pūpū	(and Te Hoata) fire demon sisters
wāhine	woman, women, female
wairua	spirit, soul
Weetbix	Kiwi brand of Weet-a-bix
Whakaari	Māori name for White Island
whānau	family
yeah-nah	Kiwi for "yes, I get what you're saying and, no, you're wrong"
Zambuck	Australian/New Zealand term for St John Ambulance officers

Acronyms:	
ABs	Abbrev of All Blacks, New Zealand's national rugby team
DPM	Disruptive Pattern Material (combat camouflage material)
EDM	Electronic Distance Meter, an instrument that sends and receives electromagnetic signals to measure the distance between fixed benchmarks on volcanic flanks
GNS	Geological and Nuclear Sciences, government department
IOE	Instructor (Offender Employment)
MCU	Multi-terrain camouflage uniform
NZDF	New Zealand Defence Force
PE	Physical Education
SAS/NZSAS	New Zealand Special Air Service, elite combat regiment

CPSIA information can be obtained
at www.ICGtesting.com
Printed in the USA
LVHW111401230220
647908LV00003B/635